DEAD END

DEAD END

Sally Spencer

This first world edition published 2019
in Great Britain and the USA by
SEVERN HOUSE PUBLISHERS LTD of
Eardley House, 4 Uxbridge Street, London W8 7SY.
Trade paperback edition first published
in Great Britain and the USA 2019 by
SEVERN HOUSE PUBLISHERS LTD.

British Library Cataloguing in Publication Data
A CIP catalogue record for this title is available from the British Library.

ISBN-13: 978-0-7278-8874-7 (cased)
ISBN-13: 978-1-84751-999-3 (trade paper)
ISBN-13: 978-1-4483-0212-3 (e-book)

Typeset by Palimpsest Book Production Ltd.,
Falkirk, Stirlingshire, Scotland.

'The body's a dead end,' Crane said. He gave the others a weak grin. 'No pun intended.'
'Good, because if there had been, I'd probably have had to kill you,' Meadows said.

PART ONE
The Hidden Grave

September 1978

ONE

I t was a dull, dark morning and heavy clouds rumbled ominously over the whole of Whitebridge and the surrounding valley.

Archie Eccleston climbed stiffly out of the ex-army cot which occupied over a quarter of the floor space in his potting shed. He felt a little giddy, perhaps because he had left the paraffin heater burning all night. He knew he shouldn't have done that – the safety instructions on the heater were quite explicit – but there had been an unseasonable chill in the air, and even with all his clothes on, he had been cold.

Yes, he admitted it, he had gone to bed with all his clothes on, but at least he'd taken his boots off (and that had to count for something!).

He slipped the boots on now, and, without lacing them, stepped outside. Once in the open air, he pulled an old flat tin out of his pocket, and extracted one of the cigarettes he'd rolled the previous evening. He lit it, and inhaled deeply.

Was it really only a few months earlier that all this had started, he asked himself, as his lungs wheezed in protest at the arrival of the grey, twisting snake of poisonous chemicals.

Yes, it was – and he could pin down exactly the point at which everything had changed.

3rd March!

Before then, everything had been perfect. The allotment had seemed just like a mini Garden of Eden to Archie – well, maybe not *quite* just like that, he admitted to himself, because if the real garden had been located in Lancashire, it would have been far too nippy for Adam and Eve to walk around bollock-naked, even in the summer. At any rate, it had been close enough to paradise for him.

His immediate neighbours had experimented on their allotments with celeriac and sweetcorn, but Archie was a traditionalist and stuck to potatoes, carrots, broad beans, onions, winter cabbages, summer cabbages, marrows and Brussels sprouts – vegetables which had been good enough for his dad, and were good enough for him.

But it wasn't just the growing things that mattered. True, there was great pride to be had from looking at your Sunday dinner plate and seeing the roast beef surrounded by vegetables that had been grown by you, but there was more to it than that – a whole process to be considered. For a start, the feller working on the next allotment wasn't just any old bod, he was your comrade. You did his weeding for him when he was sick, he shared with you that bottle of malt whisky he kept hidden behind his fertilizer bags – and when an unexpected frost got his parsnips, you felt the loss almost as much as he did.

And then, of course, there was the fact that little Patrick had loved this allotment, though there was no point in dwelling on that now.

There was no point in dwelling on that *ever* – though Archie knew he always would.

He remembered the day the letter from the council had arrived. It had been waiting for him on the doormat, in a buff envelope which proclaimed that it was official.

Inside, the letter addressed him as Mr Eccleston, perhaps to make it seem more personal, but his name had been typed by a different machine to the rest of the letter and was slightly unaligned.

This is to inform you that within the next few months the county council will be taking back the allotment (TCA 123-2) that it rents to you on Old Mill Road. This has become necessary in order to facilitate an extension of the ring road. We apologise for the inconvenience, and wish to assure you that for the time period between you losing this allotment and being allotted another one, no rent will be charged. We are also willing to bear the cost of transporting whatever structures and equipment you have from one site to the other.

They couldn't just take his allotment away, Archie had told himself. He didn't want a new one – he wanted the one he had lavished love and attention on for over twenty years. And the conversations he'd had in the Bird in the Hand pub that lunchtime had been enough to show him that he was not alone in these feelings.

They would fight the council, the allotment holders decided. They would occupy the allotments that they . . . well, that they occupied now. They couldn't live there – that much was obvious – but by careful planning they could ensure that the site was never left unoccupied, thus preventing the council from sneaking in and bulldozing it flat. It was also agreed that though their cause was just, and they couldn't possibly lose, it might be wisest not to leave any valuable tools at the allotments until matters had been resolved.

And so it was that the nightshift men were there in the daytime, the dayshift men were there at night, and the retired filled in whenever necessary.

Some wives objected, some wives were pleased to have their husbands out of the way, but most just shrugged their shoulders and said men had this unfathomable attachment to their allotments, and it was best just to let them get on with it.

And that was how it had been for the last six months – the allotment holders had protected their little kingdoms, while their backers (the National Association of Allotment Holders) had fought it out with the council in the courts.

The black van was parked just out of sight of the allotments. Sitting in the back of it, along with seven experienced bobbies, was Police Cadet L Rutter (better known to her friends as Louisa Paniatowski) who was feeling what could only be described as a mixture of excitement and terror. This, she kept reminding herself, was an actual policing operation, and *she was part of it*. True, as had been made clear to her by the desk sergeant, she was only there as an observer, with strict instructions not to participate in the action, but maybe circumstances would dictate that she had no choice but to intervene.

Idiot! she told herself. Intervention was not a good thing – a glamorous thing – it was a clear indication that something had gone seriously wrong, and the whole essence of policing was ensuring that nothing *did* go wrong. In fact, the essence of successful policing was to make policing unnecessary, and with the mum she had, she should know that better than anybody.

Her thoughts turned to her mother, who had been viciously attacked in Backend Woods earlier in the summer, and was still in a coma.

Would she ever come out of it? Her team – Colin Beresford, Kate Meadows and Jack Crane – all had a fierce belief that she would, and Louisa drew her own strength from them.

The back door of the van was opened from outside, and Louisa saw a uniformed inspector standing there. He was not alone. Standing next to him was a middle-aged civilian in a brown suit, who Louisa thought looked vaguely familiar.

'We'll be going in in exactly five minutes from now,' the inspector said. 'We're not anticipating trouble, but if we get it, I'd ask you to remember that these are not out-of-town football hooligans, they're your dad's cousin and your wife's uncle. If you've got any questions, now's the time to ask them.'

From their silence, it appeared that none of the occupants of the van *did* have any questions, and the inspector and the civilian turned and walked away.

'Who's he, Tony?' Louisa whispered to the constable sitting shoulder-to shoulder with her.

'That,' replied the constable gravely, 'is Inspector Metcalfe.'

'Oh, I know that,' Louisa replied, giving the constable a playful poke in the ribs, and wondering – even as her fingers made contact – if she hadn't perhaps gone a little too far. 'What I meant,' she continued, speaking hastily to cover her confusion, 'is who the other feller is.'

'That's Roderick Hardcastle, member of parliament for the fair borough of Whitebridge,' Tony said.

Her mum had really fancied the previous MP, Louisa remembered, and she herself had played around with the idea of him becoming her stepfather, and decided she rather liked it.

But then her mum had gone and spoiled it all by arresting him for murder!

The bulldozer and three JCB diggers stood in a line, and watching them, from behind the wheel of a Volkswagen Beetle, was a man who sometimes went by the name of Forsyth.

He looked out of place in a VW Beetle, the man sitting in the passenger seat next to him thought.

Looked out of place – hell, he *was* out of place! That suit he was wearing, for a start – you couldn't get something like that off the peg (or even made-to-measure) anywhere in the north of

England. No, that was a London suit – a Savile Row suit – unless he was very much mistaken (and Ellis Downes, who had expensive tastes he could never afford, prided himself on never making mistakes like that).

And then there was the haircut. It looked a simple cut, and it probably was, but there was an art to it which made the hair glow like sterling silver which had just undergone half an hour's vigorous buffing at the hand of a trusted servant.

I can sometimes seem pretty sharp myself – a real sophisticate – Downes reflected, but after I've been in Mr Forsyth's company for five minutes, I feel like a country bumpkin.

How old was Forsyth, he found himself wondering. Probably in his late fifties or early sixties, though he had the sort of the face that might well belong to a man in his early fifties or late sixties.

'You don't have to watch this yourself, Mr Forsyth,' he heard himself saying, sickeningly ingratiatingly. 'I can put a couple of the lads on it if you like.'

'If I like?' Forsyth repeated, without even turning his head. 'A couple of the lads?'

The man just couldn't resist the opportunity to take the piss out of the north, could he?

Oh, I bloody hate you, Downes thought. I worked bloody hard to get into grammar school, while you no doubt just wafted into Eton or Harrow or whatever other poncy public school your dad put your name down for on the day you were born. And maybe I didn't serve as an officer in the Coldstream Guards, like you probably did, but I'd not been in the army for more than five minutes before somebody spotted my obvious potential and transferred me to Intelligence.

Aloud, he confined himself to saying, 'We may be out here in the sticks, but we are trained professionals, you know, sir.'

'Are you, indeed?' Forsyth countered. 'Then what about the man who started this whole mess – the one who couldn't even follow the simple outline I left him to follow? Judd, was it?'

'Richard Judd was presented with an unexpected situation which called for a quick decision,' Downes said defensively. 'He took that decision, and the Centre has endorsed his action.'

'I'm not talking about the action per se,' Forsyth told him, 'I'm

referring to what happened next – to the chain of events that led
to my being back in this rather nasty little industrial town, when
I'd much rather be somewhere else.'

'Judd couldn't have anticipated—' Downes began.

'He *should have* anticipated it,' Forsyth interrupted. 'Any man
who couldn't have anticipated it shouldn't have been on your team.
He certainly wouldn't have been on mine.'

A police patrol car cruised slowly past the wrecking convoy,
flashing its lights. Taking that as their signal, the bulldozer and
diggers immediately fired up their engines.

'Maybe they'll be careless, and we'll just get away with it,'
Downes said hopefully.

'God give me strength,' Forsyth replied, *almost* too quietly for
Downes to hear him.

When the rumbling sound began in the distance, Archie Eccleston
was sitting outside his shed, drinking tea from a mug which bore
the message: THE BEST DAD IN THE WORLD.

Mary had bought it for him shortly after she'd given birth
to Patrick, which had been a kind thought, because everybody
else was praising her, yet instead of basking in it she found the
time to do something which said that he had a part to play, too.
He didn't know then – neither of them could even have *imagined* then – just how limited a part God – or nature, or blind
chance – had assigned to him.

It was no one's fault, and they shouldn't blame themselves, the
doctor had said as the undertaker's men were lifting the tiny coffin
into the big black hearse. Patrick had had a rare form of cancer,
and even the best care in the world – which the doctor was sure
was exactly what they'd given him – couldn't have saved the poor
little lad.

It was a week later that Mary had noticed he was still using
the mug and had exploded.

'You're not the best dad in the world any longer,' she'd screamed
at him across the kitchen. 'You'll never be a dad again . . .'

'You don't know that, lass,' he'd said tenderly.

'You'll never be a dad again, Archie, because I'm never going
to be a mum again . . .'

'Now then, lass, now then . . .'

'. . . because I couldn't stand the pain – so you can throw that bloody mug out before I smash it to pieces myself.'

He hadn't thrown it out. He couldn't bring himself to do that, even though he knew she was right and you can't be the best dad in the world to a dead boy. So instead of putting it into the bin, he'd brought it to the allotment, and it had been that mug – and this allotment – that had held him together while his marriage had been falling apart.

The rumbling was getting louder, and after carefully placing his mug on the shelf, Archie stood up and made his way down the path towards the main gate.

A few years previously, the rougher element of a visiting football team's supporters' club had demonstrated their disappointment at the result of the game (Whitebridge Rovers had murdered them!) by rampaging through the town and smashing shop windows. Then, almost as an afterthought, they had taken out their frustration on the allotments, ripping up flowerbeds and stamping on marrows (several of which had prize-winning potential). As a result, the council had enclosed the whole area with a six-foot-high wire-mesh fence topped with razor wire.

The only way to enter the allotments now was through a double gate which was of the same height and basic construction as the fence, and when Archie arrived at the gate, there were already five other men (the remaining members of the night guard), gazing through the diamond-shaped mesh at the convoy of demolition vehicles, flanked by an escort of police cars and vans, which was slowly approaching.

'They never told us they were coming,' said Roy Moores, who was a nice feller but could never have been described as the sharpest pencil in the box.

'No, they didn't tell us,' Archie agreed. 'Has anybody let the rest of the lads know what's happening?'

All the other men shook their heads.

Suppressing a sigh of exasperation, Archie reached into his pocket, and pulled out a handful of change, and it gave it to Moores.

'There's a phone box on the corner of Jubilee Street,' he said. 'Ring as many of the lads as you know have phones, and ask them all to let the rest know what's going on.'

Moores' brow pursed at the thought of being given so much responsibility.

'Wouldn't you rather do it yourself?' he asked hopefully.

'No, I can be of more use here,' replied Archie, who had just noted that the convoy had slowed to a halt, and that a man in a brown suit was making his way slowly but steadily towards the allotments.

Roderick Hardcastle was five yards from the mesh gate when he heard someone call out, 'That's far enough, Mr Hardcastle.'

He might have known it would be Archie Eccleston who'd be the one to issue the warning, Hardcastle thought.

'We need to talk, Archie,' he said.

The other man shrugged. 'There doesn't really seem to be much point in doing that, not now that you've joined the enemy.'

'I have *not* joined the enemy,' Hardcastle replied, keeping his anger under control – but only just. 'I've stood shoulder-to-shoulder with you every inch of the way.'

Archie glanced up the road. 'Doesn't look like it to me,' he said.

'I'm not here for them,' Hardcastle said, gesturing behind him. 'I'm here for you. We've lost, Archie – that's an indisputable fact – and if you refuse to bow to the inevitable, you'll only be hurting yourself.'

'We haven't lost,' Archie said stubbornly. 'There's still the High Court to appeal to, and if that fails, we'll go right up to the House of Lords.'

Hardcastle shook his head, pityingly. 'The National Association of Allotment Holders isn't prepared to pour any more money into this case, because they can see it's a lost cause.'

'Then we'll raise the money ourselves.'

'How?'

'Whist drives and raffles, and that sort of thing.'

'You could have a hundred whist drives and a thousand raffles, and you'd still not raise anything like enough.' Hardcastle switched his attention from Archie to the others. 'Come on, lads, admit defeat and let the contractors do what they need to do.'

'Will they give us a day or two to shift our sheds?' asked Ted King, raising what was, in effect, an invisible white flag.

Hardcastle sighed. 'I'm afraid they won't,' he said. 'They'll say you've already had six months, and, if I can be frank, they're as pissed off with you as you are with them.'

'We could maybe have it done by this afternoon, if we really put our backs into it,' the other man said.

Hardcastle shook his head again, wearily. 'You just don't get it, do you, Ted?' he asked. 'The council employs the contractors to put a road through the allotments, and the moment they start work, the clock is ticking. So if they can't work and it's not their fault, the council still has to pay them. Which means that if the council loses a day's work, it shells out ten thousand pounds for nothing.'

The other man whistled softly. 'It can't be as much as that,' he said.

'It's exactly as much as that,' Hardcastle insisted, though, in fact, he'd just plucked that figure out of the air.

He turned back to Archie, and saw that in the minute or so it had taken to answer the other man's question, Eccleston had produced a thick steel chain from a bag at his feet and was proceeding to wrap it around himself.

'Now come on, Archie,' Hardcastle coaxed, 'this is no time for a pointless gesture.'

Ignoring him, Eccleston threaded the two ends of the chain through both gates and then linked them together with two padlocks big enough to grace a medieval castle.

He's been practicing, Hardcastle thought. He couldn't have done that half as smoothly if he hadn't practiced it.

'For goodness' sake, Archie, how long do you think that's going to hold them up?' he asked.

'Maybe long enough for the rest of the allotment holders to get here,' Archie said.

'And what good will it do if they *do* get here?' Hardcastle wondered. 'There's enough police here to arrest you all – if there aren't, they'll just bring more in. So what's the point of it all?'

Archie wanted to explain that points didn't come into it – that you felt about these matters in your gut, rather than working them out in your head.

Of course the allotment holders couldn't stop it!

He knew that.

And of course the new strip of land the council gave them would probably be just as good – looked at objectively – as the one they'd sweated over and loved all these years.

But if they gave up just like that, without even the hint of a fight, it would be like letting the land down – turning their backs on the friable black soil which clung to them.

And he, personally, would be losing the land on which Patrick took his first few tentative steps – the land that would be marked forever with footprints which could only be seen through the eyes of love.

'Do your damnedest,' Archie snarled. 'You and the council both.'

'I've told you a dozen times, Archie, that it's nothing to do with me,' the MP said.

But as he was speaking, he was turning to face the police cars, a prearranged signal that he'd done *his* damnedest, and now he washed his hands of the whole business.

As she walked along the corridor that ran down the middle of the intensive care unit of the Whitebridge General Hospital, Ward Sister Diana Sowerbury was aware that all the nurses on ward duty were following her progress with their eyes, asking themselves what kind of sister she would turn out to be, and perhaps – and this must really be puzzling them – what the hell the hospital was doing bringing in a woman from the other side of the Pennines.

Well, they'd get the answer to their first question soon enough. She was – to use an old-fashioned term she rather liked – a bit of a stickler. She was universally loved by the doctors, since her wards always ran like clockwork, and feared and respected (in equal measure, she liked to think) by her nurses, because wards do not run like clockwork without *someone* having to suffer a little. She did not have much to do with the actual patients herself, but when she did happen to come across them, she treated them with a sterile compassion which could almost have been mistaken for the real thing. And as far as visitors went, she was quite prepared to treat them with compassion, too, as long as they stuck rigorously to her rules.

The second question her new nurses might be asking themselves was more problematic. On its most basic level, the answer was simple. She was there because she had been offered a job in the best ICU in the north of England, and she had accepted it without a second thought. On a more complex level, it was rather strange that she had been offered a position she'd never applied for, in a county she'd never even visited, and even stranger that her transfer should have been effected in a mere thirty-six hours.

The reason couldn't be her nursing skills – though she'd been a bloody good nurse and she was an even better ward sister – she was sure about that.

So it had to be because of the other thing.

She had reached the edge of her new realm, and was standing in front of the double doors which led into the main corridor and the outside world. To her left, there was a door which led into a private room which was currently being paid for by the Central Lancs police force, and looking through the window she was horrified to see that there was a man inside it wearing overalls.

She swung the door open.

'What do you think you're doing here?' she demanded. 'This is a restricted area!'

The man, who was crouched down by an electric socket in the wall, looked up at her.

'I'm fixing the circuit, Sister,' he said. 'Can't afford to have the hospital's system going down, especially in its ICU, now can we?'

And, as if to demonstrate the need for power, he indicated the bed, on which a woman connected to a number of wires and tubes lay deathly still.

'So you're from the maintenance department, are you?' Diana Sowerbury asked, still far from mollified. 'And why didn't your supervisor let me know about this?'

The man straightened up. He was quite tall, quite young and rather good looking, Diana Sowerbury quickly decided – not that any of that mattered one way or the other.

'I'm not from the maintenance department,' he said. 'To be honest with you, your maintenance department does a great job as long as nothing breaks down, but they realize – and thank goodness they do – that something like this requires the expert touch.'

He ran his finger along top of his pocket, where the words: 'Harrison Electrical – the Expert Touch' had been embroidered.

'Even if it's an external contractor, I should be informed,' Diana

Sowerbury said, unyieldingly. '*Especially* if it's an external contractor.'

The man grinned. He had a rather nice grin, she thought.

'Oh, I get it,' he said. 'You don't trust us because we were born in the wagon of a travelling show.'

Diana Sowerbury frowned. 'I'm sorry, but I'm not entirely sure what you mean.'

'Us external contractors are all gypsies, tramps and thieves – like in the Cher song.'

Diana Sowerbury didn't want to smile, but became aware that her facial muscles had betrayed her, and she was doing just that.

'Such an idea never crossed my mind,' she protested, 'but I do think I might have been—'

'Tell you what it must have been,' the electrician interrupted. 'All this was set up last week, and you were still in Sheffield then, weren't you?'

'Yes, I was,' Diana Sowerbury agreed.

'Well, there you are, then,' the man said. He picked up his toolbox, checked his watch, and headed for the door. 'Well, time and tide wait for no man,' he continued, cheerfully. 'I'll see you around.'

'Yes,' Diana Sowerbury agreed, 'I expect you will.'

She walked over to the bed and looked down at the patient. The woman was a blonde, and though it was never easy to calculate the age of someone in her position, Diana Sowerbury guessed she was somewhere between thirty-five and forty-five. Her name was Monika Paniatowski, which accounted for the rather large (though not unattractive) middle-European nose. She was well-known locally, largely due to the fact that she was a detective chief inspector, and thus her picture was always appearing in the papers. She had been discovered in the woods, with the back of her head caved in. She was in a coma, and though the specialists said she might come out of it any minute, they also accepted that she might never come out of it at all.

Diana Sowerbury wondered if Monika was aware of what was going on around her. And if she was aware, would she want to stay alive in the hope that she might make a recovery, or would she prefer to put an end to this life of perpetual ennui?

If it was me, I think I'd prefer the latter, she told herself.

'But we'll never know, will we?' she said aloud. 'Because none of us can get inside your brain.'

She turned and walked away. It was only when she was back in the corridor that she began to wonder how the young electrician – who didn't even work at the hospital – had known she'd been in Sheffield until a few days earlier.

TWO

The policemen standing behind the roadblocks at both ends of Old Mill Road were not wearing riot gear, but the shields, helmets and gas masks that comprised the gear had been unloaded from one of the vans and left in a conspicuous spot, as a visual warning that though they were not looking for trouble, they were more than prepared to deal with any that might arise.

In fact, it seemed unlikely that there *would be* trouble. True, there were at least a couple of dozen allotment holders crowded in front of the roadblock and shouting furiously at the police, but most officers could normally sense when a brick was about to be thrown, and were under no apprehension that that was about to happen here. Still, the ritual, once begun, must be played through to the end, so allotment holders bombarded the police with questions they already knew the answer to, and the policemen answered with a predictability that was almost stupefying.

'Why can't I go to my allotment?' one of the allotment holders demanded. 'This is still a free country, isn't it?'

'Well, yes, it certainly seemed to be the last time I looked,' the taciturn sergeant agreed.

'Then, I can go where I want to, can't I?'

'Yes, sir, you can – but only within reason. You see, it's our duty to protect you – even from yourself, if necessary – and it's been judged too dangerous for you to go the allotments.'

'Too dangerous! What are you worried about? That I'll be bitten by a rogue parsnip? Or that I'll be run over by a rampaging Brussels sprout?'

'With a wit like yours, sir, you should give serious consideration to going on the stage,' the sergeant said. 'But let's be honest, we both know what I'm talking about, don't we? That bulldozer could plough you into the ground and not even realize it had done it. I'm not prepared to let you risk that.'

'For Christ's sake, we take a risk every time we step through our front doors,' the allotment holder said. He glanced up at the sky. 'Looks like there's a real storm brewing up there. I could be struck by lightning, even as I'm standing here and talking to you.'

'Yes, you could be,' the sergeant agreed. 'But if you were, nobody could lay the blame for your charred remains on me.'

Louisa Paniatowski was standing close to the police van that had brought her team from the station. Though she had been informed she was on observation, no one had actually told her *what* to observe or *how* to observe it, and she was beginning to suspect that what 'observe' really meant was, 'We're lumbered with this cadet, and we can't think of anything useful to do with her.'

When she was a detective chief superintendent, she wouldn't allow that kind of thing to happen, she promised herself.

When she was a DCS, she would have a whole programme worked out which tapped into the enthusiasm and idealism of the young cadets.

If my mum heard me talking like that – all self-righteous and pompous – *she'd take the piss out of me for days*, she thought – and though she didn't mean to, she giggled.

'Is something amusing you, Cadet?' asked a voice to the left, and turning, she saw Inspector Metcalfe standing there.

She said nothing, hoping he'd just walk away.

He didn't.

'Well?' the inspector repeated. 'Is there some joke I've missed?'

'No, sir,' Louisa said, looking down at the ground.

'What are you *supposed* to be doing here, anyway?' the inspector asked.

'Observing, sir.'

'Observing what?'

'The operation in general, I think.'

The inspector gave a loud sigh of exasperation. '*I'll* give you a job if you can handle a video camera,' he said. '*Can* you handle a video camera?'

'Yes, sir, we did this course on . . .'

The inspector sighed again. 'It was a simple question and requires only a simple answer,' he said. '*Can* you handle a video camera?'

'Yes, sir.'

'Good.' The inspector reached into the back of the van and produced a video camera the size of a small aircraft carrier. 'We're using these as an experiment. What the top brass want is for us to produce training films. What I want to do is to use them to cover my lads' backs. Do you understand what I'm saying?'

'I'm not sure, sir.'

'Look over there.'

She turned her head in the direction he'd been pointing, and saw two uniformed constables carrying heavy-duty bolt cutters.

'You see what that idiot's done, don't you?' Metcalfe asked.

'He seems to have chained himself to the gate, sir.'

'Yes, he does, doesn't he? Those two officers are about to extricate him, and when they do, I want you to film it, so when the bastard claims later that we used excessive force, we can prove that we didn't. Understand?'

'Yes, sir.'

'Of course,' the inspector continued, 'if one of the officers is actually a little rougher than he meant to be . . .'

And he winked – he actually bloody winked.

'Yes, sir?'

The conspiratorial edge drained from the inspector's face.

'If such a situation does arise, then I urge you to take the greatest possible care not to erase that from the tape,' he said formally.

Then he tapped his nose twice with his index finger, in case Louisa was incapable of reading between the lines.

Archie Eccleston had chained himself to the fence in such a way that his back was against the wire, and so in order to talk to him face-to-face, the two officers had first to cut a swathe out of the wire next to the gate, and step through it.

Louisa followed them, and as she did so, she hoped they made a quick job of cutting the man free, because while the camera might *look* like an aircraft carrier, it *felt* as heavy as the Empire State Building.

Before even approaching Archie Eccleston, one of the constables
– his name was Jeff Sutton, Louisa remembered – turned to the
other four allotment holders who'd been the overnight guards.

'Top marks for trying, lads, but you must surely see that you're
on a hiding to nothing here.' He glanced down at his watch. 'It's
market day, so the Black Bull will already be open. Why don't
you go and drown your sorrows with a couple of pints of best
bitter?'

The four men exchanged looks.

'What about him?' Roy Moores said, pointing to Archie
Eccleston.

'I'll take care of him,' Sutton promised. 'Don't you worry about
that. I'll treat him better than I treat Patch, my old cocker spaniel.
Now go on, be off with you, before I feel obliged to take my little
truncheon out of its harness and give you all a tiny tap on the
noggin.'

It was not a threat that any of the men took seriously, but they
could see that he was right, and their battle had been all-but over
the moment the bulldozer turned up. So their choice, as they saw
it, was to stay and possibly get into trouble, or to sink a few beers
in the pub. It really wasn't much of a quandary, and after each of
them had given Archie Eccleston an encouraging tap on the shoulder,
they left.

The two constables moved over to the double gates, stood one
each side of Eccleston, and examined the chains which were binding
him to the gate posts.

'How many chains have you actually got wrapped around you?'
Jeff Sutton asked.

'Just the one,' Eccleston replied.

'It must be a bloody long chain,' the policeman said.

'It is.'

'It must be heavy, too. I imagine it's exhausting, carrying all
that extra weight.'

For a moment, it looked as if Eccleston might shrug, but he
was already physically and emotionally exhausted, so he contented
himself with saying, 'I'm managing.'

'What about them padlocks? They look right heavy duty, too.'

'They are.'

'And do you have the keys on you?'

'Do I look bloody daft?' Eccleston wondered. 'Because I'd have to be an idiot to have the keys on me, now wouldn't I?'

'Are you willing to tell us where the keys are?'

'Yes.' Eccleston said, and then fell silent again.

'So where are they?' Jeff Sutton asked, after perhaps half a minute had passed.

'They're at the bottom of the river.'

'If we can get this over with quickly, you can just bugger off,' Jeff Sutton said, 'but if you make things difficult, I'll have no choice but to arrest you for obstruction. And you wouldn't want that, would you?'

'As a matter of fact, that's exactly what I *do* want,' Eccleston said.

'What do you mean, lad?'

'I want you to arrest me. I want my day in court.'

Jeff Sutton cleared his throat. 'Very well, if that is what you wish, will you tell me your full name, sir,' he said.

'You already know my name,' Eccleston said. 'Or at least, you *should* do, because we've been playing on the same darts team for at least five years.'

'That doesn't matter, Arch . . . sir,' the constable said. 'If we're going to do this, it has to be done officially.'

'All right,' Eccleston said. 'Why don't you ask me again?'

'What's your name, sir?' the constable asked.

'None of your bloody business,' Eccleston told him. 'Bugger off!'

'You're just trying to make this as difficult for me as you possibly can, aren't you?' the constable asked.

The look of aggression drained away from Eccleston's face, and was replaced by something closely resembling guilt.

'I'm sorry, Jeff,' he said. 'I know I shouldn't take my anger out on you, but that allotment means a great deal to me. Ever since Patrick died . . .'

'I know, lad, I know,' Jeff Sutton said.

The padlocks *were* thick, but the bolt cutters were heavy duty and the two constables had the sort of beefy, rugby-playing strength which was required to use them to maximum advantage, so it was not long before the locks fell to the ground.

'Right then, let's get this chain off you,' Jeff Sutton said.

Eccleston had wrapped the chain tightly around him, and there were already long blue bruises forming on his forearm.

'Doesn't matter,' Eccleston said, noticing that the constables had seen them. 'Nothing really matters anymore.'

'Don't talk like that, Archie,' Sutton said. 'Look, you don't really want your day in court, do you?'

'I don't know,' Eccleston admitted. 'I thought I did, but now I think that all I really want is a good sleep.'

Sutton glanced around him. The other allotment holders were still arguing at the roadblock, and now they had been joined by reporters from the various Whitebridge and district newspapers, who were after what – in local terms – would probably turn out to be the story of the month.

'Look, they're all busy and I don't think anybody will notice if we run you home,' he said.

'I'm just so tired,' Archie Eccleston said, with the faintest of nods.

Louisa wondered whether she had videoed all she needed to, or if Inspector Metcalfe would require more. Working on the theory that it was better to be safe than sorry, she decided to keep on filming.

It was about twenty yards from the gate to Constable Sutton's car, and by the time the two policemen and allotment holder had covered half that distance, three things happened which combined together to completely derail the no-fuss ending to the incident that Sutton had been working towards.

The first of these was that another officer had opened the double gates to the allotment. The second was when the bulldozer driver, seeing that his way was clear and already (for obvious reasons) running behind schedule, did not wait for his foreman's instructions, but instead started up his machine and headed for the opening.

Archie Eccleston noticed these two things, and had a sudden thought.

'I've got to go back,' he said in a panic. 'I won't be a minute.'

Jeff Sutton would have been inclined to let him, but that was when the third thing happened.

This third thing in the unfortunate trio of events was the re-emergence of Inspector Metcalfe.

'Why isn't that man in handcuffs?' he demanded, pointing at

Archie Eccleston. 'He's already cost the council hundreds of pounds in delays and police overtime, and I want him arrested.'

'Sorry, Archie, but this is the way it has to be,' Sutton said, reaching for his cuffs with one hand and taking Eccleston's arm with the other.

'But I have to go back,' Eccleston said desperately, as he saw the bulldozer pass through the gates.

'I've been very fair with you, so don't you go making me look bad in front of my boss,' Sutton said, clamping one link of the handcuff on Eccleston's right wrist.

'Got to go,' Eccleston screamed. 'Got to go.'

And breaking free of Sutton's grip, he rushed back towards the gates.

If Louisa hadn't been looking through the viewfinder of the video camera, she might have realized what was happening a split second earlier, and avoided the collision, and if Eccleston hadn't been looking over his shoulder, he might have done the same.

As it was, Eccleston smashed into Louisa at full force, and they both went down.

For a moment or two, they lay in a confused heap – and then they quickly began to untangle from each other.

'Oh God, I'm so sorry,' Eccleston groaned. 'You're not really hurt, are you? Please tell me you're not really hurt.'

But by the time Louisa had found the breath to answer him, he'd already been dragged away by a very angry PC Sutton.

The landlord of the Drum and Monkey had grown used to hardened drinkers knocking on the door of the public bar in the hour or so before the official opening time, with the specific aim of begging him to break the rules – not to mention the law! – just this once.

'*If I could just come in and have a quick pint . . .*' was a line which often greeted him when he opened the door.

'*Sorry,*' he would invariably reply.

'*Of maybe just a half – with a whisky chaser . . .*'

'*Sorry.*'

'*Be reasonable, Harry, my throat feels as scratchy as the bottom of a parrot's cage.*'

'*Sorry.*'

The knocking this morning sounded slightly different to that of

the usual supplicants, for though there was always a desperation
behind the knocks of those early morning dipsomaniacs, there was
also an implicit awareness that if they knocked too loudly, they
might piss the landlord off, and the one in a million chance that
he might, for once, relent, would be gone.

The man hammering on the door now had no such scruples.
His knock proclaimed that he was the one who laid down the
rules, and people like the landlord had no other function in life
but to jump to it and serve him.

Well, we'll soon see about that, Harry Flynn thought, flinging
the door between the public bar and the street open.

But instead of there being one of the usual deadbeats – red-eyed,
blue-chinned, scuffed shoes – there was a man with ice blue eyes,
a well-harvested chin and shoes which almost dazzled. And to top
it all, he was wearing a bowler hat and carrying a briefcase.

'I'm Hereward Montague from Her Majesty's Department of
Trade and Commerce (Retail Section),' he said, holding out a small
leather wallet similar to the ones in which policeman kept their
warrant cards.

'Oh,' Harry said.

'Well, look at it,' Montague snapped. 'Examine it carefully.'

Harry Flynn did as he'd been told. Yes, the warrant confirmed,
this was Hereward Montague, and yes, he did appear to work for
Her Majesty's Department of Trade and Commerce.

'I'm here to do a random inspection,' Montague said.

'A random inspection?' the landlord repeated. 'Of what?'

'Of whatever I choose to inspect,' Montague said.

He took an unsignalled step forward, and in order to avoid a
collision, Harry Flynn was forced to retreat into the pub.

Montague looked around him. 'You and your wife live upstairs,
don't you?' he asked.

'Yes, we do,' Flynn told him.

But he had a strange feeling that Montague already knew the
answer.

'And is your wife in?'

'No, at this time of day she usually slips out to do a little
shopping.'

And Flynn got the distinct impression that Montague knew that,
too.

'You stay here,' Montague said. 'I won't be long.'

'I'll come with you and show you where . . .'

'You'll stay here.' Flynn said firmly.

The landlord heard the other man climb the stairs, and registered his footfalls as he inspected the living quarters. He was up there for ten minutes, and when he came down again, he inspected the lounge, the saloon bar and the toilets. When Montague returned to the public bar, he was looking grim.

'Well?' Harry Flynn asked anxiously.

'I've still got this bar to inspect,' Montague told him.

The inspector walked around the room, occasionally tapping the wall with his knuckles. Twice, he went to one of the corners and took some kind of instrument out of his pocket. The first time, the instrument beeped. The second time, it didn't.

The inspection finally over, Montague shook his head sadly from side to side.

'There's a lot needs to be done to bring this place up to standard,' he said. 'It's going to cost the brewery thousands. Still, the amount of money they're making, they won't even notice.'

'The brewery . . . the brewery doesn't own this pub,' the landlord spluttered.

'Oh, then who does?'

'Me. I bought it off them last year.'

'Well, they certainly must have seen you coming,' Montague said – and laughed. 'Talk about buying a leaking ship in the middle of the ocean!'

'I . . . I can't afford to spend thousands on repairs, not with the mortgage repayments and everything,' Flynn confessed.

A look of concern – which was both surprising and unexpected – came to Montague's face.

'My father ran his own pub,' he said. 'That's basically how I got into this line of work. And if there's one thing that makes me angry, it's the way everyone exploits the hard-working landlord.' He paused for a second, as if he were thinking. 'Look,' he continued, 'the changes I see as necessary will have to be made – there's no way round that – but I could draw up a schedule of rolling improvements, so you make a few improvements now and a few more when you can afford it.'

'Thank you,' Harry Flynn said.

'But I will need a token gesture to show good faith,' Montague said. He looked around him. 'Now what could it be?' he mused. 'I've got it – you could put a lamp bracket over that table in the corner.'

The table that he was pointing to had played a special part in the history of the Drum and Monkey, and, indeed, the history of serious crime in Whitebridge. It had been at that table that DCI Charlie Woodend had gathered his team together during some of his most important cases. And, once he had retired, it had been where DCI Paniatowski (Woodend's protégé) had worked with *her* team.

Regulars in the pub had developed a semi-proprietorial feeling for the table. Over the years, they had watched the detectives at work and then read about the arrests and trials in the newspapers, and it had begun to feel almost as if they had played a part themselves. And in a way, they *had* contributed, because though there was no reserved sign on the table, they made sure (by hint or innuendo – and when that failed by addressing the would-be encroachees in plain blunt Anglo-Saxon) that no one else used the table.

The landlord looked at the table. 'It doesn't seem particularly in the shadows,' he said.

'Well, it is,' Montague told him. 'You saw me measure it with my light meter, didn't you? And you must have heard it beep. That was because it detected a point seven five deficit.'

'So what do you want me to do, exactly?' Flynn asked.

'As I said, I want a wall light installed just above the table,' Montague told him.

'I'll get my usual electrician in,' the landlord said.

'This morning?' Montague asked.

Harry Flynn shook his head. 'He was in here last night, and he said he'll be away for a couple of days on a big job.'

'So you're talking about three days?'

'Yes, I suppose I am.'

'I'll need to inspect the work, and that can't wait for three days, because by then I'll be doing an inspection in Kent,' Montague said.

'Then I don't see . . .'

'So what we'll do is, we'll use my electrician, who always travels around with me.'

So that was what this had all been leading up to, Harry Flynn thought in disgust. All these stiff visiting cards, and talk of government regulations and light meters – all the sympathy because his own dad had run a pub – was leading to nothing more than a sordid little shakedown.

He could see now how it would pan out. The electrician would charge him much more than the work called for, and would split his haul with high-and-mighty Montague.

Flynn considered what his next move should be. As a first step, he could refuse to pay up. As a second, he could report Montague to the police and then, as his third – his coup de grace – he could take the Department of Trade and Commerce to court. But though he had friends in the force, Montague probably had some higher up the ladder. And a court action would be so lengthy and expensive that even if he won, he would have lost.

Far better, then, to bite on the bullet and give the corrupt bastard what he wanted.

'So how much will this cost?' he asked.

The question seemed to puzzle Montague. 'I've no idea,' he said. 'Pricing this kind of work does not come within my area of expertise.'

Oh please, please, don't be too greedy, Mr Montague, the landlord thought. Please ask for only a little more than I can afford.

'Couldn't you even make a rough estimate?' he asked.

'How much would you normally expect to pay?' Montague wondered.

'Fifteen quid?' the landlord said hopefully.

Montague smiled. 'Then give my man ten pounds – and a pint of bitter for the goodwill – and we'll call it dead,' he said.

He turned and walked towards the door.

'I'll get that schedule of repairs to you some time in the next month,' he said. 'I hope you'll agree with me that the light will be an improvement.'

Then he tipped his bowler hat in lieu of saying goodbye, and was gone.

Running the previous half hour through his mind, Harry Flynn found it impossible to pinpoint the moment at which Montague had changed. But changed he undoubtedly had – from a snarling tower of disapproval when he arrived to someone almost resembling a mate when he left.

The electrician turned up half an hour later. The landlord was surprised when not only was there no indication that he worked for the government on his overalls, but (quite the reverse) he had 'Harrison Electrical – the Expert Touch' embroidered over his top pocket.

'We're subcontractors,' he said, when he saw Flynn looking at it.

'Oh,' the landlord said, 'Mr Montague gave the impression that you were on his staff.'

The young man grinned. 'He does that. Makes him feel a bit more important than he is. There's no harm in it.'

When he'd finished off the job, he accepted the ten pounds that Flynn offered, but insisted on paying for his own drink.

'I was very impressed with that young man,' Harry Flynn told his first customer of the day, ten minutes later. 'Very impressed indeed.'

There were two men sitting in the van parked just up the road from the Drum and Monkey. One was wearing overalls with the words 'Harrison Electrical – the Expert Touch' embroidered over his top pocket. The other was dressed in baggy trousers and a shapeless pullover, and though neither of the articles had the word 'geek' printed on them, they might as well have had.

It was the geek who was playing with all the dials and buttons on the control panel.

'Here you are,' he said. 'Playback.'

'*We're subcontractors.*'

'*Oh, Mr Montague gave the impression that you were on his staff.*'

'*He does that. Makes him feel a bit more important than he is. There's no harm in it.*'

'Listen to that quality,' the geek said. 'I'm a genius.'

'You don't think it's anything to do with the way it was installed?' asked the other man.

'That may have helped,' the geek said, only a little reluctantly. 'So what's the pub like?'

'Not bad at all. The landlord's a good bloke, and given that it is *northern* beer, it's really quite palatable.'

'So do you think you might be going again?' the geek asked.

'Nah!' the other man said.

'Why not?'

'Well, the pub's bugged, isn't it?'

'So it is,' the geek agreed.

THREE

L ouisa Paniatowski was in what was officially known as the 'female officers' cloakroom', but was generally called the 'women's bogs'. Back in the day, when her mother had joined the force, it had been quite openly referred to as the 'sluts' room' or – even more disgustingly – the 'slits' room'. It would be foolish to claim that all such prejudice had been swept away in the years which followed, but now the male officers who had no class and shit for brains were only likely to use such pejorative terms when in the company of their caveman friends.

Louisa wasn't speculating about changing gender definitions in the modern police force – she was examining her face in the mirror. Her reflection gave her little cause for rejoicing. True, her nose was not broken, but it had swollen somewhat, as if in sympathy with her upper lip, while her right eye had opted for the giant panda look.

And it wasn't just her face which ached. Several of her ribs were bruised, too, and kept issuing a periodic reminder that they didn't appreciate being smashed into.

But what was worse than any physical pain was the damage to her pride.

She played back the scene at the allotments in her mind, inserting a script more to her liking.

She is standing there with the video camera on her hand, when she sees Archie Eccleston charging in her direction. She carefully places the camera at a safe distance, and then places herself in Archie's path. He sees her, but he is not worried, because she is a slimly-built five foot seven police cadet, whereas he is a solid man topping six feet – and he knows he barely needs to break step to fling her aside.

What he doesn't know is that Louisa has been accompanying her mother to her judo classes for the last three years, so that instead of sweeping her out of the way, as he expected to, he finds himself flying through the air and landing on his back with a sickening thud. And it is while he is struggling to regain his breath that he realizes that the little girl who is handcuffing him is the one who defeated him.

That's how it should have gone.

How it *did* go is as follows; she is looking down the viewfinder when Eccleston makes his break, and she continues to look down it – in fascinated horror – for the two or three seconds it takes for him to reach her.

And she stands there – and watches him do it!

That's right, she just stands there!

And he – looking the other way as he attempts to make his escape – doesn't see her.

So instead of being the heroine, she's a laughing stock – the girl who was just too bloody dumb to get out of the way.

Worse yet, she doesn't know what's happened to the camera Inspector Metcalfe gave her – and she's too scared to ask anybody about it.

She wonders if she'll ever live this down. She wishes she knew a great deal more about applying make-up.

But she can't stay skulking in the bogs for the rest of her shift, because if she does that she won't be just despised by others, she'll be despised by herself.

By the time she'd stepped into the corridor, she'd decided to go straight to the canteen, for the simple reason that that would ensure maximum exposure – and the sooner all the gawping at her face was over, the better – but she hadn't gone more than a few yards when she heard a voice she recognized as belonging to another cadet call out, 'Uncle Tom wants to see you!'

She stopped and turned around.

The cadet didn't look shocked, disturbed or merely amused when he saw her face, so he must have been practicing looking bland.

Louisa appreciated the effort.

'What does Uncle Tom want with me?' she asked.

'Don't know,' the other cadet told her. 'He just said that he'd appreciate it if you could slip down and see him when you have the time.'

Sergeant Thomas White was in charge of the custody suite – that section of Whitebridge Police HQ where prisoners were booked in, examined, questioned, and temporarily incarcerated. One of the custody sergeant's main tasks was to be the 'prisoner's friend', which meant that it was his duty to see that all their rights were strictly enforced, and to protect them from any abuse. It was *not* part of his job to give his detainees encouraging smiles and Polo mints, but it was in White's nature to be kind, and hence it was almost inevitable that he would become known as Uncle Tom, and that the custody suite should be referred to as Uncle Tom's cabin.

White had known Louisa as a small child, first when she had been brought into the station by her father, Bob Rutter, and later when she had accompanied her adopted mother, Monika Paniatowski. Until a few months earlier, he would have given her a bear hug, but now that she was in the force herself, he contented himself with a nod.

'By God, your face is a right mess, Louisa,' he said, grinning. 'What have you been doing? Did you fall asleep on Aintree racecourse just before the Grand National started – or have you been in the ring for half a dozen rounds with Mohammed Ali?'

'I see you've lost none of your tact, Sergeant White,' Louisa replied, but she was smiling (if a little lopsidedly), because she knew that by treating it as a joke, White was hoping to encourage her not to take it too seriously herself.

'Now I'm not putting any pressure on you,' White said, his voice a little heavier, his expression semi-serious, 'and it will be perfectly all right with me if you say you don't want to do it . . .'

'Oh, for God's sake, Uncle Tom, carry on at that speed and I'll be an old woman by the time I get out of here,' Louisa said.

White chuckled.

'You sounded exactly like your mother just then,' he said.

They both shivered, as if a sudden cold cloud had descended on them out of nowhere and was chilling them to the bone.

It was Louisa who recovered first. 'What is it you want me to do, sergeant?' she asked.

'It's not me, it's Archie Eccleston,' the sergeant said. 'He seems quite desperate to talk to you, but having seen for myself what he's done to you, I'm not so sure you'll be willing to talk to him – and I wouldn't blame you if you said no.'

'Why do you think he wants to see me?' Louisa asks.

'I imagine he wants to apologise for turning you into the bride of Frankenstein,' White said.

'You can go off people, you know,' Louisa warned him. She thought about it for a moment. 'Well, if that is what he wants to do, it would be ungracious not to give him the opportunity,' she said.

'Can we get this straight before we go any further,' Sergeant White said, across the interview table. 'You requested this meeting with Police Cadet Rutter, not the other way around. Is that correct?'

'Yes,' Archie Eccleston said.

He was probably around forty-odd, Louisa estimated. From his build he was likely an ex-rugby player, but then half the men in Whitebridge either played or had played rugby.

What else?

His hands, which he'd laid flat on the table, bore some signs of old scarring, but no evidence of recent damage, which probably meant that he'd started out doing some sort of manual labour, but had since risen in the world.

Hang on, girl, Louisa told herself, that's a bit Sherlock Holmesie isn't it?

But though she might be wrong about that, one thing she was sure the hands told her was that Archie Eccleston had not been a happy man for some time, because his nails were bitten down to the quick.

'I would also like to establish the fact that though you have been informed you are entitled to have a lawyer present, you do not wish to take advantage of that possibility. Is that correct?'

'Yes,' Archie Eccleston replied.

'Then say your piece,' White invited.

'I'm not a violent man, Miss Rutter,' Eccleston said. 'I've never hit a woman. In fact, towards the end my wife was hitting me, and I refused to defend myself.' He laughed, bitterly. 'And that, of course, only made her worse.'

'I think you really do need to get to the point,' White said – though not harshly.

'I didn't see you, Miss Rutter,' Eccleston said. 'I know you probably find that hard to believe, so I want to explain *why* I didn't see you.'

'Go ahead,' Louisa said.

Eccleston took a deep breath. 'I didn't see you because the only thing I *could* see was something very precious to me that I'd left in my shed on the allotment.' He stifled a sob. 'Something that is now probably gone forever.'

Louisa was halfway between headquarters and the allotments when the heavens opened up.

What the clouds released was not so much rain as hail, and hailstones battered down on the Cortina's roof like a thousand little toffee hammers.

Louisa slowed down immediately. It paid to be cautious, she reminded herself. And anyway, the car wasn't hers, and she really didn't fancy the idea of having to explain to her mother, once she came out of the coma, that her beloved daughter – with only six weeks' driving experience to her name – had wrapped the family Cortina around a lamppost.

She was starting to preface so many of her thoughts with that reference to her mother, she realized.

When Mum comes out of her coma, we need to talk about taking on a part-time cleaner, because the twins are becoming a real handful, and it's unreasonable to expect Mrs Holcolme to look after them and manage all the other domestic arrangements.

When Mum comes out of the coma, we'll have to decide where we're taking the boys for their first real holiday.

When Mum comes out of the coma . . .

She had to think like that, she accepted, because the idea of never sitting down with her wonderful mother again was almost unbearable.

Besides, there were the boys to consider. If her mother died – or worse, if they decided there was no point in keeping her alive, and switched the machines off – then she, little Louisa, would

have to become the twins' guardian, and as much as she loved
them, she was too young to be dragged down by that sort of
responsibility.

Far too young!

She turned onto Old Mill Road. The hail seemed to have gone
away, but the rain was no less fierce (she could tell that by the
height it bounced back up to once it had hit the puddles) and her
Cortina seemed to be the only vehicle around which was actually
moving.

She drew level with the southern end of the allotments. The
mesh-link fence was still in place here, but it hung languid and
lost now other parts of it had been removed.

The main gates (or, more accurately, the spot where the main
gates had been) lay straight ahead. When she'd been rushed away
from the allotments on a stretcher – yes, the inspector had insisted
on it, even though she'd said quite clearly and distinctly that she
was fine – there'd still been several police cars around, and dozens
of people had been pressed against the roadblock. Now, all the
people had gone, and a single patrol car remained.

Two police officers stood in close proximity to the car. They
were dressed in waterproof oilskins, but from the expressions on
their faces it seemed more than likely that a few adventurous
raindrops had managed to circumvent the oilskins, and were now
making their way down the backs of the policemen's necks.

As she parked, one of the policemen walked over to the Cortina
and tapped on the window.

Louisa wound the window down, and cold raindrops spattered
against her cheek.

The officer had obviously been about to ask her what she was
doing there, then he noticed what uniform she was wearing, and
said, 'I hope you're here to tell us we're no longer needed, so we
can bugger off back to headquarters.'

'I'd like to tell you that,' Louisa said, 'but I'm afraid I'm not
here to see you at all.'

'Then why the bloody hell *are* you here?'

'I need to get something from the allotments,' Louisa said.

The policeman gave her the sort of dour look that can only be
produced after forty years' exposure to Lancashire damp.

'What allotments?' he wondered, indicating with his thumb.

Louisa looked, and saw what he meant. The bulldozer had gone on the rampage through the site, and many of the neat little sheds had already gone.

A lorry emerged, loaded down with soil.

'Breaks your heart, doesn't it?' the constable said.

'What?' Louisa asked.

'These fellers with allotments spend years getting their topsoil right. They fertilize it religiously. They only grow things they know will help it improve. For some of them, the perfect soil is like the Holy Grail. And then what happens? Some demolition contractor comes along, and thinks to himself that he knows somebody who'll pay top whack for good topsoil. It's almost like he can't wait for the body to go cold before he starts tearing out the guts. It's enough to turn a normal decent feller into a bomb-throwing revolutionary.'

'Could you step back a bit, so I can get out?' Louisa asked.

'You're never going to go on that site, are you?' the constable asked.

'I might as well, now I'm here,' Louisa said, realising what a stupid idea it must sound to him – what a stupid idea it sounded to her!

'Listen, lass, apart from the fact that it's bloody dangerous on a demolition site – especially in the rain – you'll just be wasting your time. After the battering the site's got in the last couple of hours, whatever you're looking for will be long gone.'

He was probably right, Louisa thought. After the bulldozers, and the diggers and the lorries, how likely was it that something as fragile as a coffee mug would have survived?

But she had seen the pain on Archie Eccleston's face. And if you didn't have faith in miracles – didn't believe that you could find the mug in all that mayhem, for example, or believe that your mum could come out of her coma – then where were you?

The constable moved clear, and Louisa climbed out of the car.

'Are you sure about this, lass?' the constable asked worriedly.

'I am,' Louisa confirmed.

'Then for God's sake be careful in there.'

Louisa crossed the pavement, walked around the tubular rods which had once formed part of the gates, and stepped onto what had been a path between the allotments.

She looked around her at the desolation.

This is what the end of the world will look like, she thought – and shuddered.

Strewn around or trodden into the mud were calendars, seed packets, plant pots, biscuit tins and old cushions. Pieces of trelliswork lay on the ground like bits of a skeleton from another life. A whimsical wishing well was entangled with a miniature windmill, which itself had become attached to the sleeve of a small, unambitious scarecrow.

On either side of the path were large holes, from where the good topsoil had been gouged.

'*My allotment's on the left,*' Archie Eccleston had told her. '*The sixth one up from the gate.*'

Louisa looked in that direction. There were no huts or sheds left standing, so the chances were that his allotment had already suffered the full assault of the barbarian horde, but even if it had, there was still a chance that the mug – like the cushion and the biscuit tin – had survived.

Always do a risk assessment before you put yourself in any kind of situation, they'd told her during training – so what was the risk here?

Well, visibility was poor, and the diggers and lorries were both working against the clock and unaware there was anyone else on the site, so there was certainly a chance they'd run her down without even realising it.

On the other hand, there wasn't that much actual movement – the digger dug, the lorry waited to be loaded – and they'd already finished with the area she was interested in.

And honestly, having come this far – having already got her shoes caked in mud and her stockings and her skirt spattered with it – it seemed a real pity to turn back now.

She made her way carefully up the path. Some of the holes already had water in the bottom of them, and if it carried on raining like this, it wouldn't be that long until they were full.

She counted off the holes, and all the time, her shoes were getting heavier and heavier, as more mud adhered to them, so that by the time she reached the fourth hole, it felt as if she were wearing heavy clay boots.

She finally reached the sixth hole. This was where Archie

Eccleston had sought solace after his son's death and as his marriage had collapsed. It was here that he had drunk from the mug which had announced him as the world's best dad.

The hole which until so recently had been an allotment was about half the size of a small public swimming pool. It was roughly rectangular in shape, but the edges were irregular and the walls were steeply sloped rather than vertical.

Or to put it another way, Louisa thought, as an image of her little brothers came into her mind, it looked like Thomas' ice cream bowl, rather than James', because while James would attack his treat in a slow, organized and orderly way, Thomas would greedily scoop out the middle, and then, leaving half the ice cream still sticking to the sides, start to agitate for some new treat.

She caught sight of something yellow sticking out of the mud at the lip of the hole.

Could it be a mug?

She really thought it might be.

She bent over to take a closer look, and could see the letters 'ST DA'.

The world's best dad?

It had to be.

See, miracles did happen!

But now the trick was to extract the mug from the mud without damaging it. It might be a slow process, but it would be worth it in the end.

She heard the sound of a lorry starting up, and turned to see exactly where it was.

It must have been the shifting of her weight that upset the balance – that knocked off kilter the delicate equilibrium she had established with the earth.

But she didn't think that.

She didn't *think* anything.

She simply registered in a blind panic that she was sliding down the slope to the bottom of the pit.

She hit the water not so much with a splash as with a thud.

Because it wasn't really water at all.

It was more like a mud stew.

A mud stew which she couldn't swim in!

A mud stew which was dragging her down!

If it wasn't too deep, she was all right, she told herself.

If it wasn't too deep, she could stay here for days, if she had to.

But if it was too deep, she would drown in a sea of mud.

She had reached the bottom, and her hand came into contact with something hard – or at least, harder than this bloody mud.

She ran her hands along it, assessing its usefulness in assisting her escape. And then she realized what it was, and knew it would be no bloody good at all.

She struggled to her knees and gasped with joy as she realized that her head and upper torso were clear of the mud.

And then she heard the man's voice.

'Can you hear me?' he asked.

'Yes,' she said.

'And are you all right?'

'Of course I'm not all right,' she screamed. 'I'm practically up to my neck in shit.'

'No, I mean, are you hurt?'

'I don't think so.'

'So if I threw you the end of a rope, do you think you could wrap it round yourself?'

'Yes.'

The man threw down the rope.

'Make sure the knot's tight,' he said.

He waited while she fastened it.

'Is that secure?' he asked.

'Yes.'

'Are you sure?'

'I was the top Girl Guide of my year,' Louisa said – and then blushed, because she didn't like to brag.

'Well, stay there,' the man said. 'I'll start hauling you up in a minute.'

Stay there, she repeated to herself. What the bloody hell else am I going to do? But wisely, she did not articulate the thought.

When the man had been gone for perhaps a minute, there was the sound of an engine starting, then she felt a tug at her waist, and she was airborne.

When she reached the lip of the hole, the driver stopped the lorry, and came back to pull her free manually.

'Thank you for getting me out of there,' Louisa said. 'I'm sorry I wasn't very gracious earlier.'

'That's all right,' the driver said. 'But it's lucky I came along when I did and saw you fall into the hole, isn't it?'

On the other hand, it could be argued that if you hadn't distracted me, I'd never have fallen into the hole in the first place, Louisa thought.

'Yes, that was lucky,' she agreed.

She looked down, and saw the mug was still there.

'Do you see that mug?' she asked, pointing to it.

'Yes,' the lorry driver replied, mystified.

'Hold onto the rope, I'm going to get it out.'

'You're going to do what!'

Louisa knelt down next to the mug. If she simply pulled, she would probably break it, she thought, so she would have to do a little digging first. She scraped at the mud with her fingers, and then wiped her hands off on her filthy uniform.

'You're crazy. You do know that, don't you?' the lorry driver said.

A lot of people would have said that, she thought, especially if they knew what she had discovered at the bottom of the pit – because it was undoubtedly true that her second discovery of the day was much more important and significant than the mug, which had been the first.

But it wouldn't be more important or significant to Archie Eccleston.

She eased the mug free of the morass. It would need to be washed carefully, but otherwise it was perfect.

She climbed slowly to her feet. She'd have to do something about this mud all over her, she thought, because if it dried she'd be as stiff as the statues in the Corporation Park.

'Now, young lady – and I want no arguing about this – we're going to take you to the nearest hospital for a check-up,' the lorry driver said.

'Maybe later,' Louisa replied, and was surprised to hear how much authority there seemed to be in her voice. 'But what happens first is that I stand guard over this hole while you inform the officers out on the street that I've just found a body.'

FOUR

The first thing that Colin Beresford noted when he arrived at the former allotments on Old Mill Road was not the square white tent which had been erected over the area in which the body had been discovered, nor the fact that Dr Shastri's Land Rover was already there. No, the thing that made that initial impression was that he was nearly knocked over by a bloody large tipper truck which was picking up speed even before it left the site.

The rain was coming down fairly heavily, but not *so* heavily as to obscure the other end of the allotments, where there were at least half a dozen trucks waiting to be loaded by the mechanical diggers.

Well, we'll soon put a stop to that, he told himself.

He spotted a man in a yellow safety helmet and yellow jerkin who was frantically signalling with his hands, like a young canary learning to fly. That'd be the feller he needed to speak to.

He set off across the field, which – courtesy of the rain and the heavy plant – had become a quagmire. Even stepping carefully, he was aware he was probably ruining his new leather shoes, and on top of that, the cigarette he lit up was soon soaking wet – which somehow took the pleasure out of it.

When Beresford drew level with the fledgling canary, he tapped him on the shoulder. Closer to, he could see that there was, in fact, very little birdlike about him, since canaries are rarely over fifty, overweight, or unshaven.

'Yes?' he said, in what came close to being the least friendly tone that Beresford had ever heard.

'Are you in charge?' Beresford shouted, over the sound of a lorry which was just roaring past them.

'Yes. I'm Jed Higgins. And who the hell are you?'

'Detective Chief Inspector Beresford.'

'Really? You look too young for that. I'd have said you were only a sergeant.'

'You're going to have to close this down,' Beresford said, gesturing with his arms.

'I'm what?'

'You're going to have to close this down. I can't have you operating this close to a crime scene.'

'Oh, you can't you, can't you? Well, let me tell you, sonny, the crime scene is over there, we're over here, and since time is money, you're going to need a court order to close me down.'

'Be reasonable,' Beresford pleaded. 'By the time I got a court order, you could have destroyed valuable evidence.'

'Tough,' Higgins said. 'And a word of advice, sonny – don't think you can get round it by bringing in the big guns on this, because you'll lose. Your chief constable and me are brethren, if you know what that means.'

'Well, if you've got Mr Pickering on your side . . .' Beresford said dejectedly.

'I have.'

'Then there's nothing I can do to stop you once your vehicles have passed the roadworthy test.'

He turned, and began walking towards the tent.

'Just a minute,' Higgins called after him.

'Yes?'

'What's a roadworthy test, when it's at home?'

'It's what it sounds like. I bring the police mechanics down here, they do a fifty point test on all your vehicles, and if they pass, they stay on the road.'

'You can't do that.'

'Yes, I can. I'm empowered by the Road Traffic Act. That particular bit of legislation has been in force ever since Crane v. Meadows. And once it's underway, even Mr Pickering can't stop it.'

'All right, I'll close it down,' Higgins said. 'But I think you'll find that crossing me has been a big mistake.'

'That sounds suspiciously like a threat,' Beresford said.

'You must take it as you like.'

'We'll let it pass this time,' Beresford said. He leant forward,

so their faces were almost touching. 'But if you ever threaten me
again,' he continued, 'I'll beat the crap out of you – and to hell
with the consequences.'

It was quite a large tent, easily big enough to accommodate
two paramedics, three technicians, Dr Shastri, Beresford and two
uniformed constables. What made it feel crowded was not the
number of people but the bloody big hole in the middle of it,
which Louisa Paniatowski had used for mud diving practice.

'My mum was as chuffed as little apples when I told her what
my new job was,' one of the paramedics was telling Beresford.
'It'd be nice clean work, she said, 'not like working in a factory
or a building site. A nice clean job! Look at me!'

Beresford grinned. 'You're more like a mud pie than anything
else,' he admitted.

It must have been a hell of a job, setting up the winch over the
hole that the JCB had gouged out of the earth, then pumping out
as much of the mud and water as they could, he thought. And even
then, the real work had only just begun, because two of the paramedics had been winched down with a stretcher, and had had to
manoeuvre the body onto it. Now, the stretcher was being winched
out of the hole at the speed of a snail reaching the end of a mara-
thon – and even that didn't seem to be suiting some people.

'Slow it down,' Dr Shastri kept saying. 'Slow it down! Don't
you realize my patient gets travel sick?'

There was an appreciative chuckle, because everyone knew and
liked Dr Shastri.

Beresford's own attitude to the doctor was confused. He'd lost
his virginity at the comparatively late age of thirty, and since then
getting women into bed had been his main hobby/obsession. He
didn't keep count of his conquests, of course – that would have
been juvenile – but he believed it was somewhere around 173, and
he should, by rights, have been doing his best to make Shastri his
174th. Yet if hell froze over and – as a consequence – this undoubtedly beautiful woman offered herself to him on a plate, he would
turn her down.

He didn't know why – he just knew he would.

The stretcher reached the lip of the hole, and the technicians
swung it clear, uncoupled it, and laid it gently on the ground.

Shastri squatted down beside the body. She did not invite anyone else to join her, so no one else did.

'I would say he was about five feet ten inches tall,' she said, 'and from the fragments of clothing remaining, I would say he was wearing a suit when he died. It is hard to estimate his age, because his face, as you can see for yourselves, is as much a quagmire as the field outside this tent.'

'That couldn't have been caused by the bucket of the mechanical digger, could it?' Beresford said.

Shastri shook her head. 'I would consider that unlikely for several reasons.'

'And they are . . .?'

'Firstly, even on a long dead body, I could tell if the wounds were new. Secondly, the bucket would have done much more damage than we see here – it could well have decapitated him. And thirdly, I am convinced that the murderer did it deliberately, so that even if the cadaver was found, it could not be identified.'

'Isn't "convinced" a bit too strong a word to use at this stage of the investigation?' Beresford wondered.

'No, it is not,' Shastri replied, with a hint of rebuke in her voice. 'As a poor Indian doctor working with you clever white people, I must choose my words very carefully – and "convinced" is precisely the right word to express my degree of certainty.'

'I don't see how—' Beresford began.

'Of course you don't,' Shastri interrupted. 'But if you come and join me, you soon will.'

Beresford squatted down beside her.

'Notice the hands,' Shastri said.

'What about them?'

'Don't the fingers seem unnaturally short to you?'

'Now you mention it, they do seem short – and I can't see the nails,' Beresford said. 'Oh Jesus!'

'Yes?'

'The killer cut off all his fingertips.'

'He did indeed.'

Kate Meadows' Triumph Spitfire and Jack Crane's Vauxhall Chevette were parked on Old Mill Road, next to Beresford's Austin Allegro. It had stopped raining, but the air had a damp freshness about it totally unsuitable for a good smoke – which was why Crane had retreated to inside his car.

Meadows didn't smoke. She didn't drink, either, and she never touched the processed food which the rest of the team wolfed down during an investigation. She had only one vice (if vice it was), and that was a taste for evenings of sado-masochism with complete strangers.

Beresford emerged from the tent and walked towards them.

He waited until Crane had climbed out of his car, then said, 'It's a man, and he's dead.'

Meadows grinned. 'You seem in a good mood, sir.'

'Oh, I am,' Beresford agreed. 'After all, what better way to start the day than getting your new shoes caked in mud, and being handed a case which would have had Miss Marple reaching for the smelling salts? Now, can either of you tell me what the first thing they always drill into you during your training is?'

Meadows glanced at Crane, and that glance said, I'm the sergeant here, which puts you at the bottom of the totem pole, young Jack, so *you* answer his bloody stupid question.

'Well?' Beresford demanded.

'The first forty-eight hours of an inquiry are the most important,' Crane said dutifully.

'The first forty-eight hours of an inquiry are the most important,' Beresford repeated. 'Now that is a shame, because the first forty-eight hours of *this* inquiry passed by unnoticed three years ago. Did I say three years ago? Maybe it was five. Or ten! We won't know until the doc's played tickle and tell with her little scalpel. So what can we do while we're waiting?'

'I suppose we could get a list of allotment holders and start questioning them,' Crane said, 'but I'm not sure that's such a good idea.'

'Why?'

'Because the first thing *you* taught me in training was never to interview anybody who could turn out to be an important witness without collecting as much information as you can.'

'Correct,' Beresford said. 'And since what we actually know at the moment is nothing, we could be doing a lot of damage without even realising it. So we're stymied, and I'm open to suggestions for filling up our time.'

'We could always go and talk it over with the boss,' Crane suggested.

And the moment the words were out of his mouth, he found himself wishing he could be instantly transported to somewhere more comfortable – like the middle of Death Valley, for instance.

To suggest they talk it over with Monika was fine. Ever since she'd been discovered in a coma, they'd been going to her hospital room to discuss their cases. They didn't know if it did any good – whether the words which passed over her bed stimulated her brain or merely sounded to her like a jumble of disconnected noises – but they had been assured by her doctor that it couldn't do any harm, and that was good enough for them.

So suggesting they talk it over with Monika hadn't been a mistake – the mistake had been in calling her the boss.

It simply wasn't fair to Colin Beresford, because *he* was the boss now. Of course, that might only be temporary – and all of them, Colin Beresford most of all, hoped it was – but as long as Beresford was in charge, he had to be acknowledged as such.

'I'm sorry, sir, I didn't mean to—' Crane began.

But the other man had already raised his hand to indicate he wanted to hear no more.

There was an awkward silence that probably only lasted for ten seconds – but felt long enough to have viewed a biblical epic in – then Beresford said, 'Good idea – let's go and talk it over with the boss.'

Forsyth watched Beresford's red Allegro pull away from the curb.

'Even at this stage, I had been hoping that your friend Judd's mistake would pass unnoticed,' Forsyth said.

'He's not my friend,' Downes countered.

'Isn't he?'

'No. He's just someone who screwed up when I happened to be working in the same general area of the operation.'

Forsyth laughed. 'Ah, so now he screwed up, did he? Not an hour ago, you sounded as if you were prepared to defend his reputation – the actions he took – right up to the hilt.'

Yes, but an hour ago, you hadn't started tarring me with the same brush, Downes thought – an hour ago, I didn't think there was any chance of *his* mistake dragging *me* down.

'What do we do now?' he asked, hoping to provide a distraction.

'Now, we follow Colin Beresford and his merry band of investigators,' Forsyth said.

'Then we'd better get started, because we've already lost visual contact,' Downes said.

Forsyth laughed again, and opened the glove compartment. Within lay a bank of screens and electronic components, the like of which had never graced a Volkswagen Beetle before.

'Gifts from our cousins across the Atlantic,' Forsyth explained. 'I had a transmitter planted in Colin's car earlier in the day, and now I can find him if he is anywhere within twenty-five miles from here.' He closed the glove compartment, and the car was once again a very ordinary Beetle. 'Besides,' he continued, 'I have no need to track them at the moment, because I know exactly where they'll be going.'

Sometimes, Forsyth's arrogance was enough to tip even a discreet man like himself over the edge, Downes thought, as he heard himself say, 'You know where they'll be going?'

'Yes,' Forsyth agreed, 'I do.'

'But how *could* you know? How could you *possibly* know?'

'Oh, that's a very easy question to answer,' Forsyth said mildly. 'I know because I'm extremely good at my job.'

FIVE

Ward Sister Diana Sowerbury studied the two men and one woman who were striding rapidly down the corridor towards the nurses' desk in the ICU.

One of the males was in his mid-thirties. He moved like a man who took the admiration of women as a right, but unlike many men who fancied themselves in that way, there were some grounds for his confidence. True, he was not exactly handsome, but his features were pleasant enough. And his body more than compensated for any facial failings. It wasn't just that it was firm and well proportioned, it exuded a kind of hardness that some women

– mentioning no names! – find irresistible, Sister Sowerbury concluded – and almost giggled.

The other man was a little taller, much slimmer, and ten or twelve years younger. He was almost certainly a lover, rather than a fighter, and if Diana had been a fanciful woman – which she most emphatically was not – she might say that he looked like a poet.

But it was the woman who was the most interesting member of the trio. If all three of them were police officers – and Diana Sowerbury was almost certain that they were – then this woman would only just reach the minimum height requirement. Nor did she have the sort of body which might compensate for this lack of stature. No broad shoulders here – instead she looked as delicate as a china doll.

If she was one of my nurses, the ward sister thought, I'd be spending half my time protecting her from the others, because while all nurses were unquestionably angels in disguise, some of them could be vicious little bitches as well.

Up until this point, her face had been a blank (never put your nurses at an advantage by letting them guess what you're thinking!) but when the three visitors came to a halt, three feet away from her, she adopted a sympathetic expression, and said, 'I'm sorry, but visiting hours are between six and eight.'

'The ward sister usually lets us come and visit any time we're free,' said the hard man.

She might well have done, Diana Sowerbury thought, but you don't establish your own reputation by letting things carry on just like they always have.

'I'm sorry, Chief Inspector,' she said, with some regret. She paused. 'It is *Chief Inspector*, isn't it?'

Beresford avoided looking at Meadows, who he was pretty certain would be mouthing the words '*acting* chief inspector', and said. 'Yes, that's right. My name's Colin Beresford.'

'Colin Beresford,' Diana Sowerbury said – rolling his name around her mouth as if it were a luscious exotic fruit she were about to crunch, and at the same time resolving to look him up in the telephone directory. 'Well, Chief Inspector Beresford, whatever things used to be like here, I'm the ward sister now, and I'm afraid I've had to make a few changes in the interest of my patients' welfare. And one of those changes is that we adhere strictly to the stated visiting hours.'

'Why?' asked the china doll.

Why? Diana Sowerbury repeated to herself.

Why?

Nobody ever asked her that.

You didn't question a ward sister – especially *this* ward sister. It simply wasn't done!

'Well, is there a reason?' the china doll persisted.

'As I've already intimated, we have to consider the other patients, detective constable,' the ward sister said. 'We don't want to disturb them.'

'It's detective *sergeant*, not detective *constable*,' the china doll told her firmly. 'Detective Sergeant Kate Meadows – if you'd like to look *me* up in the phone book.'

And as she spoke, she looked first at Diana Sowerbury, and then at Colin Beresford.

It was almost as if there was a bit of mind reading going on here, the ward sister thought, uncomfortably.

'As I said,' she ploughed on, 'the last thing we want to do is disturb the other patients and—'

'Isn't the boss in a private room?' Meadows interrupted her.

'Well, yes,' Diana Sowerbury confessed.

'Then we won't be disturbing any of the other patients, will we?' Meadows asked.

It occurred to the ward sister that logically she hadn't got a leg to stand on, and that to invoke the rules simply as rules would make her look both petty and insignificant. But she was buggered if she'd give too much ground to Detective Sergeant China Doll.

'I can allow two of you in at a time – but no more,' she said, glossing over the fact that, until a minute earlier, she was allowing *none* at a time. 'So perhaps you, sergeant, might like to go down to the cafeteria, while the other two—'

'Why only two of us at a time?' Meadows demanded.

The ward sister sighed, as if to show exasperation at the laywoman's ignorance of medical matters.

'We don't want to tire our patient out, now do we?' she asked, saying the words slowly and distinctly, so that even a complete moron like Meadows would understand.

'*Our patient* is in a coma,' Meadows pointed out. 'It wouldn't matter to her if the GUS (Footwear) world famous brass band was marching around her room, playing a selection of tunes from the works of Rogers and Hammerstein.'

'Some coma patients are well aware of what is going on around them, and she might be one of those,' the ward sister responded.

'In that case, we'll save unnecessary expense by ringing Kettering and cancelling the GUS band,' Meadows said. 'That'll mean it will be down to the three of us.'

Diana Sowerbury was suddenly aware that all activity in the unit had stopped. She'd spent the morning making her mark – by which she meant whipping up her nurses into a state of terror, so that they had begun walking on eggshells for fear of causing her even the mildest displeasure. Yet these same nurses were not now gliding hither and thither, proving what good workers they could be – these same nurses were frozen to the spot, and watching her like hawks.

She shouldn't back down.

She *couldn't* back down now.

And yet—

And yet, though she didn't want to admit it, the china doll – the little waif who she had so recently imagined would need protection – unquestionably scared the hell out of her.

'I—' she began.

'I'm spitting feathers, and if I don't get a cup of industrial strength tea down my throat soon, I swear I'll turn to powder where I'm standing,' Colin Beresford said, out of the blue. 'My best plan is to head for the cafeteria. Would you care to join me, sister?'

Diana Sowerbury hesitated for a second, and then said, 'Yes, that's a good idea. You can brief me on how your work is likely to impact on my work here in the ICU.'

I wouldn't have thought she was his type, Meadows reflected, but that's only because I'd forgotten that every type is his type.

'Come on, Jack,' she said. 'Let's see how the boss is getting on.'

'How are you, boss?' Meadows asked awkwardly. 'It's me, Kate, and I've brought Jack with me.'

She looked down at the figure lying in the bed. Paniatowski had always been quite pale (which was hardly surprising given that she lived in Lancashire, where the only sure-fire way to get colour in your cheeks was to expose yourself to the harsh winds blowing off the moors!) but the chalky pallor she had acquired since the attack was enough to send shivers of apprehension running down anybody's spine.

And the tubes – the bloody tubes running in and out of her as if she were some mad scientist's experiment, rather than a person.

'Colin would have been here, but there was this sexy ward sister standing in the way – and you know what he's like when he runs into that kind of obstruction,' Meadows ploughed on.

She was no bloody good at this kind of thing, she told herself.

She could scare bullies shitless, without even breaking into a sweat.

She was a positive genius in the bedroom, provided your tastes veered towards unusual sources of pain.

But she couldn't do girly talk and she couldn't do sympathy, and even though she admired the woman in the bed – and maybe even loved her – she knew she could never express any of that convincingly.

'We've been keeping in touch with Louisa, and she's fine,' Meadows continued. 'And you mustn't worry about her finding it too much of a strain to look after the twins as well as doing her training, because your housekeeper is a bloody marvel, and when she needs a break, one of us will take over for a while.' She realized she was speaking nineteen to the dozen, and paused for breath. 'Jack is brilliant at telling the kids stories, and due to the experiences I've had with my particular hobby, I'm a dab hand at changing nappies.'

Why was she doing this? she wondered.

What was making her witter on like a demented mocking bird high on tequila sunrises?

If Monika was capable of registering what was being said to her, she'd know all this already. And if she couldn't register it, why waste the time telling her?

She studied Paniatowski's face, hoping to find evidence that even if Monika couldn't understand the words, she at least knew she was being addressed.

Nothing! It was like gazing down at a death mask.

I've been happier working on this team than I've been at any other point in my life, Meadows thought – and if the boss dies, it's all gone.

Don't you die on me – don't you *dare* die on me! she thought.

And then she realized – with mounting horror – that she had actually said the words aloud.

'Why don't you tell the boss what Louisa's been up to today?' Jack Crane suggested.

'Good idea,' Meadows said, shooting him a grateful look. 'Well, boss, it seems that our young cadet has found her first body. Was it no more than a coincidence, you ask yourself. Or does she, like her mother, have a natural gift for sniffing out stiffs?'

The hospital porter noticed the two men sitting in the front of the VW Beetle when he stepped out into the car park for a smoke.

He was supposed to report suspicious people to security, but there was absolutely nothing suspicious about these two. They had probably brought some female relative to visit a patient who was also a relative.

And as she'd been getting out of the car, she'd no doubt tried to persuade them to go with her.

'Come on,' she would have cajoled, 'our Edna will be chuffed to bits that you've come to see her.'

And one of the men would have said, 'It's you she wants to see, love. I'll only get in the way.'

But what he would really have meant would have been, 'You'll feel right at home in there. Any woman does. But I'm a *man*! I don't like hospitals. They turn my insides to water.'

And the woman would finally have given up, and left the men in peace, listening to the cricket on the radio.

The hospital canteen was a little too antiseptic for this to be a truly romantic first date, but it was what there was, and it would have to do.

Ward Sister Sowerbury was certainly a quarry worth a little hunting, Beresford thought, looking at her over his coffee. She was tall for a woman, and a little too broad for many men's taste, but she was muscled without being over-muscular, and though he had not stroked it yet, he could tell her skin would feel wonderfully soft.

'How long have you been nursing?' he asked her.

Diana Sowerbury smiled knowingly at him. 'It's thirteen years since I qualified,' she said, 'and in case you're counting, that makes me thirty-four.'

'I wasn't counting,' Beresford said.

Diana's smile broadened. 'I feel I can trust you,' she said.

'You *can* trust me,' he assured her.

'And would you like to know *why* I feel I can trust you?'

'Is it because I've got an honest face?' Beresford asked hopefully.

'No, it's because I can tell when you're lying. You *were* counting the years, weren't you?'

'Maybe a little bit,' Beresford admitted sheepishly. 'So, have you always worked in Lancashire?'

'Changing the subject?' Diana Sowerbury asked.

'Definitely,' Beresford agreed.

'I used to work in Yorkshire, and before that I was in Singapore and Gibraltar,' Diana said, and when she saw Beresford raise a quizzical eyebrow, she said, 'I was in the army. That's where I did my training.'

'So what brought you to Lancashire?' Beresford wondered.

'I'm surprised you even need ask that question,' Diana said.

'Really? And why's that?'

'Because I thought that as far as you Lancastrians were concerned, there are only two kinds of people in the world – those who *live* in Lancashire, and those who (whether they admit it or not) *want* to live in Lancashire.'

'Fair point,' Beresford said, complacently.

The story the smoking porter had concocted for himself was not *quite* a hundred percent off the mark, in that the men in the VW were, in fact, listening to the radio – though it was certainly not the cricket which was holding their attention.

'There are a number of questions I think we should be asking ourselves,' Meadows was saying through the speaker. *'For a start, why did the killer choose the allotments as a place to get rid of the body? It certainly isn't the first place I'd think of. Was the victim local – or was he not? If he wasn't local, why did the killer go to so much trouble to disguise him?'*

'*And if he was local, did anyone report him missing?*' asked a second – male – voice.

'*Exactly, Jack,*' Meadows said. '*The chances are that if he was a local man he* was *reported missing, since there are very few people around who absolutely nobody would miss. But we haven't got the time, or the resources, to go through the records of every man who's disappeared in central Lancashire in the last twenty years. So what we desperately need is for Doc Shastri to tell us how long he's been dead.*'

'*It's time to go,*' a third voice announced. '*Say your goodbyes.*'

'*Would you like to . . .*'

'*No, I'll wait in the corridor.*'

There were a few seconds of silence, then Meadows said, '*We're all finding this hard to take, but it's hardest of all for Colin, because he's been your friend for a long time.*' Another pause. '*There's not one of us that doesn't believe you can come out of this, boss.* Not one of us!'

There was the sound of footsteps, and a door closing.

'How touching Lady Katherine can be when she puts her mind to it,' Forsyth said.

'Why do you call her that?' Downes asked – and the moment the words were out of his mouth he knew he'd fallen into one of those little pits full of sharpened bamboo poles that Forsyth seemed to take such delight in setting in his path.

'I call her that because that is what she is,' Forsyth said. 'Didn't you know? Haven't you read the files?'

'It isn't in the files,' Downes said.

'That's right, it isn't,' Forsyth said, as if he had forgotten that detail. 'Several years ago, when she was still just about one of us, she used her influence to have that removed.'

'One of us?' Downes asked, hating himself. 'Was she in the service?'

'Not *that* us! I'm talking about the establishment – the people who matter,' Forsyth said airily. 'She hasn't got the same influence now. Oh dear me, no. Once you've chosen to step outside the charmed circle, there's no going back – you simply have to learn to live in the outer darkness.'

'With people like me,' Downes said, as if challenging him to be rude enough to confirm it.

'Yes, with people like you,' Forsyth said easily. 'Look, here comes three-quarters of the finest crime-fighting team in Lancashire.'

The two men watched as the team progressed across the car park.

'I meant what I just said, you know,' Forsyth told Downes. 'A lot of people might judge Colin Beresford to be plodding, but he would prefer to describe himself as dogged, and so would I. Lady K; she's fearless and recognizes no boundaries – physical or mental – which is why she is often able to find out things that completely elude others. Jack Crane is very bright and has a sweeping imagination. Put all that together with Monika Paniatowski's over-arching leadership and vision, and what have you got?'

'DCI Paniatowski is in a coma,' Downes reminded him.

'What you've got,' said Forsyth, ignoring the comment, 'is a team to be worried about. And I am.' He paused for a moment. 'I think we'd better pay Monika a visit ourselves.'

Ward Sister Diana Sowerbury studied the two men walking down the corridor towards the ICU. The younger one had clearly dressed in a way which he imagined would make him look smart and classy, she thought, and he probably just about succeeded. On the other hand, the other man – the one with the hair like spun silver – didn't really have to try, because there was something about him which ensured he would be classy if he were dressed in a dustbin bag.

The two came to a halt at Sister Sowerbury's desk.

'I do hate to disturb you, Sister,' Forsyth said in a voice quite unlike his ordinary one, 'but I'm only in this lovely town for a few hours, and while I'm here, I would so like to take the opportunity to see my niece.'

'What's her name?' Diana asked.

'Minnie Mouse.'

The sister frowned. 'As you are no doubt aware, we have no one of that name here, and if this is your idea of a joke . . .'

'Oh, good heavens!' Forsyth said, holding up his hands in mock horror. 'Did I say Minnie Mouse?'

'You know you did.'

'I must have been having a senior moment there. You see, I've known her since she was a child, which is why I still call her Minnie Mouse, and she still calls me Uncle Goofy. Everyone else knows her as Monika Paniatowski.'

Diana considered her options. If she turned him down, that might suggest to her nurses that she was very much in control. On the other hand, it might just suggest that she was the kind of woman who found it easy to bully an old age pensioner like this man, but immediately caved in the face of police intimidation.

If she let him in, however, she would be signalling that she had changed her mind on the visiting rules for humanitarian reasons – and that it had nothing to do with the fact that she had been scared of Kate Meadows.

She chose the latter course, though with the proviso that she wouldn't make it look *too* easy.

'Strictly speaking I shouldn't let you in, but if you can produce some proof of identification, I will allow it,' she said grandly.

'Some proof of identification, some proof of identification,' Forsyth muttered. 'Ah, yes, I have my driving licence.'

'That would be fine,' Diana Sowerbury said.

Forsyth reached into the inside pocket of his suit jacket, and took out an expensive wallet. He flicked it open and took out a driving licence, which he offered to the ward sister. Then, at the very last moment, he pulled back.

'Wait a minute, that's no good,' he said.

'I can assure you that if it really is your driving licence . . .'

'Oh, it's my driving licence all right. It says Charles Masterton, and I'm Charles Masterton, so it must be mine.'

'Then that's all that's required.'

'But it doesn't say I know Minnie Mouse, you see,' Forsyth said, clapping his hands. 'I could just as easily be one of those sick individuals who like to look at people in comas – and if I was, you'd never know, would you?'

'I'm sure you're not that sort of person,' Diana Sowerbury said.

And she was thinking, what's happening here? He's supposed to be the one who's trying to persuade me to let him see the patient, but instead I'm the one who's trying to persuade him.

'I tell you what might do it,' Forsyth said, opening another section of the wallet and pulling out a photograph. 'Take a look at this.' He handed Diana the photograph. 'It was taken in my garden, just after Minnie joined the police.'

The ward sister looked at the picture, and Downes glanced at it over her shoulder.

The garden in which the photograph had been taken had an immaculate lawn which was bordered by flower beds. In the middle of the lawn, a fountain bubbled. There was nothing in the photograph which said that this was just a very small slice of a much larger garden, but you knew from the composition that that was the case.

In the foreground were three people smiling with quiet contentment and with their arms draped over each other. Forsyth (or Masterton, as he apparently was for the moment) was at the left-hand side, and a middle-aged woman was standing to the right. In the middle was a much younger Monika Paniatowski.

The picture was faked – Downes was sure of that – but it had been so skilfully done that it would be almost impossible to *prove* it was a fake.

It hadn't been necessary to produce it, because the ward sister had been quite prepared to let him through on just his driving licence.

But then, this whole pantomime had little to do with the ward sister – it had been put on for the benefit of E Downes, bag carrier and shit eater.

Look at me, Forsyth had been saying – when I want to be a little old man, I can convince even a trained medical professional that that is exactly what I am.

Look at this photograph. It was complicated and expensive to produce, and there was only a very small chance I'd ever really need to use it – but I had it made anyway, because I *can*.

'She was a lovely young girl, don't you think?' said doting, doddering Uncle Goofy.

'Very nice,' Ward Sister Sowerbury said, without a great deal of warmth or enthusiasm. She looked around. 'Nurse Coombes!'

'Yes, sister?'

'Take this gentleman and his friend to see DCI Paniatowski.'

SIX

Once the nurse had left the room, Forsyth walked over to the bed and, using his little finger, delicately lifted Paniatowski's right eyelid.

'Is there anybody in there?' he asked, in the mock-fearful voice of a cartoon character trapped in the cellar of a haunted house.

He stepped away from the bed.

'It doesn't look as if anyone is home, but appearances can be deceptive,' he said. 'Monika has only said one word since she was admitted here, but that single utterance was enough to point the dogged Inspector Colin Beresford in the direction of her attacker – I'm sorry, what I meant to say was that single word was enough to point the dogged *Acting Chief Inspector* Colin Beresford in the direction of her attacker. Can you even *begin* to work out what that tells us about her mental state, Downes?'

Do you know what, Downes said to himself, I've just about had enough of this cat and mouse game. Sod my prospects, and sod my pension, I'm not going to take this anymore.

'Since you seem to have cornered the market in infallibility, why don't *you* tell *me* what it means?' he asked.

Forsyth chuckled. 'So you're finally fighting back,' he said. 'I wondered how long it would take you.'

'What do you mean?' Downs asked.

'You surely don't think I was baiting you without purpose, do you?' Forsyth asked. 'I never do anything without purpose.' He paused. 'Oh, I admit there's some pleasure to be gained from squeezing something until it squeaks, but my main aim here is to ensure you *don't* squeak.'

'I don't know—' Downes began.

'I'm toughening you up,' Forsyth explained. 'I don't want you dragging me down, and so I'm helping you to prepare for dealing with the people you'll have to deal with if – as may very well happen in this particular disaster of a project – the excrement hits the rotating cooling units.'

'What's wrong with simple English?' Downes asked. 'Why don't you just say when the shit hits the fan?'

'Then again,' Forsyth said, clearly ignoring the comment, 'everything I've just told you could be piffle, and I might simply be playing another – entirely different level – of mind games with you.' He strolled over to the window. 'But to get back to the matter in hand – what Monika proved when she all-but named her attacker was not only that her mind was still working, but that she was still conscious of the world around her.' He swung round and returned to the bedside. 'The question is, has her mind deteriorated since then, or is she still as sharp as she ever was – because if she is, then we both have cause to fear.'

'I think you may be over-estimating her,' said Downes, feeling newly emboldened – or perhaps feeling that he'd been given permission to *act* as if he felt that way.

'Oh, that's what you think, is it?' Forsyth asked.

'Yes. All right, she knew the name of her attacker – but that was because she'd seen him. Finding a connection between the body at the allotments and something that happened in the past is quite a different – and much more complex – matter. That would challenge someone at the top of their game. And just look at her – at the top of her game, she is not.'

'An interesting viewpoint,' Forsyth mused. 'Over the years, I have come into conflict with Monika three times, and, as was almost inevitable, I have come out on top.'

'Of course you have,' Downes said, making only half an attempt to hide his sneer.

'The reason it was almost inevitable was because I had the full power and authority of the state behind me, which is something which – I need not remind you – we do not have at this time and for this project. But even though Monika's David did not even come close to bringing down my Goliath, she came closer than anyone else has, and even scored a few minor victories along the way. She has a remarkable brain, you see, full of sharp corners and jagged edges.'

'What?'

'Most brains don't really know how to deal with information – they can store it, they can modify it, and they can pass it on, but they can never really *use* it. It's a bit like a conduit system, if you'd care to think of it that way – you feed excrement in at one end, and it flows smoothly through the system before emerging, only slightly watered down, at the other end. But a brain like Monika's – or like mine, for that matter – isn't content with that. The sharp corners stop the flow, the jagged edges hook the detritus and hold it up for examination. "What exactly is this fragment of information?" the brain asks. "How does it differ from this other fragment? And do the two of them considered together tell us something important?" Do you see what I'm getting at?'

'Yes,' Downes said.

Forsyth knelt down beside the bed, almost as if he were in prayer.

'What is that brain of yours doing now, Monika?' he said, in a voice which was suddenly soft and almost kindly. 'Is it at rest? Is there nothing in there but the electrical hum of a tired old refrigerator on the lowest possible setting – or, after what Kate Meadows has told you, are you already asking yourself if the body in the allotment can be fitted into a larger scheme of things?' He raised his hand and gently stroked her cheek. 'Is it possible that one day in the near future, when all your team are gathered around you, you will open your mouth and say "Arthur Wheatstone"?' He looked up at Downes. 'I fear Monika's brain,' he said, 'and if you have any sense, then so will you.'

'If you're so worried about her, why not just kill her?' Downes asked sarcastically.

'Do you really think I haven't considered that as a solution?' Forsyth asked mildly. 'But my masters won't hear of it for the moment.'

Forsyth was playing his games again, Downes thought. Well, he was getting the hang of that himself.

'Why won't your masters approve?' he asked. 'Is it because she's a fairly high-ranking police officer?'

'Well, her rank certainly comes into it,' Forsyth replied, 'but I wouldn't say that is the main consideration. My masters like all the tidying up to appear to be either an accident or from natural causes, you see. Out on the street, it would be simplicity itself to have her knocked down by a runaway lorry, but it would be hard to explain the presence of a juggernaut on the third floor of a large hospital. And as for natural causes – well, she's being closely monitored by a team of expert doctors. Any of the methods we've used to fake a natural death in the past would be very quickly uncovered.'

'So as long as she stays in here, she's safe?' Downes asked.

'As long she either keeps her mouth shut or doesn't start saying the wrong words, she's safe. But if she does start saying the wrong words – or if there's even a *possibility* she could say the wrong words – it may be necessary to take her out first, and worry about the consequences later.'

Jesus God, this was real! Downes thought.

In a way, he was surprised that he was surprised. After all, he already knew about Arthur Wheatstone and the man in the trench, so he was aware that people got killed as a result of deliberate decisions taken by other people. But he'd been on the periphery of that, and it had all seemed so distant – a tale told around the campfire as the whisky bottle was passed from man to man.

This, on the other hand, was painfully close! This was a woman lying on a bed a few feet from him, a woman who he might be told to . . .

But no, Forsyth would never ask him to do that!

'*You* killed somebody once, didn't you, Monika?' Forsyth asked, scouring her face for a reaction as he spoke. 'Did you know that, Downes?'

'It's not in the file,' Downes replied, almost world-wearily.

'No, it isn't in the file,' Forsyth agreed. 'But it happened, all right. She did it to protect her old boss, Charlie Woodend, although it has to be said that *when* she did it, he was not in any immediate danger.'

'Then why isn't it—?' Downes began.

'Horse trading,' Forsyth interrupted. 'I wanted something from Charlie Woodend, and he wanted something from me.' He moved, so he was examining Paniatowski from a slightly different angle. 'Yes, you killed to protect good old Charlie, so you can't really complain if Downes here kills you to protect me, now can you, Monika?'

Her face remained as still and lifeless as it had been before he began speaking – but that proved nothing.

'We'll laugh about all this one day, Monika,' Forsyth said. 'Or, at least, *I* will.'

* * *

When she first regained consciousness – no, *not* consciousness, because you had to have at least a few more parts of you working before you could call it consciousness . . .

What *should* she call it then?

The first time she had regained *awareness* – yes, that was about right – the first time she had regained awareness, she had thought she was dead.

And why wouldn't she have thought that? She couldn't move, couldn't see, couldn't speak, and maybe that was what death was – a brain floating on an airbed in a perfectly calm sea for all eternity.

But then a nurse had entered the room – or maybe not, maybe her brain had invented the nurse to keep from absolute despair.

It had only been when Louisa had spent some time with her that she'd finally accepted unconditionally that she was alive – if that was what you wanted to call it.

She had tried to keep track of how much time had passed by registering any conversations she heard:

'My French neighbours were making a hell of a lot of noise last Thursday.'

'Well, what do you expect? It was their independence day, after all.'

So the previous Thursday had been the 14th of July.

And how many days had passed since then?

Three – which made it the 17th.

Or was it four?

In the end, she had given up on the present, and sought some kind of escape in the past.

She remembered what she had been told of her father's last heroic and pointless cavalry charge – Polish horses against German tanks.

She relived the life she and her mother had led after the invasion – wandering all over Europe, hiding first from the Nazis and then from the Red Army, begging food where they could, stealing it where they couldn't, but always hungry . . . always so very, very hungry.

She recalled her mother's second marriage and her stepfather's unwanted attentions, forced on her in the middle of the night.

She experienced anew the black despair she had felt when she was told Bob was dead, and the sheer joy that adopting Louisa had brought her.

Yet though she had lived a life crowded with events, memories of it were not enough – even when viewed from a startling new angle – to banish the ennui which had become a constant companion.

She had come to realize that she was not afraid of death, for though she had battled against her childhood religion for most of her adult life, she had finally – with the miracle of her pregnancy – begun to embrace Mother Church once more. Now she believed in a merciful God (albeit one with a particularly black sense of humour) and was confident that beyond the grave, she could look forward to a life of everlasting things-could-be-worse.

So the growing fear which had been eating away at her insides was not about dying, it was about *not* dying – about lying there helpless for another thirty or forty years, until Death finally came to harvest her.

And now, a minion of the forces of darkness (let's call him Satan's little helper, she thought – and was both surprised and pleased that she could still make a joke of it) had been to visit her and hinted that he was looking for a way to terminate her.

She was not sure how she felt about that.

On the one hand, he could bring her the death she had been praying for.

On the other, she was suddenly more optimistic about her chances of recovery.

The two might have evenly balanced out but for a third element, which she suspected was petty and childish, but nonetheless seemed to be flashing like a gaudy neon sign in the very forefront of her mind.

She didn't want Forsyth to win!

It was a ludicrous thing for a woman in a coma to be thinking, and yet she could feel herself drawing strength from it.

He had exposed a weakness, and if she were ever to be in a position to take advantage of it, she needed to prepare now.

'Is it possible that one day in the near future, when all your team are gathered around you, you will open your mouth and say "Arthur Wheatstone"?'

Arthur Wheatstone!

Of course!

Forsyth had been very much in evidence when the paramilitaries had been secretly training on the moors, and he had been constantly popping up (like an evil jack-in-the-box) during the coal strike, yet there had been no sign at all of him during the Arthur Wheatstone investigation.

Yet she should have known – *she should have bloody known* – even though she hadn't seen him. She should have been able to sense his presence – should have able to pick up a hint of the scent of evil which trailed behind him – because that case had his fingerprints all over it.

Arthur Wheatstone.

She had never even heard of him until that morning in April – four years earlier – when she had arrived at his house.

PART TWO
The Hanging

April 1974

SEVEN

Monika Paniatowski hated being called as a witness. It wasn't so much that she resented some oily barrister suggesting that she was cither a liar or a fool – and, as a bonus, that she was possibly bent. It wasn't even that some of the older judges expressed surprise that a little lady like her could actually be a chief inspector, and sometimes interrupted the proceedings to make sure they'd actually got that right.

No, what really got her goat was the time it took! Very often, she would not be called on the first day of the trial she'd been summoned to attend, either because the questioning of another witness had taken longer than expected, or because the judge adjourned early (perhaps, she would speculate maliciously, because he had an urgent appointment with a high-priced prostitute who would shout gross obscenities at him while he ate food out of a dog bowl on the floor!).

It was such a waste of resources – such a waste of *her*! While she fretted in the corridors of Lancaster Castle, crimes were being committed on her patch which needed a serious looking into.

She was on her way to Lancaster Crown Court at about half-past six that crisp morning in early April, when a bulletin over the police radio informed her that there was a break-in in progress in Barrow Village.

The village, set just inside the moors, was not too far off her current route, she thought, and since it was at the very edge of the Whitebridge policing area, it was highly unlikely that any of the regular patrol cars would be closer to it than she was.

Of course, this might mean she was late for court, but though the judge might hate the fact, he certainly wasn't going to rebuke her for catching a criminal.

And how delightful would that be?

'DCI Paniatowski,' she said into her microphone. 'I'm about a mile from the village, so I'm going in – but I'd appreciate it if you could send me some reinforcements.'

She approached Barrow Village from the south side. The village drew its name from the fact that it was located on Barrow Moor, though where the moor got its name from was anybody's guess. The hamlet's name instantly conjured up images of old stone buildings covered with ivy, smoking chimneys, and ancient residents with blackthorn walking sticks and clay pipes. Nothing – the new arrival would quickly learn – could be further from the truth, for though a few of the houses could claim a history, the major part of the village was made up of a new housing estate.

The houses on this estate were all detached. They had double garages and dormer windows in their sharply sloping – almost alpine-like – roofs, and most of their owners were drawn from the moderately prosperous middle class.

The break-in was reported to have occurred at No. 23 Blackthorn Way. Paniatowski parked at the other end of the street.

As she walked down Blackthorn Way, she checked around her. All the front rooms of the houses she passed were in darkness, though a few of the upstairs bedroom lights were on. Most of the activity, however, seemed to be occurring at the backs of the houses, in the kitchens and breakfast rooms.

It was a strange time of day to commit a robbery – just as it was getting light – Paniatowski thought. But then maybe the burglar knew something she didn't.

As she drew level with No. 23, the door to the house opposite opened, and a tall man in a heavy wool dressing gown walked down his garden path and onto the street. He moved well for an old man, Paniatowski noted, but old was what he obviously was.

'Are you the law?' he asked.

Yes,' Paniatowski confirmed.

He took a step closer to her. 'My name's Martin Cole. I'm the one who phoned you. Can I see your warrant card please?'

Paniatowski produced her warrant card, and held it out for him to see. Most people would have given it no more than a glance, but Cole went over it line by line, and then went over it again, before nodding that he was satisfied.

'Tell me what you saw,' Paniatowski said.

Cole spread his legs and clasped his hands behind his back. 'At around twenty past six, I saw a man casing No. 23, which is the home of Arthur and Elaine Wheatstone,' he said.

'What do you mean by "casing" it?' Paniatowski asked.

'He was walking around it in a meaningful manner, looking up at the windows, and assessing how difficult it would be to force the doors.'

'How do you know?' Paniatowski wondered.

'How would *you* know?' Cole countered.

'You're ex-job,' Paniatowski guessed.

'That's right,' he agreed. 'I was a detective sergeant – and then inspector – for over thirty years. And you are the famous DCI Paniatowski. I suppose we should feel honoured that you've come to deal with such a petty crime personally. Why, I remember—'

'Describe the man to me,' Paniatowski said, interrupting him before things got too cosy.

'He's around 35 years old, six feet tall and weighs about twelve stone. He has brown hair, cut so short it's almost a crew cut. He's wearing a check sports coat, check trousers, and what I think are moccasin shoes. His outfit may not be to my taste, but it wasn't cheap, either.'

'It doesn't sound like the sort of clothes a burglar would choose when he was out on a job,' Paniatowski said sceptically, because while she had no doubt that he had once been a policeman, he could well have chosen in his retirement to make a hobby out of being a nutter.

'It is a strange outfit,' Cole said, steadily and firmly, 'but that's what he's wearing.'

'You seem to have had plenty of opportunity to observe him,' Paniatowski said, still unconvinced.

'I did.'

'Where were you watching him from?'

'My bathroom. I was having a pee – which can be a protracted business when you get to my age.'

'Do you always look out of the window when you're having a pee?'

'Usually.'

'Why?'

Cole grinned sheepishly. 'Because it's a lot better than looking down at my faded glory,' he said.

'Did you actually see him enter the house?' Paniatowski asked.

Cole shook his head. 'He disappeared around the back.'

'So you can't know for sure that he's inside.'

'No, but that's where my gut says he is.'

'Are the Wheatstone family at home?' Paniatowski wondered.

'There's only the two of them – Elaine and Arthur. Elaine's away visiting her mother, but Arthur's there.'

'When was the last time you saw him?'

'I saw him twice last night. The first time was around seven. I was taking the dog for a walk, and he was standing in the garden.'

'I would have thought it would have been a bit cold for standing in the garden,' Paniatowski said.

'It was – but Elaine doesn't like him smoking in the house, you see.'

'When was the second time you saw him?'

'About eight o'clock, when he opened the door for his visitors.'

'Did you see them from your bathroom again?'

'That's right.'

'Tell me about them.'

'One was about five feet ten, the other was at least six four.'

'You sound pretty sure of their heights.'

'I am. They were standing next to Arthur, you see – and I know how tall he is.'

'What were they wearing?' Paniatowski asked, promising herself that if Cole described them as wearing something exotic, she'd be back in her car and on her way to Lancaster.

'They were both wearing anoraks, and either jeans or dark trousers,' the ex-bobby said.

'When did they leave?'

'I can't say for sure, but their car – a blue Vauxhall Victor – was gone by the time I went for my eleven o'clock pee.'

'How tall is Arthur Wheatstone?' Paniatowski asked.

'Five eight.'

'And is he in shape?'

'No, he's a bit of a weed, to tell you the truth.'

So what we have here is a large burglar who doesn't seem particularly worried about getting caught in the act, and a house-holder who can – at best – only make a poor job of defending himself, Paniatowski thought.

It could turn out to be a very nasty situation.

Paniatowski clicked on her radio, but there was only static.

Bloody moors! she thought.

She turned towards Whitebridge, and listened for the sound of police sirens in the distance.

Nothing.

'From what you've told me, Mr Wheatstone could be in danger,' Paniatowski said to the old man. 'I'm going to go in there.'

'I'll come with you,' Cole said.

Paniatowski grinned. 'Really, Inspector Cole?' she asked.

Coles shook his head in disbelief. 'What am I thinking?' he asked. 'For a moment back there, I forgot I wasn't young. How about, as an alternative course of action, I stay here and raise the general alarm if needs be?'

'That's a much better plan,' Paniatowski agreed.

'Are you sure you'll be all right?' Cole asked, concerned.

'Certain,' Paniatowski told him, 'I've got a black belt in judo – and if he causes me any trouble, I'll wrap it round his neck and throttle the bastard.'

Once the decision was made, there was no point in delaying any longer.

Paniatowski sprinted across the road. The front door of No. 23 was locked, and there was no sign anyone had attempted to force it.

She moved a couple of feet to the left, and risked a glance into the living room.

No sign of a burglar there. No sign of the homeowner, either. The living room was as neat and tidy as if the Wheatstones were expecting guests to turn up at any minute.

She moved rapidly around the side of the house, past the bin, to the back door. There was no more sign of life in the kitchen than there had been in the living room.

She tried the kitchen door. It wasn't locked.

There was a single plate, a knife and fork and a wine glass in the sink. No evidence of any pans, so maybe Wheatstone had eaten some convenience food he'd heated up in the oven. The toaster was cold, the kettle was cold, and there was a nearly full bottle of milk in the fridge.

The utility room led off the kitchen, but Paniatowski could see at a glance that there was nothing of interest in there.

She checked out the living room, and then the small study which lay off it. The study was full of technical books and journals which all seemed – on a first fleeting impression – to be concerned with aeronautics.

Paniatowski made her way up the stairs. There was a master bedroom with an en suite, two more bedrooms and a second bathroom. The beds in the guest bedrooms had not been made up, and though there were sheets and blankets on the bed in the master bathroom, it had not been slept in.

Monika checked the en suite. Both the soap and the towels were completely bone dry.

So what had she learned?

She had learned that Mrs Wheatstone was away, and Arthur Wheatstone had had two visitors the night before, but they were gone by eleven, and unless he had washed up after they'd gone, he'd offered them no refreshment. He himself had had something to eat, and drunk at least one glass of wine. But he had not slept in his bed, nor had he had any breakfast.

As for the intruder with the crew cut, there was no indication – despite ex-Inspector Cole's gut feeling – that he had ever entered the house.

There was one more space to check – the garage.

She went downstairs again, crossed the kitchen, and entered the utility room.

She reached for the handle of the door that led into the garage, and then hesitated.

You were told never to go into a situation like this without backup, she reminded herself.

But what exactly was a *situation like this*?

A well-dressed man breaks into the house in the middle of the countryside just as night is ending.

Why?

Why, why, why?

And if it was important enough for him to take such a risk, was it important enough to kill for?

She had her judo, that was true. But he might have a gun, and it was generally acknowledged that although the ability to use an opponent's own weight against him is a great asset, it isn't much defence against a bullet.

As she flung open the door to the garage she was screaming out her name and rank, not because she thought those two things would make any difference if he'd decided to shoot her, but because loud words – any *loud* words – can create moments of confusion – and actions taken in those moments can be life-saving.

There was only one person in the garage as far as she could tell, and he would never present a threat to anyone, ever again.

He was a skinny man – 'a bit of a weed' as ex-DI Cole might have said – and he was wearing grey flannel trousers and a brown cardigan.

He was hanging from the central concrete beam which ran the length of the garage. His tongue was hanging out, but though the crotch of his trousers was heavily stained, there was no pool of urine on the floor. Just behind him, on its side, was one of those small stepladders which people use when they need to reach high shelves.

She supposed the next thing she should have done was check his pulse, but she knew that would be pointless. Even so, under normal conditions she would probably have done it, but these were not normal conditions, because she didn't know where the bloody man in the check jacket was.

She heard the footfall behind her a split second before she felt the sharp blow on the back of her head.

For a moment, everything went black, but she was still aware enough to put her hands in front of her to break the fall which she accepted as inevitable.

Her palms hit the floor, her wrists were jarred, and her eyes opened again. She saw a pair of check trouser legs, and heard the sound of the up-and-over garage door being lifted. Then the early-morning light flooded into the garage, and the trouser legs were gone.

As Paniatowski struggled to her feet, the man was already dashing down the road.

He probably had his car parked at the other end of Blackthorn Way, she thought, and if she didn't catch him by then, she would have lost him forever.

And then – blessed relief – she heard the police sirens.

She turned and faced the oncoming car, waving for it to stop.

It drew up beside her.

'DCI Paniatowski,' she said to the driver, waving her warrant card at him. 'Get in the back.'

'I'm sorry, ma'am, but are you sure . . .?'

'Get in the bloody back,' Paniatowski repeated. 'Go on – move it!'

The driver hesitated a split second more before deciding that while she might well be deranged, she was still a *DCI*, which meant that she had licence to be pretty much whatever she wanted to be.

Once the driver had climbed into the back, Paniatowski took his place at the wheel, and slammed the gear into a racing start. The car roared up Blackthorn Way, leaving a small whirlwind of gravel behind it.

They reached the end of the street just in time to see the man in the check trousers pulling away in a Jaguar XJ.

'Get on the radio,' Paniatowski said. 'I want every police vehicle in Lancashire on that bastard's tail.'

The Jag shot off towards the Lancaster road. By the time it reached the edge of the village, it was doing nearly eighty.

Even though the Vauxhall Vectra that Paniatowski was driving had been souped up, she knew that once they were out on the moors, where there were countless side roads following the old peddlers' routes, they could soon lose him.

'Get patched through to Chief Superintendent Snodgrass and tell him I want roadblocks set up on all roads that lead off the moor between Bolton and Lancaster,' Paniatowski told the constable in the passenger seat. 'Tell him I'd normally get it cleared with the chief constable, but right now I'm too busy chasing somebody who might just turn out to be a murderer.'

The village was already five miles behind them – and the needle on the speedometer was nudging a hundred and ten – when they saw the sign stating there were roadworks ahead.

In front of them, the Jaguar's brake lights went on, and there was a screech of tyres as the car slowed.

She slammed on her own brakes, and the rear end of the Vectra did a rattling mambo before juddering to a halt.

She could see now what his problem was. The road was just about wide enough for two cars – or two lorries, if they were very careful – to pass each other, but half the road was currently occupied by a steamroller, and the other half was operating a reversible flow system. On their side, the single lane was blocked by a bread van, a milk lorry and a tractor, all waiting for the lights to change. Even worse news, from the Jaguar driver's viewpoint, was that two police cars were just approaching the other side of the roadworks.

Paniatowski manoeuvred the Vauxhall so it was across the road, cutting off the Jag's retreat.

'Shall we go and get him, ma'am?' asked the constable on the back seat.

'No,' Paniatowski said. 'He's very likely to be dangerous, so we'll wait for the reinforcements.'

'Roberts and me can handle him easily, ma'am,' the constable said, doing his best not to sound disappointed.

He was like a little kid who'd been denied his football, she thought, and almost laughed. Yet alongside that amusement there was envy, because in putting a damper on his enthusiasm, she was also leaving the younger Monika – who scorned the boring, the predictable and the safe – even further behind.

And then she remembered that she had virtually hi-jacked the car she was sitting in, and had driven it at high speed when she was probably suffering from concussion – and while she felt she should certainly censor herself for taking such an irresponsible action, it still made her feel a whole lot better.

'What's your name?' she asked the constable.

'Butler, ma'am.'

'I'll tell you what we'll do, PC Butler. We'll give the rest of the lads five minutes to get here, and if they're still not here by then, you'll get your wish to go over there and have your heads kicked in.'

'You're a bloody star, ma'am!' Butler said enthusiastically.

'Easy, Johnno,' Roberts cautioned him.

'Sorry, ma'am,' Butler said, blushing. 'I didn't mean to be cheeky or anything—'

'He's moving,' Paniatowski interrupted him.

He was. The man in the check jacket had got out of the Jag, and was walking slowly and casually towards the Vauxhall.

'Ma'am, do you think we should . . .?'

'I'll get out of the car first,' Paniatowski said firmly. 'I don't know what I'll do after that – that will depend on him – but whatever I do, I'll want you just behind me. Have you got that?'

'We could be in front of you, if you thought that might be better ma'am,' Butler said.

He wanted to protect her, bless his little cotton socks – and she couldn't have that.

'When I give an order, Butler, I don't expect it to be questioned by a lad who still thinks his pubic hair is a bit of a novelty,' she growled. 'Do you think your tiny brain can grasp that fact?'

'Yes, ma'am,' Butler mumbled.

'Then I'll get out of the car first, and you stick close behind me.'

Paniatowski got out of the Vauxhall, and quickly took up a position in front of the bonnet. She did not need to check whether Butler and Roberts were with her – she could hear their short, excited breaths.

The man was still advancing on them, keeping to a regular pace, looking neither left nor right,

'That's far enough,' Paniatowski said.

The man came to an immediate halt. Paniatowski studied his face, looking for guidance as to what he might do next, but his neutral expression gave absolutely nothing away.

'We're going to arrest you now,' she said. 'It would be pointless to resist, and pointless to attempt to escape. Either of those things would only make things worse for you in the long run.'

The man smiled, slowly turned around then clasped his hands together in the small of his back.

You're an idiot, Monika, Paniatowski told herself.

And what makes you an idiot?

The fact that it's taken you so long to work out that this feller is an American.

EIGHT

By the time Paniatowski got back to the dead man's house, a whole caravanserai of official vehicles was parked outside. She checked them off in her mind: Meadows', Crane's, and Beresford's cars; the Scene of Crime Officers' van; and four patrol cars, parked across Blackthorn Way at an angle to serve as ad hoc roadblocks.

The only two vehicles needed to complete the scene were Dr Shastri's Land Rover, and an ambulance.

The constables who had arrived in the patrol cars were now out on the pavements, dealing with the neighbours.

'Move along please.'

'We will be taking all your statements later, I promise you.'

'There's really nothing to see.'

It was true – there was nothing to see but the same brick walls they must have seen day after day.

Ah, but it was different now. There had been a sudden dramatic death in the house, and now the very brickwork had a fascinating evil about it.

Paniatowski wondered if she should consult Dr Shastri about the blow she had received to the head, but apart from a continuous dull ache and the occasional shooting pain, it was causing her no problems at all, so taking care of it could be postponed until later.

Once she was inside the garage, the first thing Paniatowski's eyes were drawn to – inevitably – was the body, but then she scanned the rest of the place, and saw a number of randomly scattered cardboard boxes, which looked as if they might once have been part of an orderly pillar.

And that was exactly what they had been – a pillar of boxes behind which the American was hiding until he burst out and struck her on the head, probably with the spanner which was lying in the floor.

Beresford looked at the body and then at Paniatowski. 'I realize that the feller you arrested was probably committing some kind of crime by even being here,' he said, 'but I wouldn't have thought it was a serious enough crime to interest us.'

'What about him?' Paniatowski asked, jerking her thumb in the hanging man's direction.

'It's a suicide, isn't it?' Beresford asked.

'Is it?' Paniatowski wondered. 'Then where's the note?'

Beresford looked around him. 'We haven't found one,' he admitted.

'Suicides almost invariably leave the note close by,' Paniatowski pointed out. 'Some of them even pin the notes to themselves.'

'True,' Beresford agreed, 'but there's always the exception that proves the rule, isn't there? The note might somewhere else in the house. Or he may have written it as a letter, and posted it to somebody. He might even not have left one at all. Some people don't.'

'It was brass monkey weather up here on the moors last night, yet according to Inspector Cole from across the road, our Arthur here was out in the garden, smoking a cigarette, because his wife doesn't like him smoking inside. That's the action of a man who plans a long-term future.'

'Or it could be the action of a man who's simply a slave to habit,' Beresford countered. 'He's always smoked in the garden, so he did it without thinking about it.' He paused. 'I'm not saying you're wrong about suicide, boss – but somebody has to put up the alternative argument.'

'Agreed,' Paniatowski said. 'Then answer me this – if you'd decided to top yourself and it was your last night on earth, what would you have to eat?'

Beresford made a face. 'I'm not sure that I'd be able to fancy anything,' he said.

'I would,' Crane said. 'I'd have a dozen fresh oysters from Normandy, a few Coquilles Saint-Jacques, and a goose pâté from the Dordogne, with fresh French bread to accompany it.'

'Jesus!' Beresford said, in disgust. 'Even if you were planning to kill yourself, there's still no excuse for pushing stuff like that down your throat.' He shook his head in wonder. 'There are times when I think you're from a different planet from the rest of us, Jack.'

'You're missing the point, Colin,' Paniatowski said.

'Am I?'

'Yes, I rather think you are. One of you would be too nervous to eat anything, one of you would want go on the binge of a lifetime. What neither of you would do is treat it like a normal day – what neither of you would do was leave one plate and one knife and one fork in the sink.'

'You may be right,' Beresford said, though still sounding dubious.

'And we can see he wet himself, but there's not even the hint of a puddle on the floor,' Paniatowski said.

She noticed a coil of rope wrapped around a wall bracket which was identical to that wrapped around Arthur Wheatstone's neck – and that gave her an idea.

'How tall are you, Colin?' she asked.

'Five feet eleven,' Beresford said, puzzled.

'And what about the dead man?'

'It's hard to be exact, but I'd guess he's about three inches shorter than me.'

'Take the step ladder he was standing on, and stand on it yourself,' Paniatowski said.

'But that will contaminate the evidence,' Beresford protested.

Paniatowski laughed. 'There'll be nothing at all to contaminate,' she told him. 'Whoever strung Arthur up will have been sure to wipe it clean.'

'Let's just hope you're right about that,' Beresford grumbled, 'because the last thing I need is to be given a rocket, and then sent on a course to improve my evidence collecting skills.'

'You won't be,' Paniatowski promised him.

Beresford picked up the stepladder, moved it some way from the corpse, and stood on the top of its three steps.

Paniatowski handed him the coil of rope. 'There's a small gap between the beam and the ceiling,' she said, 'Can you thread the end of this rope through it?'

'I should think so,' Beresford said.

And then he discovered that even on tiptoe, he couldn't reach the top of the beam.

'Maybe I can thread it through even if I can't reach the spot myself,' he suggested.

And perhaps he could have done, if he had been dealing with something stiffer and more inflexible – like wire – but the rope was floppy, and without the help of a fakir (sitting cross-legged on the floor, and charming it with his flute) there wasn't any way it could be fitted through the narrow gap without a hand to guide it.

'He must have used another – longer – ladder to stand on while he threaded the rope through,' Beresford said.

'Then where is it?' Paniatowski asked.

They all looked around the garage. There was no sign of any ladder.

'My good friend DI Cole, whose word I am coming to rely on more and more, says that Wheatstone had two visitors last night, and one of them was at least six feet four,' Paniatowski said. 'So we are faced with two possibilities. One; Arthur Wheatstone decides to

commit suicide, but he doesn't leave a note, or smoke in the house
(which he knows will annoy his wife). He has a simple meal – nothing
at all special – then gets a ladder, takes it to the garage, threads the
rope through and takes the ladder away again. Possibility two; he's
murdered by someone tall enough to thread the rope through.'

'It's possibility two,' Crane said.

'It has to be,' Beresford agreed.

The corpse was lying on a wheeled stretcher, and Dr Shastri had
just spent five minutes examining it.

Now she turned to Paniatowski, and said, 'You would no doubt
like me to tell you when this poor unfortunate soul died, wouldn't
you, Chief Inspector?'

'If it's not too much trouble,' Paniatowski agreed.

'Oh, it is no trouble at all,' Shastri told her. 'As a humble and
unworthy Indian doctor, I regard it as both my duty and my privi-
lege to dedicate my simple talents to your service.'

Paniatowski grinned. 'Have you thought any more about taking
up that job you were headhunted for by Stanford?' she asked.

'Alas, my mind would agree to be transported in an instant to
that great temple of learning, but my body refuses to consider the
move,' Shastri said. 'It has got used to the cold and damp of
Lancashire, and would suffer withdrawal symptoms were I to take
it to a more civilized climate.'

'So when *did* he die?' Paniatowski asked.

'Taking into account his temperature and the extent of his rigour
(plus several other factors I would not even dream of boring you
with), I would say that he died between seven o'clock and eleven
o'clock last night,' Shastri said.

DI Cole had seen his visitors arrive at eight, but their car had
been gone by ten. That would fit in neatly with what Shastri
had just told her, Paniatowski thought.

'But did he die by hanging?' she asked.

'Ah, there you have me,' Shastri replied. 'He certainly shows
several signs of having died in that manner, but until I open him
up with my little scalpel, I will not be able to say with any degree
of certainty.'

'I'd like a report as soon as possible,' Paniatowski told her.
'Shall we say this afternoon?'

'You may say what you like, but it will be ready when it is ready,' Shastri said sweetly. She smiled at Beresford. 'Your boss is a tyrant,' she told him. 'But then her boss, Charlie Woodend, was a tyrant, too. And no doubt when Monika has been safely dispatched to the Home for Retired Gentlewomen, you will be just as monstrous to me.'

'No doubt,' Beresford agreed.

'So,' Shastri said, turning to the two waiting ambulance men. 'Would you two gentlemen be so kind as to convey my new friend to the mortuary?'

A small crowd had gathered out in the street, and its persistence was rewarded by the sight of the stretcher being loaded into the ambulance.

'I want this village squeezing like a lemon,' Paniatowski said, running her eyes over the spectators. 'I want to know if any unfamiliar faces have suddenly started appearing in Barrow. I'm most interested in the big man who DI Cole saw last night, but I also want to know about the man who was with him – and, of course, the American in the Jaguar XJ. Is that clear, Colin?'

'Yes, boss,' Beresford said. 'I've already commandeered the village hall, and as soon as I get reinforcements from Whitebridge, I'm on it.' He paused. 'Can I ask a question?'

'Of course.'

'You seem to be assuming that the big man is the murderer.'

'I am. He's the only one who was tall enough to have threaded the rope between the beam and the ceiling.'

'Yes, but maybe the killer had a ladder, in which case he wouldn't need to be tall at all.'

'There was no ladder. We looked.'

'And doesn't that strike you as strange? Can you think of any other garage you've been in where there wasn't a ladder?'

Actually, she couldn't, Paniatowski thought.

'But I still don't see what you've got against our tall man being the killer,' she said.

'The fact that he *is* tall,' Beresford countered. 'Listen, what a killer wants most of all is to slip away unnoticed, but that's hard to do when you're exceptionally tall, which is why I'm willing to bet you that most known contract killers are under six feet tall.'

'You've got a good point,' Paniatowski conceded, 'but within hours of him arriving at the house, Arthur Wheatstone was dead.'

'Yes, and even before he'd gone through the door, he'd been spotted,' Beresford said. 'If he really was a killer, wouldn't he have been more careful?'

'Maybe he underestimated just how nosy a small village can be,' Paniatowski said, though it seemed a weak argument even as she was propounding it. 'I also want all the information you can obtain on Arthur Wheatstone and his wife, as well. Were the Wheatstones happy? Did Arthur have any particular friends they knew of – or enemies? Was he involved in any disputes with neighbours with adjoining properties? Did he have a gambling habit? Was he a peeping tom?'

It was all pretty standard stuff, and Beresford nodded.

'What about the Yank who you surprised in the garage?' he asked. 'How does he fit into all of this?'

'I don't know,' Paniatowski admitted. 'The only really clear impression I've got is that he didn't try too hard to get away.'

'What do you mean – didn't try too hard to get away? First he hits you on the back of the head, then he's driving away like he's in an action movie.'

'Yes, but I think that was his first panicked reaction. By the time we hit the roadworks, he'd calmed down, and he surrendered.'

'I'm not sure it's so much a case of him calming down as him not having much choice.'

'But he did have a choice. He could have driven off into the moors.'

'Isn't the road raised at that point?'

'Yes, it's a flood protection measure.'

'So he'd have had to drive down a pretty sharp embankment. I can't think of many people who would have tried it.'

'I would have, in his position,' Paniatowski said.

'Yes, boss, but with the greatest respect, you can be a bit of a raving madwoman sometimes,' Beresford said.

'True,' Paniatowski admitted, trying not to look too pleased. 'But there's more to it than that. When he surrendered to me, it was like it was a bit of a joke,' she persisted. 'He wasn't worried at all, and everybody who gets arrested is worried to some extent – even if they're innocent.'

NINE

Paniatowski knew Chief Superintendent Snodgrass to nod to, and they had undoubtedly had a few meaningless conversations at the social events they had both been expected to attend, but that was about the limit of their contact.

Snodgrass had been brought in from outside a couple of years earlier, to tighten up rural policing. He was ex-army, and station rumour had it that he had been in the commandos, and had killed men with his bare hands. Paniatowski paid it no mind. She had all-but-stopped listening to rumour since a single dinner with a middle-aged priest from Ghana sparked the story that she was having an affair with the Nigerian vice consul.

Since Snodgrass's remit was the highways and byways of rural Lancashire, Butler and Roberts – her gung-ho companions of earlier that day – were his men, so when she saw him striding across the car park at police headquarters, her first thought was to put in a good word for his lads.

Her second thought was to leave it for another day, because Snodgrass was not just striding – he was striding *furiously*. And there were other signs she was picking up on – his bulky frame seemed swollen well beyond its normal size, and his face (framed by his square head) was the colour of bubbling lava.

Yes, he was mad all right, Paniatowski thought, and pitied whoever would be on the receiving end of his rage.

That was when she realized he was heading straight for her.

Snodgrass came to a halt directly in her path, so that short of stepping around him – which would have been very undignified – she had no choice but to come to a halt too.

'Can I ask you a question, DCI Paniatowski?' Snodgrass bellowed. Then, without waiting for a reply, he continued, 'What the bloody hell gives you the right to go sticking your big bloody nose into my patch?'

This simply couldn't be happening, Paniatowski thought.

Senior officers might occasionally shout at junior officers.

They shouldn't, but they did. But never – *never* – did one senior officer bawl out another, as Snodgrass was doing now – and the fact that he was doing it in a public area only made things worse.

'For God's sake, sir, get a grip!' she said. 'Remember who you are – and where you are.'

'Barrow Village is my patch, and I don't expect to find CID on it without a very good reason,' Snodgrass continued, but maybe something of what she'd said had got through to him, because now he had lowered his voice a little. 'Did you have a very good reason for being on my patch, Detective Chief Inspector Paniatowski?'

'Yes, sir, I heard on the police radio that there'd been a forced entry into a house in Barrow Village . . .'

'And you're investigating burglaries now, are you? I thought you fancy twats at CID didn't get off your arses unless there was at least a double murder to investigate.'

'I happened to be driving past the village—'

'And you thought you'd go and find a simple suicide, and turn it into a murder.'

'With respect, sir, what makes you think Arthur Wheatstone's death was a suicide?' Paniatowski asked.

'It's my men out there, doing the donkey work for your Inspector Beresford, you know,' Snodgrass said. 'And do you think that my men wouldn't let me know what's happening on my patch?'

'Are you saying that they're telling you that it isn't a murder?' Paniatowski asked.

'I'm telling you, Chief Inspector, that your thirst for newspaper headlines at any cost is pleasing no one,' Chief Superintendent Snodgrass said. 'I'm telling you that you've made an enemy of me, and I'm not the only one, because nobody likes an officer who can't be a team player.'

And without waiting for a response, he turned sharply on his heel and marched away.

Meadows was already back at the CID suite.

'What's the matter, boss?' she asked, when Paniatowski walked in. 'You look like you've seen a ghost.'

'No, it feels more like I've been hit by a truck,' Paniatowski said. 'Are we any closer to establishing our suspect's identity?'

'Not really,' Meadows said. 'He had no documents on him, nor were there any in the car.'

'What about the car itself?' Paniatowski wondered. 'That must have told us something.'

'You'd think so, wouldn't you,' Meadows agreed. 'But it was hired from a rental firm near Manchester airport.'

'So he must have shown them some identification before they'd hand over the car.'

'I'd assume so, but I don't know that for a fact, because they're not answering the phone.'

'Then why don't you ask the Manchester police to do us a favour and pop round there?' Paniatowski suggested.

'I did,' Meadows said. 'And when they got there, they found it was shut.'

'But it's a car hire *business*!' Paniatowski exclaimed.

'I know.'

'If they're shut, then not only can they not rent out any cars, they can't process the returns, either.'

'I agree with you,' Meadows said, 'but the fact is that they'd closed.'

'Do the Manchester police know when this was?'

'According to the tobacconist next door, they were already open when he got there at six . . .'

'Isn't that very early to be opening up?'

'No, because they do a lot of their business with people who've flown into the airport, so they have to be there when the planes land.'

'There's no strike at the airport is there?'

'No, it's running normally.'

'They were open when the tobacconist got there at six. Did he happen to notice what time they closed up?'

'He thinks it was around half past seven.'

Or, to put it another way, about the time we had the suspect hemmed in at the roadworks, Paniatowski thought.

'I'm going to question the American,' she said.

'On a scale of ten where one is a good idea and ten is a bad one, that's about a thirteen,' Meadows said.

'And why's that?' Paniatowski asked.

'Firstly, because you don't know enough about him to start questioning him,' Meadows told her. 'And secondly, they're never going to prosecute him for his attack on you if you have anything more to do with the investigation.'

It made sense, Paniatowski thought, but her gut told her he was never going to be charged with the attack anyway, and that if she didn't talk to him now, there wouldn't be another chance.

The door of the interview room opened, and the prisoner and escort entered.

'Please take a seat,' Paniatowski said, and the American sat down opposite her and Meadows.

'You don't object to being interviewed by two women, do you, Mr . . .?' she asked.

The American said nothing. Instead, he looked at them, sitting across the table from him, with a sort of bland lack of interest.

He was around thirty-five, Paniatowski estimated, and if she'd had to guess, she'd have said he was college educated and had a middle management post in some large corporation.

So what the hell had he been doing in Barrow Village at six o'clock in the morning?

'This is my colleague, Sergeant Meadows,' she said aloud. 'I'm DCI Paniatowski – the woman you crept up behind and struck on the back of the head with a spanner.'

No reaction. Not guilt – not even an acknowledgement that the attack had taken place.

Paniatowski switched on the tape recorder, and reeled off the prisoner's rights and the rest of the required rubric.

'I will ask you once more if you would like legal counsel,' she said, just in case he claimed later that, confused by a foreign environment, he hadn't known what was going on.

The prisoner said nothing.

'For the purposes of the recording, I need you to state in words whether or not you need a lawyer,' Paniatowski said.

The prisoner shrugged slightly, as if to indicate he didn't give a shit about *her* needs.

'I will take your silence as indicating that you have no objection to proceeding,' she said.

Still nothing from her prisoner.

'What's the matter?' she asked. 'Don't you trust English lawyers? Would you prefer one more like Perry Mason?'

This time, his face did register a little surprise.

Paniatowski laughed. 'What's the matter, Hank?' she asked. 'Oh, I'm sorry, you don't mind me calling you Hank, do you?'

The mask had slipped back into place.

'I think he's wondering how we know he's an American,' Meadows said.

'Oh, that's easy to explain,' Paniatowski said. 'For a start, there are your clothes. I mean – honestly! – the kindest way to describe them is as a little brash for our English taste. But the real giveaway was that when you surrendered to us, you put your hands behind your back. We handcuffed you the way you were expecting, because we didn't want you to know – at that particular moment – that we'd sussed you out. But if you'd been British, we've have handcuffed your hands in front of you.'

'Would you like to talk to Hank about what the future holds for him?' Meadows suggested.

'I don't see why not,' Paniatowski agreed. 'We may charge you with the murder of Arthur Wheatstone, Hank, but if we can't get you for that, you will certainly be charged with an assault on – and perhaps attempted murder of – a senior police officer. You'll be going to prison – there's no way round that now, I'm afraid – but how long you serve will depend on the exact nature of the charges. I should also mention that you could serve all your time over here, away from your family, or it could be arranged that you serve most of your time in the USA. It's up to you.'

With a brilliant lack of timing, a uniformed constable chose that moment to appear in the doorway.

'Yes?' Paniatowski snapped.

'Sorry to disturb you, ma'am, but his lawyer's here,' the constable said awkwardly.

'It can't be his lawyer,' Paniatowski said. 'No one even knows he's here.'

'He gave me this,' the constable told her.

He handed Paniatowski a card which said:

Oliver Staines
Solicitor

There was also a Manchester address, and a phone number.

'I want to see my lawyer,' said the American, in a voice which, to Meadows, suggested jambalaya and grits.

'What lawyer?' Paniatowski asked.

'The one on that card.'

'Do you even know his name?'

'I don't have to. You have to give me that card, and all I got to do is read it off.'

He was right, Paniatowski thought and suppressing a sigh (because she saw no reason why the prisoner should get the satisfaction of hearing it), she handed the card over.

'I'd like to see my solicitor, Oliver Staines,' the American said.

'He's not your solicitor,' Meadows said. 'You'd never even heard his name until you read it off that card.'

'Maybe you're right,' the prisoner agreed, 'but I've read the name now, and he is my solicitor – and nothing else is worth a plugged nickel.'

They weren't quite sure what to expect from a man who was happy to be known as 'Staines' but Oliver of that ilk was immaculately turned out in a herringbone suit, white shirt, Oxford university tie and shining black shoes. He was carrying an attaché case in one hand, and when Meadows and Paniatowski stood as he entered the room, he waved his free hand carelessly through the air and said, 'Oh please, don't get up for me. It makes me feel so awkward.'

'You're a funny man, Mr Staines,' Paniatowski said.

'Very funny,' Meadows said, and her voice had a growling edge to it – the sort of noise a Scottish lynx might make while it was working out which bit of naked flesh it was about to dig its teeth into.

'But you must realize that we're not getting up because we hold you in such high esteem,' Paniatowski continued. 'Believe me, nothing could be further from the truth. We're standing up so we can vacate the room, and so give you the privacy that you need to confer with your client.'

'But I don't need to confer with him,' Staines said. 'This is such a simple matter to resolve that I could have sent one of the clerks to do it.'

'Really?' Paniatowski said. 'Maybe you'll start to treat matters a little more seriously when I tell you . . .'

'That Robert here bopped you on the head with a spanner? Oh I already know all about that.'

'How do you know?' Paniatowski demanded.

'Oh, sources,' Staines said, making that annoying gesture with his hand again.

'You called him Robert,' Meadows said jabbing her fingers though the air, in the general direction of the American's heart.

'That's right, I did call him that, and by some happy coincidence, it happens to be his name,' Staines said. 'May I introduce you to Robert K Proudfoot III. Take a bow, Robert.'

And Proudfoot did indeed go through the motions of a flowery bow.

'I feel I should point out that you were extremely foolish to conduct the investigation into, and the interrogation of, the man who attacked you,' Staines said. 'If it had ever got to court, the defence would have torn it to pieces in minutes.'

'Have you misplaced the word "allegedly"?' Meadows wondered.

'I beg your pardon,' Staines said.

'Most of you shyster types are very careful what you say,' Meadows pointed out. 'You say, "My client allegedly did this." "My client allegedly attended this meeting." "I've put my umbrella up because it's raining – allegedly." But you're right up front about it. You say, "My client took this spanner, and he belted DCI Paniatowski on the back of the head."'

'Well, so he did,' Staines said expansively. 'And he's very sorry about it, aren't you, Robert.'

'Yes,' Proudfoot said.

'But it really doesn't matter what Robert says or doesn't say, because he's never going to be charged with anything.'

'Want a bet?' Meadows asked.

'Yes,' Staines said, seriously, 'but before I take your money, you'd better read this.'

He opened the attaché case, took out a single piece of paper, and laid it on the desk. The two women read it.

'This says that it's from the American Consulate,' Paniatowski said. 'Is it real?'

'Most authentic,' Staines confirmed.

'And what it says is that Robert Proudfoot III is a member of the American diplomatic corps.'

'Correct. He has diplomatic immunity, so he can steal, rape – even kill – and all you can do is deport him.'

'How do we know the man mentioned in the document and the man sitting at this table are the same man?' Meadows asked.

Staines reached into his attaché case again, produced a shiny new American passport, and handed it Meadows.

The detective sergeant flicked through it, then handed it back.

'Good enough for me,' she said, with obvious displeasure.

'So how long has Proudfoot been a diplomat?' Paniatowski asked.

'I wouldn't know,' said Staines, with a grin. 'But possibly not long.'

'A couple of hours?' Meadows guessed.

'As I said, I wouldn't know.'

So that was why Proudfoot had run, and why he had refused to say anything once he'd been caught, Paniatowski thought – because he'd been stalling while other people worked out a way to pull him out of the shit.

'Can I take my client back to Manchester, now, Chief Inspector?' Staines asked.

'If I want to see him again—' Paniatowski began.

'You can't,' Staines interrupted.

No, Paniatowski thought, she didn't suppose she could.

It was half an hour after Staines and his client had left police headquarters that the call came through.

'Hello,' said a cheery voice, 'it's your favourite solicitor on the line.'

'Mr Staines,' Paniatowski said wearily, 'after this morning, I can think of several words I might use to describe you, and favourite isn't one of them, so say something to grab my attention quickly, or I'm hanging up.'

'I think we should meet, because you'll hear something – as we solicitors love to say – to your advantage.'

'I don't think so,' Paniatowski said.

'Your loss, toots,' Staines told her.

The comment made her laugh, and the laugh made her relent.

'Where shall we meet?' she asked.

'I'm in a pub called the Grapes,' he said.

'I'll be there in two minutes,' she told him.

Staines was sitting at a table in the corner of the snug. On the table were a pink gin and a vodka.

'I asked the barman if he had any idea what DCI Monika Paniatowski drank, and he said every self-respecting barman in Whitebridge knew that she drank vodka,' he said.

Paniatowski sat down. 'Where's Robert Proudfoot Part Three?' she asked.

'I sent him off with my driver, to get some food,' Staines said.

'So we could have our little tête-a-tête?'

'Exactly.'

'And what is it that we need to get our heads together over?'

'I think it would be a mistake to focus too heavily on the part the Americans played in the incident in Barrow Village,' Staines said.

'The *murder* in Barrow Village,' Paniatowski corrected him.

'The murder, then.'

'Are you here to warn me off?' Paniatowski asked, starting to get angry. 'Are your American clients annoyed I'm not dancing to their tune?'

'No, not at all,' Staines protested, holding his hands up. 'I'm not here for them – I'm here for you. I want to help you.'

'Why?' Paniatowski wondered.

'Honestly? Because I fancy you and I'm trying to win your favourable opinion.'

'Oh, that's how you think it works, is it?' Paniatowski asked. 'You convince me you're on my side, and then we head for the nearest hotel?'

'No, no, of course not,' Staines protested. 'I want to bed you eventually, of course, but I'm perfectly content to play the long game.'

Paniatowski laughed again. It was nice being with a man who made her laugh.

'All right, why do you think the Americans have nothing to do with what happened in Barrow Village?' she asked.

'I never said that they had nothing to do with it – merely that they did not play a major part.'

'Go on.'

'They knew about it before you did – that's obvious, since Proudfoot got there before you. But I don't think they knew *much* earlier.'

'What makes you say that?'

'Because if there'd been time, they'd have sent someone from London up to Barrow Village, rather than rely on a man who'd just landed in Manchester after travelling all night on the red-eye.'

'And is that what they did?'

'Yes, assuming that Proudfoot was acting on behalf of his government in Barrow Village, rather than as an individual.'

'So Proudfoot didn't land until early morning?'

'That's right.'

'I assume the reason the car hire company closed down was so we wouldn't have any details ourselves before the consulate got its documentation completed.'

'I think I've gone as far as I'm going,' Staines said.

'But you're their agent, so you must know.'

'I'm not their agent. I'm a freelance solicitor. Have mediocre law degree – will travel. I fix things for people, but I never do anything illegal, and I never knowingly do anything political.'

'It was you who offered the car hire company a lot of money to close down for the day, wasn't it?' Paniatowski asked.

Staines stood up. 'If I call you in a few weeks and ask you to go out to dinner with me, will you think about it?' he asked.

'Yes, I'll think about it,' Paniatowski said.

Staines' eyes suddenly flooded with sadness. 'And then you'll say no,' he said.

'And then I'll say no,' she agreed.

'But why?' Staines asked. 'Am I not charming? Am I not good looking?'

'You're both of those things,' Paniatowski said.

'So then why?'

'I think the world you live in is a bit too complicated for me,' she said.

He shrugged, philosophically. 'There are times when I think it's a bit too complicated for me, too,' he admitted.

TEN

I t was twelve-thirty when the call came through.

'Hi,' said the voice on the other end of the line, 'this is Janet Goodman speaking.'

The wheels in Paniatowski's brain whirled round.

Janet Goodman . . . Janet Goodman . . .

Ah, yes, nice woman. She was an usher at Lancaster Crown Court, and they'd lunched together a couple of times when Paniatowski had been appearing . . .

Shit, shit, shit!

She'd had an excellent excuse for arriving late – but once Proudfoot had been arrested, she'd had no excuse at all for not handing the investigation over to someone else.

She'd have to grovel to the judge. She knew that.

She'd probably get a heavy fine for contempt of court. Well, she'd just have to find the money from somewhere.

But what was really tearing into her guts was the thought that she might lose this murder case.

'Are you there, Monika?' Janet Goodman asked.

'Yes, I . . .'

'His Honour is not pleased with you,' Janet said severely. 'He has instructed me to inform you that the only way you can compensate for your disgraceful conduct is to sleep with him.'

'What!' Paniatowski exploded.

Janet Goodman chuckled. 'Had you there, didn't I? You've nothing to worry about. One of the witnesses recanted overnight, so the prosecution's case has collapsed.'

'You evil witch!' said Paniatowski, through a smile that was half grin, half relief.

'No need to thank me – it's been my pleasure,' Janet said. 'I'll see you in court.'

At a quarter to one, as Paniatowski entered the public bar of the Drum and Monkey, she was thinking that it already felt as if it had been a long day.

Beresford and Meadows were sitting at the team's table. Judging by how much best bitter Beresford still had in his pint glass, they had been there for around ten minutes and had still not attempted to kill one another – which was good.

Actually, relations between the two had never reached the extreme of making homicide seem a distinct possibility – but they had been bad enough. And even now, animosity could still flare up between them occasionally, because though they did genuinely like each other, Beresford thought that Meadows did not have enough respect for rank, and Meadows was bloody certain that Beresford didn't have enough respect for liberated women (with the exception, of course, of his boss, but since she was – in his eyes – almost a goddess, that didn't really count).

Paniatowski bought herself a tonic water (Louisa was making her cut down on alcohol) and walked over to the table.

'So what have you got?' she asked.

'Arthur Wheatstone worked for British Aircraft Industries,' Colin Beresford said.

'It was really thoughtful of you to sugar the pill,' Meadows said, as Paniatowski's stomach did a series of somersaults that would have scored a perfect ten at the Olympics.

'It doesn't *necessarily* have to have anything to do with spying,' Beresford replied. 'Take the Verity Beale case as an example.'

Ah yes, the Verity Beale case, Paniatowski thought.

That murder had occurred back in Charlie Woodend's day, when she'd been his sergeant. Verity had had links to both BAI and the nearby American air force base and, as the investigation proceeded, Woodend's team had come close to suspecting that virtually everything that happened – from a cuckoo being heard in the woods to a minor car crash on the High Street – was part of some huge CIA-MI5 conspiracy to muddy the trail.

And in the end, much to their chagrin, it had had nothing to do with spooks at all.

In the end, it had just been a simple case of jealousy.

Yes, but there had been no Robert Proudfoot número tres – with his early-morning visiting habits and American embassy connections – involved in that case.

'What else?' Paniatowski asked Beresford.

'Mrs Wheatstone is away in Cumbria, visiting her sister. The Cumbrian police have contacted her, and they'll bring her back to Whitebridge sometime this afternoon. I'll stick around till she gets here, and conduct the interview myself.'

He could do it, Paniatowski thought. He could do it very competently and thoroughly. But the poor woman had just lost her husband, and might appreciate the gentleness of Jack the Poet, rather than the blunt directness of Shagger Beresford.

'You'll be more useful back in Barrow Village,' she said. 'Jack Crane can handle the Wheatstone interview.' She turned to Meadows. 'Has Arthur Wheatstone's name been released by the media yet?'

'No,' the sergeant replied. 'I thought you'd want it kept quiet till you'd done a bit of spade work, so I asked the local radio and television people if they'd hold off until the evening newspapers come out.'

'Did they agree to?'

'Yes.'

By doing so, the radio stations would be giving up their one advantage over the newspapers.

'Do you think they'll keep their promise?' Paniatowski asked.

'Oh, yes,' Meadows said. 'I went out of my way to ask them *very nicely.*'

And it would be a brave man or woman who turned down a request that Meadows had made 'very nicely', Paniatowski thought.

'Have you given the media a picture?' she asked.

'Yes, this one,' Meadows replied, taking a photograph out of her pocket and sliding it across the table. 'I found it in the house, and the neighbours say it's a good likeness.'

The man in the photograph looked somewhat different to the way he had when suspended from the beam in the garage or laid out on a stretcher – and it wasn't just because his eyes weren't popping or his tongue hanging out.

Inspector Cole had described Wheatstone as a bit of a weed, but that, it turned out, had been no more than a big man's disdain

for someone who did not conform to his idea of manliness. It was
true that Wheatstone was neither tall nor broad, but he had the
sort of figure that some people would still describe as dapper. And
he was good-looking too – not that spectacular jump-off-a-cliff-
just-to-get-his-attention good-looking, but certainly the sort of
good-looking which most women would probably give at least a
second glance.

Paniatowski took a sip of her tonic water.

Did people really drink this for pleasure? she wondered.

'What will you be doing this afternoon, boss?' Beresford
asked.

'What I *thought* I'd be doing was talking to Doc Shastri, but
she rang me to say her report won't be ready till later – or maybe
even tomorrow.'

'That's a bit of a nuisance,' Beresford said. 'Couldn't you chivvy
her along a bit?'

'Could *you*?' Paniatowski asked.

Beresford grinned. 'Fair point.'

'So what I'm going to do instead is to visit the British Aircraft
Industry's plant, accompanied by my beautiful assistant, and see
if we can ascertain why anyone should wish to bring a sudden
and dramatic ending to the temporal existence of Arthur Wheatstone.'

'I love it when you talk dirty,' Beresford said.

Mrs Wheatstone sat across the table from Crane in the less austere
and disapproving of the station's two interview rooms. She was
dressed, in his opinion, how any woman of taste in her mid-thirties
should be dressed. Her tailored jacket was a deep cornfield gold,
and blended perfectly with her cream blouse and her rich brown
skirt. She had a colourful silk scarf around her neck, and was
wearing tan shoes which he suspected were hand-stitched.

Simple, elegant, perfect.

The person *inside* the clothes, however, did not stand up anything
like so well to inspection.

There were huge bags under her eyes, and a positive roadmap
of broken veins in her cheeks. Her skin had left the soft-as-velvet
period far behind, and was rapidly heading towards its industrial
sandpaper stage. Her nails were bitten down to the quick, and her
fingers were stained with nicotine. She was a mess, and not a

recent mess – not a mess created by the announcement of the recent tragedy.

'Firstly, may I say how much I admire your bravery in the face of this terrible news,' Crane said.

'Thank you,' Mrs Wheatstone replied, looking down at the table as if too modest to accept a compliment.

'What have you been told about your husband's death, Mrs Wheatstone?' Crane asked.

'Only that he's dead,' the widow said. 'But since I'm here in a police station, I assume it wasn't natural causes.'

'Nothing is officially established until after the inquest,' Crane said, 'but no, I think we can say it wasn't natural causes.'

'And, by the same logic, it won't have been an accident, either – not unless it was the kind of accident that someone can be held criminally responsible for.'

'No, not that either,' Crane agreed.

A sudden look of horror appeared on Mrs Wheatstone's face.

'Oh, my God, it wasn't suicide, was it?' she gasped. 'Please tell me it wasn't suicide.'

Neither the boss nor Colin Beresford considered it could be suicide, but until Dr Shastri had put her official stamp of approval on the murder theory . . .

Crane reached across the table, and took Mrs Wheatstone's hands in his.

'If it does turn out to be suicide, you must not blame yourself,' he said. 'And you mustn't blame your husband either. It is easy to condemn someone who's taken their own life as selfish and cowardly, but until we've walked a mile in their shoes, we have no idea what pressure they were under.'

Mrs Wheatstone pulled her hands away.

'Where did that crap come from?' she asked. 'Did you read it in a book, or do they actually waste tax payers' money teaching it to you?'

'I . . . err . . . I was just trying to be helpful, and the words, which I thought would help, were my own.'

'I hope that when you're chatting up women you've got a better line of patter than that – because if you haven't, you might as well reconcile yourself to a life of celibacy.'

'I thought . . .' Crane said.

'You thought that I would be devastated if Arthur had topped himself. And so I would be. But it's not about lost love, not about my own sweet darling being taken from me by his own hand, how will I ever go on without him by my side . . . blah, blah, blah.'

'Then what *is* it about?' Crane asked.

'It's about the life insurance, moron! If that arsehole has gone and killed himself, then I get nothing.'

'Except for a big house and – no doubt – some stocks and shares,' Crane said, realising he was losing his objectivity, and not giving a toss.

'Yes, there are stocks and shares, and it is a big house,' Mrs Wheatstone agreed. 'But it's not enough. He could leave me the Royal Borough of Kensington and Chelsea, and it still wouldn't be enough.'

'You really hate him, don't you?' Crane said.

'A brilliant deduction, young sir! You ought to be a detective.'

'But you didn't kill him? Or have him killed?'

'Ah, so it is murder! That's a relief!'

'Yes, murder is the most likely cause of death.'

'How was it done?'

Crane hesitated for a moment, then said, 'It's most likely that he was hanged.'

'Where?'

'In the garage.'

'Then it's got to be murder, hasn't it? Because my short-arsed husband could never have reached the beam without a ladder!'

'And there weren't any in the house, were there?' Crane asked.

'No, there were not.'

'Why?' Crane asked.

'Why what?'

'Why weren't there any ladders? Every home has a couple of ladders lying about.'

'You were asking me whether or not I'd killed my husband, and the answer is "not",' Mrs Whitestone said. 'I should have, but somehow I just didn't have the get-up-and-go. People who marry for money always have a good reason for bumping off their part- ners, I suppose. But I was a fool, you see – I didn't marry him for money, I married him for love.'

'You're avoiding my question about the ladders, aren't you?'
Crane said.

'Yes, I am,' Mrs Whitestone agreed.

'Then answer this question – who can you think of who might
want your husband dead?'

Mrs Whitestone smiled. It was a sad, poignant smile.

'I could tell you,' she said, 'but why should I humiliate myself
when there are so many other people willing to do it for me?'

ELEVEN

The British Aircraft Industry's main site had started life in
the early years of the century as a small airfield in the
countryside, where rudimentary aircraft could take off and
land, and rudimentary repairs could be carried out by mechanics
who were developing their skills largely through trial and error.
It had been developed by Sutton Aircraft, a company which could
almost guarantee that its planes would not come apart in mid-air.
Sutton was swallowed by Whalley Air, Whalley Air fell victim
to a hostile takeover by Northern Aeronautics, Northern
Aeronautics amalgamated with Plaintree Weapons Systems . . .
and onwards and upwards, with new stationery and new logos
every time.

As the business expanded, so did the company's need for more
land. The farmers who owned it protested that their families had
worked it for generations, and to part with it would be like cutting
out their own hearts. Then the money on the table reached dizzying
amounts, and the farmers began to wonder who actually *needed*
a heart, anyway.

'There's a lot to dislike about the Russkies, but they're not all
bad,' one chairman of BAI was recorded saying in an unguarded
moment. 'After all, if they weren't so set on world domination,
there'd be fewer ex-farmers with money to burn, and we certainly
wouldn't be trading at anything like £27.30 a share.'

The site was located 10 miles due west of Whitebridge and 21
miles south-east of Blackpool. It was said that if you stood on top

of one of the company's huge hangar workshops, you could not only see Blackpool's famous tower, but also the big wheel on the South Shore Pleasure Beach.

It was also said that a young apprentice had once done exactly that, and after a secret trial had been sentenced to twenty years in a maximum-security prison for damaging property deemed essential to the defence of the realm. It was a good story, but like all good stories, the spinner of the tale would invariably back its authenticity by claiming that though he hadn't known the apprentice himself, he had known someone who had known someone who had.

What *was* indisputably true was that BAI was absolutely vital to the economy of the North-West. It employed eleven thousand workers on its site, as well as indirectly providing work for another sixty thousand who worked for companies servicing its needs. It had excellent industrial relations, and as long there were nations which wished to protect themselves from harm whilst also threatening harm to others, its future seemed rosy.

Paniatowski had not rung for an appointment – people who were usually available suddenly became unavailable at the prospect of being visited by the police – but had simply turned up and announced to the receptionist in the administration building that she would like to speak to the head of personnel on a matter of some urgency.

'I'm sorry,' the receptionist said, with a look of deep regret she could only have learned to conjure up on some kind of training course, 'but Mr Steel is in France at the moment. Would you like to see Mr Jackson, his deputy, instead?'

'Is he a man with a sharp, incisive mind?' Meadows asked.

'No,' the receptionist said. She looked confused. 'What I mean is, he's Mr Steel's deputy.'

'Yes, we'll see him instead,' Paniatowski said.

Mr Jackson was waiting for Paniatowski and Meadows as they stepped out of the lift. He was around forty years old, slightly plump and balding. He was the owner of a very unsuccessful moustache.

'Welcome, ladies,' he said. 'I am blessed indeed to be visited by two such charming creatures.'

Kate's really going to love this feller, Paniatowski thought, and the cat-like growl at the back of Meadow's throat confirmed her suspicion.

Jackson led them into his office. It had a window which looked out over the car park, and furniture which was high-quality veneered. Paniatowski guessed that his boss – Mr Steel – would have hardwood furniture and a view over the country-side, and that there were days when Jackson could almost convince himself that life hadn't short-changed him.

A pretty blonde with her hair in ringlets stuck her head in through the open doorway.

'The bubbly is cold enough now, Geor . . . Mr Jackson,' she said. 'Would you like me to bring it to you, or would you prefer to wait until . . .?'

'Would you two ladies like to join us in a glass of champagne?' Jackson asked.

'Is it a celebration?' Paniatowski asked.

'Yes, as a matter of fact, it is.'

'Then we'd be delighted.'

'You'd better add two more glasses to the tray then, Valerie,' Jackson said.

He still hasn't asked us why we're here, which is the *first* thing he should have done, Paniatowski thought – and the fact that he hasn't is why he's the man with the veneer furniture.

'There is one little favour I must ask you,' Jackson said.

'Yes?'

'You mustn't tell anyone about this little celebration until five o'clock, when the official announcement will be made.'

'No one will get a peep out of us,' Paniatowski promised.

And she was thinking that whatever the good news was, the simultaneous announcement of the death of Dr Arthur Wheatstone might possibly take the edge off it.

Valerie reappeared with the champagne. Jackson made a great show of opening the bottle with his thumbs, and his secretary gave a cute little squeak of fear when the cork flew out.

'You can pour, Valerie,' Jackson said, with an oily flirtatious-ness. 'You're so good at pouring.'

And he gave her bottom a friendly pat.

Was he showing off, or was it simply that he'd drowned any inhibitions he might have had in a pre-celebration celebration?

Whichever it was, he wasn't exactly endearing himself to Kate Meadows.

The secretary poured four glasses and handed them out.

'I'd like to propose a toast,' Jackson said, 'To the good ship BAI, may she stay afloat forever.'

The secretary repeated the toast with enthusiasm, and Paniatowski repeated it with mild embarrassment. Meadows took a sip from her glass, decided it was the sort of champagne that people who knew nothing about champagne thought was rather good, and spat it back into the glass. She walked over to the window, and disposed of the contents of her glass in a convenient rubber plant. She was glad she'd given up alcohol.

'Good heavens, you've drunk all yours already,' Jackson said to her. 'Can Valerie pour you another glass?'

Meadows simpered. 'No, thank you,' she said. 'After two glasses I become quite giggly.'

The day I hear Kate giggle, Paniatowski thought, is the day I'll know that the Four Horsemen of the Apocalypse are waiting just around the corner.

Sensing that Meadows was moving into attack-dog mode, she'd been about to muzzle her, but now she decided that the best way to interrogate someone like Jackson was to let her sergeant loose on him.

'So what are we celebrating?' she asked, sensing that Jackson would burst if she didn't invite him to say his piece.

'We have a partnership with a French company called Roussillon Aéronautique,' Jackson said. 'We have been developing a fighter plane called the Faucon.' He grimaced. 'We would have preferred to call it the Falcon, but you know what the French are like, don't you?'

'*Oui!*' Meadows said.

'Anyway,' Jackson continued, ignoring the remark, 'there's no point in building a first-class plane if no one wants to buy it – and for quite a while it seemed as if no one would. I don't mind telling you, I had some sleepless nights.'

'So you were shitting yourself at the thought of the company going belly up,' Meadows said.

Valerie giggled awkwardly, because only George – only Mr Jackson – was allowed to use naughty words.

Jackson himself seemed suddenly to have realized that in the interests of telling a dramatic story, he had been far from prudent.

'No, I never thought it would ever be anything like as bad as that. We don't just build aeroplanes. We're a very diverse company. We help submarines to navigate their way under the polar ice cap. We make it possible for democratic governments not only to detect hostile missiles, but to neutralize them.'

'Democratic governments!' Meadows repeated. 'So you only sell to democracies, do you?'

'We also sell to governments which are striving to *become* democratic. Our technology buys them the time they need to develop their democratic institutions,' said Jackson, probably quoting a line straight out of the company prospectus. 'At any rate, the point I'm making is that we don't just depend on one or two products for our survival. But it is true that if we hadn't sold the Faucon, I would have had to lay off quite a number of highly skilled workers.'

You wouldn't have had to lay off anybody – your boss would, Paniatowski thought. And it's more than possible that one of the casualties would have been a surplus to requirements deputy personnel manager.

'Who did you make the sale to?' she asked.

'Saudi Arabia. The Saudis had been very reluctant to have anything to do with the project, and then, out of the blue, they placed a very substantial order. I like to think of myself as a rational man, but I have to admit that this does seem a little like a miracle.'

'Interesting!' Paniatowski said briskly. 'Now, the reason we're here is that there are a few questions we'd like to ask you.'

'Oh!' Jackson said, in mock surprise. 'And here was me thinking you'd come to sell me tickets for the policemen's ball.'

'So if you wouldn't mind leaving us,' Paniatowski said pointedly to Valerie.

'It must be serious if you want my Girl Friday to leave the room,' Jackson said, in one of those film-trailer voices.

'Yes, it is,' Meadows told him. 'You can leave the tray for now,' she said to Valerie, who was collecting up the glasses.

'It won't take a minute,' the secretary said.

'You can leave it for now,' Meadows repeated, in a voice which said it was rather more than a request. She turned to Paniatowski. 'Would you like us to sit down, ma'am?' she asked.

'What a good idea,' Paniatowski agreed, sitting down in one of the visitors' chairs.

'And there's your chair, Mr Jackson – the nice mock-leather one behind the desk,' Meadows said.

Jackson knew something was going on here, but he wasn't quite sure what. He was beginning to wish he hadn't had all that brandy while waiting for the champagne to chill.

He was drunk, he realized. He was bloody well drunk!

Being careful not to crash into the furniture, he negotiated his way around the desk, and sat down.

'So what can I do for you?' he asked, trying to sound serious.

'Do you know an Arthur Wheatstone?' Paniatowski asked.

'Well, yes, he works here.'

'Do you know the names of everyone who works here?' Meadows wondered.

'Of course not. There are over eleven thousand people, so I couldn't possibly be expected to know them all.'

'And yet you know Wheatstone. Why is that? Has he been causing you problems?'

'No, he's never caused any problems, as far as I know.'

'So you must share an interest? What is it? Do you both enjoy swimming with sharks? Do you share a mistress?'

'No, nothing like that. As I said, I can't be expected to know the name of everyone who works here, but I do know everyone above a certain level.'

'And what level might that be?'

'I suppose I know everyone who has a key to the executive toilets and eats in the executive dining room.'

'So Arthur's an executive, is he?' Meadows said.

'Yes, in a way. But I wouldn't exactly call him management, because he's more on the technical side of the business.' He paused, as if a new thought, quite unconnected with his ego, had managed to find its way to the forefront of his self-obsessed brain. 'Why are you asking me all these questions?' he demanded. 'Has something happened to Arthur?'

'What exactly does he do?' Meadows asked, as if he'd never spoken.

'Now look here, I just asked you . . .'

'What exactly does he do?' Meadows insisted.

'I can't tell you that,' Jackson said, wiping away the sweat that had been gathering on his brow.

'Why? Is it because you're so low in the pecking order of this place that you don't even *know*?'

'I am *not* low in the pecking order,' Jackson said furiously. 'I review all the files. I know what everybody does.'

'So why can't you tell us?'

'Because, you idiot, I've signed the Official Secrets Act.' A look of real horror came to Jackson's face. 'I'm so sorry,' he whined. 'I never meant to . . .'

'You're right, I am an idiot,' Meadows said.

The horror was replaced by incredulity. 'You are?' Jackson asked.

'A complete idiot,' Meadows said humbly. 'You see, it never really occurred to me that the work Arthur Wheatstone was doing might be secret.'

'Everything that happens here is secret,' said Jackson, who seemed to believe he was back on top.

'So has Arthur been working on this fighter plane of yours?'

'I can't tell you,' Jackson said, still confident but becoming cautious again. 'I'd be in breach of the act.'

'He hasn't been working on it, has he?' Meadows teased. 'I can see it in your eyes.'

'No comment.'

'Nah, he hasn't been working on it,' Meadows said. 'That's a definite, one hundred percent nailed-down certainty.'

'I never told you that,' Jackson croaked, almost panicking. 'You can't say you got it from me.'

'So where does that leave us?' Meadows mused. 'Well, since he wasn't working on the French project, he must have been working with the Americans, instead.'

'Now you look here . . .' Jackson began, raising a warning finger, 'you can't just go . . .'

'Missiles, is it?' Meadows asked. 'Blow up the world with the push of a button? Or is it navigation equipment, in case the Yanks want to sneak up the river to Moscow?'

'I'm saying no more,' Jackson told her, as he folded his arms firmly across his chest.

'That's probably how he got to know Robert Proudfoot, isn't it?' Paniatowski asked.

'Who?'

'Robert Proudfoot.'

'I've never heard of the man, and I'm not going to answer any more questions about the company without my lawyer being present,' Jackson said.

Meadows and Paniatowski exchanged the briefest of glances, yet it was enough for them to agree that while this line of questioning was dead, they might squeeze a little more interesting information out of him if they switched to talking about the crime.

'You never asked us why we were asking questions about Arthur Wheatstone,' Paniatowski said. 'Well, now's your chance to question us.'

Jackson hesitated, as if he suspected some kind of trap.

'Go right ahead,' Paniatowski said encouragingly. 'You've no need to worry about Sergeant Meadows – she's pretty much used up her supply of venom for the day.'

'What's . . . what's happened to Wheatstone?' Jackson asked.

'What do you think might have happened to him?'

'Has he been hurt?'

'It's a bit more serious than that.'

'He's dead?'

'Well, that is the next step.'

'Was it an accident, then?'

'I'm a sergeant, and my boss is a DCI,' Meadows pointed out. 'Do you seriously think we'd be wasting our time investigating an accident?'

'So it's suicide, then?'

Paniatowski felt the hairs on the back of her neck stand up.

'Now why would you assume that the next step beyond accidental death is suicide, I wonder?' she asked.

'It's surely the sort of assumption anybody would make,' Jackson said defensively.

'I wouldn't make it,' Paniatowski said.

'Me neither,' Meadows echoed.

'Well, it wasn't an accident, and it wasn't suicide, either,' Paniatowski said, studying Jackson's face closely. 'He was shot.'

'Shot!' Jackson repeated.

'You sound surprised.'

'Well, yes, I must admit I am. It's not the sort of crime you think of as happening round here.'

'Actually, we still don't know how he died, though we suspect he was strangled.'

'So what was all that shooting bollocks about?' Jackson demanded.

'I wanted to see how you reacted.'

'Does that mean I'm a suspect?'

Paniatowski laughed. 'Mr Jackson, you must surely realize that everyone in central Lancs is a suspect.'

'But you're not sitting across from everybody in central Lancs, are you?' Jackson asked.

'And I have to say, I'm quite surprised at the way you're reacting to the news of a colleague's death.'

'As I told you earlier, I really didn't know Wheatstone well,' Jackson said, 'and I'm simply not the kind of man to shed buffalo tears.'

'Crocodile tears,' Meadows said.

'Come again?'

'If you're wishing to illustrate insincere emotion, then the phrase you're looking for is crocodile tears, not buffalo tears.'

'Are you taking the piss?' Jackson asked.

'Absolutely,' Meadows told him.

TWELVE

Put Dr Shastri in a sari and white clinician's coat and she looked like a beautiful Indian model hired to do a hospital photo shoot. Add large glasses, perched on the end of her nose, as they were now, and she looked like a *very sexy* beautiful Indian model.

'The reason I have kept you waiting so long, my dear Monika, is that there was one nagging question that I didn't have an answer to,' she said.

'And now you *do* have an answer,' Paniatowski said.

Shastri shook her head. 'No, but I am beginning to think that I will never have an answer, and that I might as well give you what I can.'

'All right,' Paniatowski agreed.

'Your victim died as a result of asphyxia, the asphyxia itself being as a result of hanging.'

'But he couldn't have killed himself,' Paniatowski interrupted. 'He simply couldn't have reached the beam.'

'Did I say he had killed himself?' Shastri asked sternly.

'No, but . . .'

'Then, as they say around here, if tha' wants to learn somethin', tha' should keep tha' trap shut till I've finished,' Shastri said, riding roughshod over her normally exquisitely polished vowels with a broad Whitebridge accent.

Paniatowski grinned. 'Sorry,'

'And so you should be,' Shastri said, grinning back. She laid some photographs on the desk. 'These are pictures of the victim's throat.'

There was a dark band of bruising around the throat, where the rope had bitten in, cutting off his air.

'What is wrong with that?' Shastri asked.

For a moment, Paniatowski could see nothing wrong. Then she said, 'It's very regular.'

'Just so! A man may be truly determined to hang himself, but once he feels himself walking on air, he will struggle for the few seconds available to him. He can't help it – he is gripped by the human instinct for survival. This struggle will inevitably spread the area of the bruising. In some cases, it is hardly noticeable – a little wider here, a little more irregular there. In others, it is obvious he has fought like the very devil, and you can see bruises where he has tried to get his fingers between the rope and his neck. I even had a case where a man managed to dislocate his jaw. There is no sign of extended bruising here, which means he did not struggle at all.'

'So he was unconscious when he was strung up?'

'He may have been unconscious, or he may have been conscious but paralysed. I cannot say for sure.'

'But you do think he was doped?'

'I *know* he was doped. There are bruises on his arms where he was held down, and beneath one of them is the tiniest of pin pricks.' Shastri paused for a moment. 'And now you are going to ask me what drug was used, aren't you, Monika?'

'Yes.'

'I do not know. I can find no trace of it in his system.'

'You mean, it's not there anymore?'

'No, I mean that none of the standard tests will identify it.'

'And why's that?'

'I don't know. It's possible it's a newly discovered poison, in which case it will probably have come from South America. Then again, it might have been created by a rogue scientist, probably as a by-product of his work on a new synthetic opiate.'

'So let me see if I've got this straight,' Paniatowski said. 'The whole fake suicide was an incompetent disaster from start to finish – yet the killer somehow managed to get his hands on a Rolls Royce of a poison.'

'That would seem to be the case,' Shastri agreed.

'Could this drug be the reason there was no pool of urine on the floor?' Paniatowski asked.

'Yes, that is possible,' Shastri conceded, 'It could also explain why his bowels were not evacuated.' She picked up her notebook. 'Now what else do I have for you? A few hours before he died, your victim ate a vindaloo curry which I suspect – from the quality of the material – came from a packet.' She crinkled her pretty nose in disgust. 'Why would anyone eat vindaloo from a packet?'

'It takes all sorts,' Paniatowski said.

'There was evidence in his lungs of a kind of compost which *Forensic Science for Ambitious Little Indians* tells me is often associated with growing pot plants. Did your victim have a greenhouse attached to his home?'

'No, he didn't.'

'Then perhaps he has a friend with one, and finding this friend will lead you to the murderer. I offer this suggestion free of charge, and with no thought of future reward.'

'You're very kind,' Paniatowski said, with a smile. 'Anything else?'

'He had also drunk two glasses of wine.'

'Did he have a drinking problem?' Paniatowski asked.

'No, Monika,' Shastri said. 'Why would he have a drinking

problem? He was not, after all, a police officer! In fact, I would say from the evidence of his liver that he was in excellent shape for a man of his age.'

'You treat your body like a temple – and then you get murdered,' Paniatowski said. 'Just goes to show, doesn't it?'

'If that is intended to get a rise out of me, it will fail,' Shastri said severely. 'I have given up trying to save you, Monika, and hence I no longer lecture you on your health.'

'No, you don't,' Paniatowski agreed. 'Now you've trained Louisa up to do it, you've no need to.'

'She is a good girl,' Shastri said, with a fond smile. 'And now, since I have no more to tell you, I will escort you off the premises.'

'Why do you need to escort me?' Paniatowski asked. 'Are you afraid I'll nick something from this lovely mortuary of yours?'

'Of course not,' Shastri said. 'But one can never be too careful with the constabulary.'

As they walked towards the door, Shastri said, 'I should not even have been on duty today, you know.'

'Why's that?' Paniatowski asked.

'I have a list of approved locums, and one of them – a man who has only just left the army – is always pestering me to let him fill in for me. He says it would help to plug an important gap in his curriculum vitae – and I suppose he is right.'

'His problem is, he's never going to get his foot through the door because you've got an aversion to taking time off,' Paniatowski said.

'That is generally true, but today would have been special,' Shastri said. 'There was a concert of Indian Carnatic music in the Free Trade Hall in Manchester this afternoon. The performers are famous throughout India, and though I applied almost as soon as the tickets became available, they were all sold out. I was naturally very disappointed, but then someone, an admirer, perhaps . . .' She paused. 'Or do I flatter myself when I say I have admirers?'

'You know you don't.'

'At any rate, whether he was an admirer or not, someone sent me a ticket – one of the best seats in the house. So I rang this doctor and I asked if he'd fill in for me, and he said he'd be delighted. Then this morning, he rang me up at eight thirty to say he couldn't fill in for me today. At eight thirty! And five minutes later, I got another call, telling me there was a cadaver waiting for me in Barrow Village. It's almost as if he'd been given the details, and decided he just couldn't be bothered with that particular corpse.'

'Maybe that was exactly what it was,' Paniatowski suggested.

'No, because he never knew about it. The call which came into the mortuary would have been transferred to him if he'd been available, but since he wasn't, it was switched directly to me.'

'Well, it's certainly a mystery,' Paniatowski said as she stepped out of the main door.

'But no doubt you think it's a very small one in comparison with the one you're involved with.'

'Well, yes,' Paniatowski admitted, caught off-guard.

Shastri grinned. 'There are no small mysteries,' she said, deliberately misquoting Stanislavski, 'only small investigators.'

Paniatowski entered the public bar of the Drum and Monkey at twenty past nine.

'What's it to be tonight, Chief Inspector?' the barman called out. 'Tonic water or vodka?'

She knew what Louisa would say – but then Louisa wasn't trying to crack a murder, was she?

'Vodka,' she heard herself say. 'Make it a double.'

Meadows was already there, and a couple of minutes later, Beresford walked in.

'Where's Crane?' Paniatowski asked.

'He was booked to read his poetry at the Bamber Bridge Institute,' Beresford said. 'If he'd cancelled, it would have been the second time, so I told him we could do without him tonight.' He paused, uncertainly. 'I hope that's all right.'

'It's fine,' Paniatowski said.

Jack Crane was probably a better police officer for his poetry, although if you followed that argument to its natural conclusion, Meadows was a better officer for her sado-masochism. And maybe she was. Who was to say? It was hard to see how Colin's ambition to sleep with every available woman in Whitebridge improved his performance (out of bed) but maybe his carnal hunting instincts made him a better bobby.

And me, she thought. What about me?

Maybe she should take up watercolour painting or pottery.

But she knew that wouldn't work. She wasn't one of those people who resented work getting in the way of her interests. It was quite the reverse, in fact, and she could just picture herself moulding a pot and wishing the phone would ring to summon her to a nice juicy murder.

'How are things in Barrow Village going, Colin?' she asked.

Beresford took a sip of the pint that the barman had started to pull for him the second he walked through the door.

'It's one of the cleanest houses we've ever had to deal with,' he said. 'Four bedrooms, three bathrooms, a kitchen you could cater a wedding from, and only four sets of prints lifted so far – all of them identified.'

'The victim, his wife, their cleaner . . .' Paniatowski speculated.

'That's right.'

'What about the fourth set?'

'They're yours.'

Of course they were, Paniatowski agreed.

'What else?' she asked.

'As is already obvious from the prints, they weren't the most neighbourly of couples. They kept themselves to themselves, but their rows were so loud that people in houses several doors up the road were aware they were going on.'

'What were these rows about?'

'That, they couldn't hear – or are not prepared to admit they could, because that would suggest they were nosey parkers, rather than innocent bystanders. But they do say that the rows went on for hours, and when they ended, Arthur Wheatstone would some-times drive off, and they wouldn't see him for a couple of days.'

'Is there anything else to be learned from the house?' Paniatowski asked hopefully – but without much hope.

'Could be,' Beresford said. 'We'll see what the SOCOs come up with in the morning.'

'Fine, let's move on,' Paniatowski suggested. 'Did anybody in the village notice any unusual activity last night?'

And she was thinking, dear God, was it only last night it happened, and only fourteen hours since I found the body? It seems like half a lifetime ago.

'Don't get too downhearted, because we've only managed to doorstep half the village today, but—'

'But no,' Paniatowski interrupted.

'But no,' Beresford agreed. 'The only person who's seen the very big feller and his partner is your mate ex-Inspector Cole, and if I was you, boss, I'd start asking myself if he's really that reliable.'

'He's reliable,' Paniatowski said firmly. 'I had my doubts at first, but everything he told me has panned out, so if he says he saw a big feller and a little feller, then they were there.'

A man entered the bar and headed straight for their table. He was around forty years old and mildly reminiscent of Kirk Douglas, Paniatowski thought, although he was a little darker than Douglas. He was wearing a stylish leather jacket, and had an impressively chunky gold ring on his index finger.

'Chief Inspector Paniatowski?' he asked, holding out his hand. 'I'm Greg Steel.'

Paniatowski shook the hand. Steel had a firm grip, but not a grip of steel, which was reassuring.

'Do you think we could have a few moments in private, Chief Inspector?' he asked.

'I don't see why not,' Paniatowski told him. 'There's a free table over there. I'll join you in a moment.'

'Who's he?' Beresford whispered once Steel had gone.

'He's the head of personnel at BAI.'

'And what does he want?'

'That's just what I'm about to find out.'

Steel was smoking a Benson and Hedges, and Paniatowski looked at it with lust in her heart. She'd been trying to cut down – Louisa again – but when he offered her the packet, her hand seemed unwilling to resist.

'I'm sorry not to have met you at the plant,' Steel said, as he lit her cigarette, 'but I was on my way back from France.'

'Ah yes, signing the deal for the new super fighter.'

Steel laughed. 'George Jackson may have tried to give you the idea that we in personnel are the core around which all else in the company revolves, but I have no such illusions. Have you ever heard the expression, "I'm talking to the engineer, not the oily rag"?'

She laughed. 'Yes, I have.'

'Well, I see us very much as the oily rag.'

'And yet here you are, taking up both my valuable time and your own,' Paniatowski said.

He chuckled. 'Did George pull that Official Secrets line on you?'

'Yes, he did.'

'He loves that. It makes him feel so important. But he can't always distinguish between what's secret and what isn't, so I'm here to answer some of the questions that he wouldn't.'

'And voluntarily, too,' Paniatowski said.

He smiled again. 'That's right.'

There was definitely a tingle of electricity between them, Paniatowski thought, but she'd given up falling for men connected with cases she was investigating.

Still, no doubt Louisa had been right when she'd said that what her mother needed was a permanent man (Louisa was right about most things, the cocky little bitch), and maybe when this case was over . . .

'So what do you want to know?' Greg Steel asked.

'Oh yes,' Paniatowski said, arriving back in real life with a jolt. 'Jackson refused to say whether or not Wheatstone was working on the new Anglo-French plane that you've just sold to the Saudis.'

'He wasn't.'

'Then what was he working on?'

'He was working on a project for the Americans, and—'

'What? Are you telling me that you're building planes with both the French *and* the Yanks?'

'Not exactly,' Steel said. 'We're equal partners with the French, despite the fact that the plane has been given a French name. And the Americans don't like that one bit.'

'They don't like it that the plane's got a French name?'

'No, they don't like it that we're partnered up with the French. The Americans like to be in control of everything, you see, which is one of the main reasons that President de Gaulle took France out of NATO. Now they're truly independent, and the Yanks are so annoyed they don't even send them a birthday card anymore. And working on this plane makes *us* semi-independent – at least in this one sphere – and the Americans don't like that, either.

'But we still work with the Americans on the other plane?'

'No, it's very much an American plane, and we don't work *with* them, we work *for* them. Essentially, we're subcontractors, or, to put it in its most basic terms, day labourers. We labour for the Americans, they pay us, and what is produced is theirs.'

'Exactly what kind of work was Arthur Wheatstone involved in?' Paniatowski asked.

'It's something very complicated involving string and lots of elastic bands,' Steel said, with a smile.

'In other words, you won't tell me.'

'In other words, that really is where the Official Secrets Act begins to raise its ugly head.'

'But you can tell me who he was working with?'

'Oh yes.'

'And you'll have no objection to me questioning them?'

'As long as it doesn't touch on their work, you can question them about anything you want to.'

'Have you heard of an American called Robert Proudfoot?' Paniatowski asked, doing her best to disguise the fact that she was studying him for some reaction.

'No, I don't think so,' Steel said.

And either he was a bloody fine actor or he was telling the truth.

'What made you ask that?' he wondered.

'He wasn't working alongside Wheatstone?' Paniatowski asked.

'And again, what would make you think that?'

'Well, since we've already established that Arthur *was* working with the Americans . . .'

A sudden look of realisation came to Steel's face. 'I see where you're going wrong. This is all Hollywood's fault,' he said.

'What do you mean?'

'In the movies, you've got all the scientists together in one big lab, and they're all looking puzzled. Then one of them says something like, "If nothing else is working, why don't we try using bat testicles, a xylophone and a left-handed ballpoint pen?" The others say it's worth a shot, and in the next scene you've got them all huddled over a big box with flashing lights and tubes. Well, maybe it did work like that once, but not anymore. Everything is done through computer-aided design these days. He probably never met the Americans he was "working" with, and chances are that any practical work to test his theories will have been carried out in specialized laboratories in Wisconsin or South Carolina.'

'So he was a *theoretical* scientist,' Paniatowski said.

'Yes, I think I can admit that much,' Steel conceded.

'So he, and the people he works with, wouldn't have been able to lay their hands on any rare chemicals?'

'What makes you ask that?'

'Just something the police doctor said.'

'I don't want to tell you how to do your job—' Steel said.

'Now there's a relief,' Paniatowski interrupted him.

'. . . but it seems to me that in searching for a motive for his death, you're concentrating perhaps a little too heavily on his professional life.'

'So what is it about his private life that I should look into?' Paniatowski wondered.

'I'd rather not say,' Steel said.

'You don't do coy well,' Paniatowski told him.

Steel grinned, self-consciously. 'No, I don't, do I?' He put his hands together, almost as if he were in prayer. 'My problem is, you see, that I have certain suspicions about certain actions that certain persons may have taken, but it does not go beyond that – certainly not far enough to convince me that I should point the finger at another man.' He paused. 'Or, indeed, at a woman.'

'You have a civic duty to tell me what you know, Mr Steel,' Paniatowski pointed out.

'But not to reveal my merest thought, Detective Chief Inspector Paniatowski,' Steel countered. He stood up. 'I will leave you with one question that may assist you in your inquiries,' he said. 'And it is this; why would Wheatstone and his wife want to live out there in the middle of the moors? And before you say it, it isn't because he couldn't afford anything like as nice a house in town. The truth is, he could afford it easily. So what made him choose to live where he did? Or was it his choice at all?'

And then, with a parting gesture which resembled either touching his forelock or offering a mock salute, he was gone.

The regional news went to town on the murder, as was only to be expected. Camera crews had been up in Barrow Village all day, and the result was short film clips of the Wheatstone house, the neighbours' houses, the community centre (which Beresford had commandeered as his incident room) and surrounding moorland.

There was also an interview – of sorts.

DI Beresford – half a dozen microphones in front of him – is looking far from at his ease.

'Is it true, DI Beresford, that the murderer attempted to make it look like a suicide?' asks a disembodied voice.

'The statement we issued earlier said we suspected foul play,' Beresford answers. 'That does not automatically mean that there was foul play, or that what we are dealing with here is a murder disguised as a suicide.'

'But what do you think*?' the voice persists.*

'I think *there may have been foul play,' Beresford says.*

'Don't you think the public has the right to know what's going on?' another voice asks.

'Yes,' Beresford says, 'but it also has the right to expect that when it does get the information, it will be carefully verified fact, rather than wild speculation.'

'Do you think that Arthur Wheatstone's murder has something to do with the fact that he was a famous scientist?' another voice asks.

'Was he?' Beresford says. 'I hadn't heard of him until this morning. Had you?'

'Well, no,' the reporter admits.

'Can't have been that famous then, can he?' Beresford asks. 'And there you go again, talking about "murder" when all I've said is "death".' He checks his watch. 'We expect there to be a press briefing sometime tomorrow. Until then, no further information will be released. Thank you all for coming.'

'Who's a pretty boy, then?' Meadows asked. She put her hand to her mouth as if she'd just realized she'd made a big mistake. 'Sorry, that really wasn't very respectful, was it? What I should have said was, "Who's a pretty boy then, *sir!*".'

'Your problem, Sergeant Meadows, is that you've never had to do what I do, so you just don't appreciate how bloody difficult it is.'

'Shut up, the pair of you!' Paniatowski said. 'I want to watch this.'

On the screen, the anchorwoman was leading into the next story.

'It is ironic that on the same day as this tragedy, BAI should have heard some of the best news it has had for a long time,' she says. 'Let's go over now to Peter Hayes, our transport and commerce correspondent, who, I know for a fact, considers himself something of an expert on all matters aeronautical.'

The screen splits, with the anchorwoman on the left side and Hayes on the other.

'I was just telling our viewers what an expert you are on the aircraft business,' the anchorwoman says.

Hayes tries to smile, and doesn't quite make it.

'That was very kind of you,' he says, 'but then your kindness is legendary. There are people in the studio who hide when they see you coming, because they just can't take any more of your kindness.'

'In the morning, they'll both do their best to pass all this off as playful banter which they didn't get quite right,' Meadows said, 'but it's much more personal than that.'

'Yes, it is,' Paniatowski agreed, hiding a smile. 'Now perhaps you'll start to understand what it's like having to nanny the pair of you.'

'Oh, come on, boss,' Meadows said.

'It's nothing like that,' Beresford protested.

'So, feel free to correct me if I've got this wrong,' the anchorwoman says, 'but didn't you tell us a couple of weeks ago that there was no way on earth that this deal could go through.'

'I think I said that the plane didn't have what the Saudis wanted,' Hayes says, gritting his teeth.

'Not enough ashtrays, perhaps?' the anchorwoman prods.

'Yes, it could be something like that,' Hayes says. 'On the other hand, it could be a sophisticated navigation system which allows them to operate at low level, at night, even when they are not in communication with their base.'

'Is that what they wanted?' the anchorwoman asks.

Hayes sighs. 'Nobody knows, because it's all been kept secret,' he explained, 'but the general consensus among the experts is that it has to be something like that.'

'So it's no more than a guess?'

'I suppose so, but it's an educated one.'

'It all sounds very complicated and sophisticated.'

'*It is.*'

'*It can't be that complicated if BAI couldn't provide it two weeks ago, but now they can.*'

'*You refuse to understand, don't you? You're just a . . . oh, I just give up on you.*'

'Well, that was more than just a clash of personalities,' Beresford said. 'That was a lovers' tiff in cinemascope.'

'Directed by Cecil B DeMille, with Charlton Heston as the reporter, and Bette Davis as the anchorwoman,' Meadows chipped in.

'Do you think either of them will still have a job by this time tomorrow?' Beresford asked.

'The woman will be gone, but the man will probably survive it, because, after all, he *is* a man.'

'Now, now, let's not let our prejudices paint a false picture of the world,' Beresford said.

'Oh, get stuffed,' Meadows replied, though without rancour.

It was nice to hear the children playing together quite happily again, Paniatowski thought. But the news bulletin had disturbed her, and the fact that the contract had been signed the same day the body was discovered was disturbing, because she didn't like coincidences.

But was it a coincidence, after all? Was it right to try and link a purely local murder with a deal spread over two continents and worth millions – perhaps billions – of dollars?

Let's not see it as any more than it is, she told herself. Let's not get dragged into conspiracy theories, like we did last time.

On the screen, the anchorwoman was talking rather pleasantly to a man who had walked all the way from New York to Los Angeles.

It was four o'clock in the morning when the van pulled up at the gates of the Old Mill Road allotments, and two men – both dressed in black jumpers and black trousers, and wearing black rubber gloves – got out. As the van was pulling away, one of the men was already inserting his allotment holder's key in the lock.

Even at that time of day, it was risky entering by the gate, which was why the shorter of the pair had suggested that they cut the wire round the back, instead.

The taller man had looked at him as if he were mad.

'We are aiming for a light touch,' he said. 'We aim to be in and out, and no one the wiser. If we cut a hole in the fence, we might as well leave a big sign next to it saying, "We were here".'

'People might think it was just kids.'

'And they might not. We can't take the chance, so we'll use the gate.'

Once they were inside, they picked their way carefully between the plots until they reached the potting shed which was not really a potting shed at all.

The door was padlocked, and the padlock would have to be cut through, but they had been aware of that beforehand, and had brought a replacement lock of exactly the same kind with them.

The shorter man sheered through the padlock with bolt cutters, and dropped it into the bag his partner was holding open.

Once inside the shed – with the shutters down and the door closed – they could afford the luxury of switching on their torches.

'Well bugger me sideways!' exclaimed the smaller man, who had not been there before.

His partner, who had been anticipating just such a reaction, chuckled. 'Yes, it's quite a set-up, isn't it?'

'Did he use it much?'

'It depended on the circumstances, but there've been times when he's used it six or seven times a week.'

'And was it always the same . . .?'

'No, not always.'

'You've got to take your hat off to him, haven't you?'

'Is that the kind of thing that you admire a man for?'

'Well, you know . . .'

'Look around you,' the taller man said. 'How tidy would you say it was?'

'Neither that tidy nor that untidy,' the shorter man decided.

'Then that's how we'll leave it when we've finished – neither that tidy nor that untidy.'

'Surely, nobody will notice a bit more mess here and there, will they?' the shorter man asked. 'I mean, the first thing they'll see is what I saw, and after that their minds will be so blown that they won't want to bother with the details.'

'Most people *won't* notice,' the taller man agreed. 'Maybe there's only one man in a hundred who *can* see things as they really are – but he's the only one who actually matters to us.'

'OK,' the smaller man said, sounding unconvinced.

'Do you see that cupboard?' the taller man said.

'Yes.'

'Turn it round carefully. Pinned to the back of it, there's an envelope marked Top Secret. I want it.'

The other man did as he'd been instructed. 'Yeah, you're right!' he said. 'There is a brown envelope. How did you know it would be there?'

'I knew it was there because I put it there.'

'You broke in and put it there?'

'Yes.'

'And now you're breaking in and taking it away again?'

'Yes.'

'Why?'

'Because things didn't quite turn out in Barrow Village as they'd been intended to. Could I have the envelope, please?'

The shorter man handed him the envelope, then said, 'What's that in the corner?'

'I don't know. Why don't you investigate?'

The smaller man crouched down and poked the thing with his finger. 'Ugh,' he said, rapidly rising again and looking at one finger of his gloved fingers in disgust. 'It's a French letter. A *used* one.'

'Excellent,' the other man said. 'We'll leave it where it is for our little Catholic copper to find.'

THIRTEEN

She sensed the tension in the air the moment she walked through the side door of police headquarters next morning. It was a special sort of tension, of real significance only within the world of local policing – the police bubble. It had been there – this tension – when Chief Constable Marlowe had resigned in disgrace, when the whole shift had been informed that Bob Rutter was dead, and when Charlie Woodend (who everyone assumed they'd need wild horses to drag out of the place) had quietly announced that he was jacking it all in and going to grow geraniums on the Costa Blanca.

As she walked briskly up the stairs (Louisa discouraged her from taking the lift) she wondered what the source of the tension was this time.

She did not have long to wait for an answer. In fact, she'd only just entered the CID suite when one of the clerical officers – a bright girl called Linda – said, 'Have you heard about Chief Superintendent Snodgrass, ma'am?'

An image of Snodgrass from their encounter the day before immediately flashed across her brain

A big man, using his size – as all bullies do – to intimidate.

'Can I ask you a question, DCI Paniatowski? What the bloody hell gives you the right to go sticking your big bloody nose into my patch?'

'What about him?' she asked.

'He's left.'

'Left?'

'To join another force.'

'I thought you fancy twats at CID didn't get off your arses unless there was at least a double murder to investigate.'

He wouldn't be missed, at least by her, she thought. But before they could finally be rid of him, there'd be the receptions and parties, and she'd almost wear out her smiling hypocrite mask.

'Who's collecting for the gift in this department, and how much is everyone chipping in?' she asked, bowing to the inevitable.

'There isn't going to be a gift, ma'am.'

'But when there's a party . . .'

'There won't be a party, either.'

'But when someone goes . . .'

'Chief Superintendent Snodgrass isn't *going*, ma'am – he's *gone.*'

'Gone?'

'As in "left" ma'am – hit the trail, taken the bus to Bradford, sailed off into the sunset—'

'Yeah, yeah, I get it,' Paniatowski interrupted, thus stemming Linda's seemingly endless flow of images of departure.

Senior officers didn't just leave at the drop of a hat, she told herself. Before they could even think of relinquishing their posts, they had to untangle all the strands of activity which had inevitably been drawn into their web. In some cases, it was so complex that they had to stay on for a few months, to help their successors to navigate the labyrinth.

The only reason a senior officer ever left in a hurry was that he had been dismissed and would, in all likelihood, soon be standing in the criminal dock, but Linda had already made it clear that wasn't the case with Snodgrass.

So what the hell *was* happening to Snodgrass?

'If you want to give him a personal present – just from yourself, like – you could always send it to his new posting,' Linda suggested.

'And do you know where that might be?'

'*Should* I know?' Linda asked cautiously.

'Probably not,' Paniatowski said. 'So where is it?'

'It's the same job as he had here, but in Hertfordshire.'

Not a demotion, then, but not really a promotion, either.

'I'm telling you that you've made an enemy of me, and I'm not the only one, because nobody likes an officer who can't be a team player,' Snodgrass had told her.

Well, it would seem from the way things had turned out that someone wasn't entirely chuffed with him, either.

All jobs probably had some unpleasant aspects attached to them, Dick Judd thought, as he unenthusiastically turned over the soil on his allotment. Yes, but the difference between his job and other jobs was that while lorry drivers could admit they hated loading and unloading, and teachers were allowed to complain about all the out-of-school marking, he had to pretend he actually enjoyed working on his allotment in the same way as the three scientists from BAI (Horrocks, Jennings and Wheatstone) so obviously did.

Two scientists, he corrected himself.

Not three – two.

Because while the late Arthur Wheatstone had revelled in dirt and clearly loved planting his seed, that had nothing to do with the allotments.

There was no sign of Horrocks or Jennings that Saturday morning, although they always came on a Saturday – a bit of weeding and a bit of watering, then off to the Bird in the Hand, for a couple of pints with the rest of the weekend gardeners. Perhaps they'd stayed away as a mark of respect, Judd thought, or maybe they were genuinely upset at their colleague's death.

But that was no good to him, was it? He wasn't supposed to know any of them that well. *And* he was supposed to love his gardening time, so it would have looked bloody odd to all the other gardening nutcases if good old Dick hadn't turned up today.

He just wished the scientists had taken up some other hobby – model making, for example. He was sure he could have produced a cracking Spanish galleon made entirely out of toothpicks, if he'd been given the opportunity.

But they hadn't done that. They were at the top of the evolutionary tree, involved in work that ninety-nine point nine percent of the population couldn't even begin to understand, yet they chose to spend their free time involved in the same manual drudgery as their ancestors had been involved in thousands of years ago.

Morons!

Tired of his allotment – bloody tired, so tired that if he never saw an allotment again, it would be too soon – he looked around for some distraction which he could still legitimately classify as work, and his eye fell on Archie Eccleston, two allotments away, who was sitting on a stool outside his potting shed and smoking a roll-up.

Judd ambled over to Eccleston's allotment, remembering to examine the allotment before he even spoke to the other man.

(That was how these people were. They'd notice that you'd planted radishes first, then – maybe – that you'd accidentally chopped your own foot off and were bleeding to death).

The left-hand side of the allotment, he noted, was a virtual metropolis of plants, with carrots waving their tails defiantly in the air and lettuces which were smugly green.

The other side of the allotment, however, Judd thought, was a desert.

No, not a desert, he corrected himself.

How could it be a desert with such fertile soil?

He didn't know what to call it, and the truth was, he didn't give a monkey's toss anyway!

'You've been busy,' he said, in his best hearty, fellow-allotment-holder voice.

Eccleston picked up a mug with **THE BEST DAD IN THE WORLD** written on it. He raised the mug carefully to his mouth, and took a sip.

'I always give it a thorough going over before I plant anything new,' he said. 'There's them as think they can get away with less, but I've never believed that myself.'

'And you're quite right, too,' Judd agreed. 'That's the trouble with people today, they haven't got the self-discipline or the moral fibre that they used to have before . . .'

He pulled himself up as he realized that Dick Judd, allotment holder, was on the point of merging with Richard Judd, right-wing agitator.

He didn't like Richard Judd very much, he thought – but at least Richard didn't have to dig gardens.

The poetry reading the night before had started out a great success, because the audience, though few in number, had been fans of the art (as they needed to be if they were to spend the entire evening in a draughty hall). They'd asked some intelligent questions and made some perceptive comments. There was a general feeling that culture was being experienced, and though it would have been wrong to call them 'snobby' and 'smug' it might not have been too far off the mark to describe them as 'self-approving.'

And then some idiot at the back had asked the wrong question.

'Didn't I see you on the telly the other day?'

'Poets rarely get on the television,' Crane had said evasively.

'No, I'm sure it was you,' the man persisted. 'You were with that woman detective. Now what's her name? It's foreign sounding.'

'Paniatowski?' a woman a couple of rows in front of him suggested.

'That's right – Pontovski. You were with Inspector Pontovski.'

The evening had gone downhill from that point, for though he was interesting to them as a poet, he was fascinating as a man who had rubbed shoulders with murderers.

Well, that was all behind him now. It was a new morning, he was in Barrow Village close to the scene of the crime, and he was out to prove that whatever his failings as a poet, he could be shit-hot at his day job.

He knocked on the door of number 45, and his knock was answered by a small, round woman with mischievous eyes and a nice smile.

'You're too late, love,' she said, when Crane showed her his warrant card. 'Your mates have already done me.'

And then she laughed, and her breasts, denied movement either to the left or right by an ironclad bra, wobbled dangerously up and down.

'You're Mrs Moore, are you?' Crane asked.

'That's right.'

'And also living in this house are Mr Fred Moore . . .'

'My husband – the Lancashire tripe magnate! He's had more cows' stomachs across his market stalls than I've had . . . well, never mind that. He was interviewed when he got back from the market, last night.'

'Philip Moore and Mary Moore . . .'

'The seed of his loins, and the fruit of my womb. They're away in boarding school – Fred wants to turn them into a lady and gentleman. I think Philip's the one he's hoping will turn out to be the gentleman.'

'And a Walter Wicks.'

'My dad.'

'It appears that he wasn't interviewed.'

'He was having his sleep when your lads came round, so I asked them if they could come back later. Well, I seem to have traded them in for you, and I'm more than pleased with the bargain.' Her face grew a little more serious. 'Listen, it's not that I want to get rid of you – you grace my home with your golden presence – but you'll be wasting your time talking to my dad. I love him to pieces, but even I have to admit that he's doolally.'

'I'm a bit doolally myself,' Crane said. 'Maybe we'll have a meeting of minds.'

On the whole, Whitebridge disapproved of tall buildings (as it tended to disapprove of anything it didn't have much of), but people were generally positive about the Red Rose Tower, if only because it served to remind any passing Yorkshireman that the final result of the Wars of the Roses had been Lancashire 1 Yorkshire 0.

The tower was located in the upper part of Whitebridge, so the views – especially from the flats on the higher floors – were impressive. They didn't come cheap, these flats, but then the building had a full concierge service, an indoor pool and a gymnasium.

Given that it was on the right side of town for the BAI plant, it was not really surprising that two of the company's unmarried male scientific staff should call it home, but Meadows certainly raised an eyebrow when she realized that two of the men working on the American project – John Horrocks and Philip Jennings – were not only living on the same floor, but had adjacent apartments.

Choosing at random, she pressed Jennings' bell, but after the third ring she heard the door open behind her and a voice say, 'If you're looking for Philip, he's just taking a coffee break with me.'

Meadows turned. The man who addressed her was in his late thirties. He had wispy fair hair and a slightly piggy nose (it could so easily have been an unattractive face, yet for some reason it wasn't) and he was wearing a cravat.

A cravat!

No one in Whitebridge wore a cravat, especially at that time on a Saturday morning!

'So who are you?' he asked.

'I'm Kate Meadows and I'm a—'

'A model!' John Horrocks interrupted her. 'You just have to be. Well, we are honoured. This might well be the most bijou residence in Whitebridge, but we still don't get many . . .'

'I'm a detective sergeant.'

The look of pleasure immediately drained from Horrocks' face, and was instantly replaced by a wariness.

'This is about Arthur's death, isn't it?' he asked.

'Yes, it is,' Meadows admitted.

'We knew we were expecting someone – but certainly not you,' Horrocks said, almost petulantly. Then he shrugged and replaced his defensiveness with a smile. 'Well, now you're here, you'd better come inside and have a cup of coffee,' he said.

'Yes,' Meadows agreed, 'I suppose I'd better.'

Mr Wicks had wild white hair and eyes that still retained much of their childhood innocence.

'Did our June tell you I was a loony?' he asked, when Mrs Moore had seated them in the lounge, put a plate of biscuits between them, and taken her leave.

'No, she most certainly did not,' Crane said.

The old man laughed. 'Then she will have used another word – perhaps one not quite so stark. What was it? Doolally?'

Crane joined in with his laughter. 'Yes, it was,' he admitted.

'She's a good girl, but she can't tell the difference between a loony and an eccentric,' Wicks said. 'I myself am an eccentric.'

'I gathered that,' Crane said.

'I see the world differently to the way most people see it,' Wicks told him, 'and sometimes, if it doesn't make sense, I retell it, so it does. My world is a much more exciting one, but also, I like to think, a much kinder one.' He paused. 'Perhaps I was being unfair to June, earlier. There is a very narrow line between loony and eccentric, you see, and sometimes I topple over and fall on the wrong side of it.'

'You're a poet,' Crane said, with genuine admiration.

'Am I?' the old man asked. 'I must admit, I don't recall ever writing any poetry.'

'It doesn't matter,' Crane said dismissively. 'It's what you are, and you can't do anything about it.'

And what you're supposed to be, said a voice in his head, is a policeman.

He cleared his throat. There was no real need to, but it made him feel more official.

'Could you tell me about your next-door neighbours?' he asked.

Mr Wicks nodded. 'Arthur Wheatstone didn't speak to other people, unless they spoke to him first, and even then, he'd only grunt. I used to think he was angry with life in general, and then I learned that was not so.'

'How did you learn it?'

'I needed new glasses, and June took me into Whitebridge. We went to a pub, and he was sitting at a table at the other end of the room. He was with a group of people, and he was laughing and joking. So, you see, it wasn't life he hated, it was life in this village.'

'So why did he live here?'

'I don't know.' Wicks looked around him. 'Some people say

he was murdered and some people say he killed himself. Which was it?'

'He was murdered.'

'I thought so.'

'Why?'

'Because through suicide, he would be robbing the world of a most wonderful person.'

'You don't have a very high opinion of him yourself, do you?' Crane asked.

The old man shrugged. 'How could I possibly have a high opinion of pond scum?'

'So tell me about *Mrs* Wheatstone,' Crane suggested.

'She changes form,' Wicks said, 'though whether that is through her own power or because of some spell he cast on her, I cannot say.'

'What forms does she take?'

'She has been a cat, and once she was an owl, but mostly she takes the form of her own kind.'

'What do you mean?'

'I have seen her transformed into a tall, dark woman, a short blonde woman, and a woman who was neither tall nor short and had red hair.'

'When do these transformations occur?'

'At night, when everyone is asleep.'

Crane smiled. 'So if everyone is asleep, how do you know about them?'

'Everyone but me, I should have said! June will not let me out on my own, because she is worried that I'd wander off or fall into a river and drown. And maybe she's right. So I always have her with me when I leave the house in the daytime.'

'But at night . . . when everyone is asleep?'

'I have a key that June does not know about. I do not go far. Some nights I will walk a little way up the street, other nights I will stay in the back garden. It is being able to go out when I want to that is important.'

'I understand that,' Crane said.

'It is when I am in the garden that I see her in a new shape. When she is the owl, she perches on a tree at the end of the garden and hoots. When she is the cat, she prowls the garden. Once, to show me just how confident she was, she brushed up against my leg.'

'What about when she takes the form of another woman?' Crane wondered.

'She always does that in the house. And sometimes – though this is never my intention – I see her naked flesh.'

'Must there be certain conditions in order for these transformations to take place?' Crane asked.

'What do you mean?'

'Well, must there be a full moon, or is it always when the moon is new?'

'It has nothing to do with the moon.'

'Then it must just be random.'

The old man shook his head. 'It cannot be random because life is patterns and patterns are life,' he said. 'We talk of the circle of life . . . the circle of life . . . life in a circle . . .'

'Don't upset yourself,' said Crane, feeling an uneasy combination of guilt and alarm. 'It's not important. It really doesn't matter.'

'Yes, there is a pattern,' the old man said triumphantly. 'Of course there is a pattern. I was a fool not to see it earlier.'

'What is it?' Crane asked.

'The transformation cannot take place while her car is in the village!' the old man told him.

FOURTEEN

There were two armchairs in John Horrocks' living room, but no sofa. One of the armchairs was occupied by Philip Jennings. He did not look entirely comfortable in it, but that was hardly surprising, Meadows thought, because he was probably around six feet five tall – and a lot of that was leg. He was wearing lemon-coloured trousers and a lemon V-neck sweater, with nothing on underneath it.

'Well, don't both you boys look smart – and on a Saturday morning, too,' she said, once Horrocks had performed the introductions.

Many middle-aged men would have taken umbrage at the

comment, but Meadows had guessed they'd be pleased, rather than annoyed, and she could see that she was right.

'Why don't you sit in John's chair, Kate,' Jennings suggested.

'Yes, why not,' Horrocks countered. 'I can always sit cross-legged on the floor, can't I?'

Jennings laughed. 'Or you could fetch a straight-backed chair from the dining room, while you're waiting for the coffee to percolate.'

'So what did your last slave die of?' Horrocks asked, and gave a little chuckle himself.

Meadows sat down in the proffered chair. 'What can you tell me about Arthur Wheatstone?' she asked Jennings.

'Very little,' Jennings said. 'You see, we may all have worked on the same Project with a capital P, but there were different projects within it, so we didn't overlap.'

'Oh come on!' Horrocks called from the kitchen. 'You can surely do better than that!'

'I don't like to speak ill of the dead,' Jennings mumbled.

'I didn't hear that,' Horrocks said. 'Would you mind repeating it?'

'I said, I don't like to speak ill of the dead,' Jennings said loudly.

'There's no need to shout,' Horrocks told him. He walked back into the lounge carrying a tray. 'You don't like to speak ill of the living, either – and have you any idea how infuriating that can be?' He placed the tray down on the coffee table next to Meadows. 'Help yourself to cream and sugar.'

Meadows poured herself a black coffee and took a sip. Some of her colleagues (I'm looking at you, Colin Beresford! she thought) would expect any coffee John Horrocks made to be weak and feeble, but they'd be wrong.

'Excellent coffee, John,' she said. 'And am I right in thinking that if I'd asked you the question I asked Philip, I'd have got a different answer?'

'You are,' Horrocks agreed. 'Arthur Wheatstone was a complete prick.'

'In what way was he a prick?'

'In what way wasn't he?' Horrocks asked. 'He was as unpleasant as he could be to everyone he came into contact with—'

'To every *man* he came into contact with,' Jennings interrupted.

'I stand corrected – to every *man* he came into contact with. It was as if he always needed to show them who was top dog.'

'It was calculated unpleasantness,' Jennings said. 'He'd work out where you were weakest, and go for it.'

'How was he unpleasant to you?'

'He said I was so tall I was a freak – and there was no other word to describe me. He said that all John's friends had already noticed it, and that when he noticed it himself –' he buried his head in his hands – 'he would leave me.'

Horrocks put his hand on Jennings' shoulder. 'There, there,' he cooed softly, 'we both know that is never going to happen.'

'What did he say to you?' Meadows asked Horrocks.

'He used a variation on the same theme. He said gay relationships never lasted, so I could look forward to dying alone.'

'But he was different with women?'

'Oh yes,' Horrocks said. 'While he was chasing them, he treated them like goddesses.'

'But once he'd finished with them, they didn't really exist as far as he was concerned. He couldn't even make the effort to be nasty to them.'

So there was plenty of motive there, Meadows thought – the only problem was that this just didn't feel like a woman's crime.

'Anything else?' she asked.

'I don't know what his work on the project is like – it's presumably all right, or he'd have been fired by now – but we have an allotment, you see, and—'

'Wait a minute,' Meadows said, 'you two have an allotment?'

Horrocks frowned, and then the frown changed into something closer to regret.

'I had great expectations of you, Kate,' he said, 'but when push comes to shove, you'll go with all the old clichés, won't you?'

Shit, shit, shit! Meadows thought.

'It was a temporary slip,' she told him. 'Please give me another chance.'

Horrocks nodded. 'You were nice about my coffee, so why not? Some people think it's strange that people who design the weapons of war should have an allotment, but we don't. You can't do any harm with a radish, and all a spring onion can do is bring you pleasure.'

'You were going to tell Kate about Arthur Wheatstone's allotment,' Philip Jennings said.

'Yes, that's right. If somebody reports that your allotment isn't up to standard, then you're called to appear before the committee . . .'

'The secretary of which happens to be . . .' Jennings said with a smile and a sweeping gesture of his arm.

'The secretary of which happens to be me,' Horrocks said, in a voice beloved of self-martyrs since the dawn of time. 'All right, I know. If there's a committee anywhere, I'm probably on it.' He paused to draw breath. 'Anyway, Arthur Wheatstone came up before the committee, and he was as awkward as you might have expected him to be. It's my allotment, he said, I can do what I want with it. No, you can't, we told him. If your allotment's deemed to fall below standard, we can take it off you. Well, he said, we could try, and he laughed in our faces. But he stopped laughing when I showed him the Act of Parliament that gives us the power to do just that.'

'But did he pull his socks up?' Jennings asked rhetorically. 'Did he buggery. What he did do instead was hire a team of landscape gardeners to do it for him. Can you imagine that – paying someone to tend an allotment?'

'The other allotment holders were furious,' Horrocks said. 'You see, there's a waiting list for allotments, yet here was a man who clearly didn't want the one he'd got. So I checked through all the regulations *and* the Act of Parliament, and came to the reluctant conclusion that there was nothing we could do about it.'

'So what *is* his game?' Meadows asked, although she already had her own theory.

'If he didn't want the allotment for growing things on, he must have wanted it for the shed,' Horrocks said.

'Any idea what's in that shed?'

'Not a clue,' Jennings said. 'Most people leave their shed doors open if the weather's half decent, but his is always firmly closed. And it's a big shed – the biggest that's allowed.'

Meadows stood up. 'Thanks for your time,' she said.

'It's been our pleasure,' both men said, simultaneously.

At the door, Meadows stopped and turned around.

'Actually, there is one more question I'd like to ask you,' she said, 'but it's more for my own curiosity than any other reason, so you don't have to answer if you don't want to.'

'Go on,' Jennings said.

'It's obvious from the way Philip acts that this is his flat as much as it's yours,' Meadows said to Horrocks. 'In fact, I'd be willing to bet that you don't even use the flat that's in his name.'

'Oh, you'd be surprised how often it comes in useful,' Horrocks said, unconvincingly.

'Oh, come on, fellers, trust me,' Meadows said.

'Why should we?' Horrocks asked.

'Because I'm not as straight as I seem.'

'What does that mean?'

'It means that on my nights off, I go by the name of Zelda and wear a rubber mask,' Meadows said.

The two men looked at each other, then grinned.

'If virtually anyone else had told me that, I don't think I'd have believed them,' Jennings said.

'So?'

'You're quite right. We don't use that flat at all.'

'So why do you have it? You surely don't think it fools anybody, do you?'

'It fools those who need and want to be fooled,' Horrocks said.

'And what does that mean?'

'The people who watch us know the government doesn't like homosexuals working in the defence industry.'

'It doesn't?'

'No. It thinks they are too unstable and too open to blackmail.'

'But homosexuality is legal. It has been since 1967.'

'And there's nothing to stop Roman Catholics becoming prime minister – but we haven't had one yet, have we?'

'At the same time, while they might not trust us, they need us,' Jennings said. 'The defence industry – which has very little to do with defence, as you'll appreciate – is one of the treasury's biggest earners.'

'So the local spooks are on the horns of a dilemma,' Horrocks said. 'If they say we're unreliable, the government will remove us, and then, later, blame them for the loss of revenue. If they say nothing, and one of us blurts out secrets one night to a drunken Russian sailor who's giving him a seeing to – and said sailor turns out to be neither a mariner nor drunk – then the government will accuse our minders of incompetence.'

'The second flat gives the spooks an excuse,' Jennings added. 'They can say we had our own individual flats, so there was absolutely no indication that we were gay.'

'Why would you do that for them?' Meadows asked.

'It's not for them, it's for us. We want to stay here, and as long as we give them this fallback position, they're likely to let us.'

'How many spooks are there in Whitebridge?' Meadows asked.

'How long is a piece of string?' Jennings countered.

The man who had probably killed Arthur Wheatstone had been exceptionally tall, Meadows thought as she was walking back to her car. Philip Jennings was also exceptionally tall, and hated Arthur Wheatstone. Most police officers would have been delighted to put these two things together.

But she was not most police officers. She did not believe for a moment that Philip would have been capable of hauling a paralysed Wheatstone up to his garage ceiling and then stand watching while he died.

Even so, it was clear that she should go straight to her boss, and present her with all the facts, alongside her own reservations.

But if she did that, Paniatowski would want to interview Philip herself, or at least get Colin Beresford to do it. And, to be fair to her, she would be quite right, because that would be in line with standard procedures.

So there it was – tell the boss, cover her own back.

It was the only sensible course – and she knew she was not going to do it.

FIFTEEN

Half an hour before the first press conference of the investigation was due to take place, Paniatowski got a phone call from the chief constable.

'I'll be there when you have your little battle with the media,' he said. 'In fact, I'll be taking the lead. Do you have any objections to that, Chief Inspector?'

'No objections, sir,' Paniatowski replied, giving the only answer possible. 'It's just that I don't really see the need to—'

'Fine,' Baxter interrupted. 'Have you checked through the widow's statement?'

'The widow won't be at the press conference, sir.'

'She won't?'

'No, sir.'

'The press will find that very strange.'

'I realize that, sir,'

'So *why* won't she be there?'

'DC Crane has advised me that having her there would be very counter-productive.'

'Is that what he said? Counter-productive?'

'No, what he actually said was, "It's not that Mrs Wheatstone doesn't want her husband's killer caught. She does – but only so that she can give him a big wet kiss".'

'I see,' the chief constable said. 'And you trust Crane's judgement?'

'I trust the judgement of everyone on my team, sir. They wouldn't be working for me if I didn't.'

'You've always been an absolutist, haven't you, Monika?' Baxter said. He sighed. 'I'll see you in half an hour.'

'Yes, sir.'

Paniatowski put down the phone, and sighed herself.

She'd met George Baxter when she'd been on secondment in Yorkshire, and had instantly thought of him as a huge ginger teddy bear. She'd been broken hearted at the time, and allowed herself to drift into an affair with him. The affair had ended long before Baxter had applied for the Whitebridge job – it had been his decision, taken when he had finally acknowledged that however hard she tried, she could not make herself love him in the same way as he loved her.

They had managed, since Paniatowski's promotion, to work well together, because they were both fair-minded people and good police officers, but Baxter had never been able to quite suppress his feelings of hurt and betrayal – just as she had never been able to quite suppress her feelings of guilt – and that meant they were forever operating on a knife edge.

In the twenty-four hours since the murder, the story had grown and grown, so though the room was not as full as it would have been if the crime had taken place in the south (where murder really mattered!) there were several London journalists and a couple of camera crews from the national stations, to supplement the local reporters and television people.

Baxter opened the proceedings, and then handed matters over to his DCI. Paniatowski outlined the details of the discovery of the body and stated that the police were treating it as a murder.

'If you knew him, and have observed him behaving in any way strangely, please let us know,' she concluded. 'It doesn't matter how trivial it might seem to you, it could be of great value to us. If you've seen anyone watching him or following him, please let us know. Don't worry about looking a fool, because let me assure you that you won't look that way to us.' She paused and checked her watch. 'There's just time for a few questions.'

'Do we know what poison was used on him, Chief Inspector?' one of the local reporters asked.

No, they bloody didn't, despite the fact that Dr Shastri had been up for most of the night working on it.

'For operational reasons, we are not prepared to reveal the name of the drug at this stage of the inquiry,' Paniatowski said.

'Is it possible that he was a spy?' asked a man in a leather jacket, who was from the BBC in London, and was thus automatically the alpha male in the press pack.

Paniatowski had anticipated such a question, and had come up with a line which, while it didn't actually answer the question, at least sounded as if it had.

'We have no evidence—' she began.

'I can state categorically that Russian intelligence had nothing to do with this case,' Baxter interrupted her.

Paniatowski resisted the urge to turn towards him and demand to know what the hell he thought he was doing – but it wasn't easy.

'And before you accuse me of sophistry, let me assure you that the same holds for the East German Stasi, the Bulgarian Committee of State Security and any of the other Eastern Bloc agencies you care to mention,' Baxter continued.

The surreptitious smile at the corners of the BBC man's mouth was only there for a second, but it told anyone who was watching him closely – and Paniatowski was – that there was nothing he liked better than making provincial policemen seem stupid on camera.

'That's a great deal you seem to be assuring us of,' he said.

'It is,' Baxter agreed, like an innocent who had no idea he was walking into a trap.

'And may I ask you what you base your assurance on?'

'Indeed you may. I base it on a conversation I had with the Home Secretary not half an hour ago. And in case you're wondering where *he* got the information from, he assured me it came from his various heads of security – MI5, MI6 – clever people like that.'

'Oh,' said the BBC man, not quite sure where to go next.

The rest of the journalists fell silent, savouring this moment at which the top dog had – in front of their very eyes – stepped on his own bollocks.

Paniatowski stood up.

'Thank you for coming, ladies and gentlemen,' she said, taking advantage of the pause. 'You'll be informed by the chief constable's secretary when the next press conference will be held.'

'Neatly extricated, Chief Inspector,' Baxter said, as they strode away from the press conference, down the corridor that led to both of their offices.

'Thank you, sir,' Paniatowski replied. 'Was it true?'

'That I spoke to the Home Secretary about half an hour ago. Yes, that was true.'

'And did he tell you there was no Russian involvement in this murder?'

'Yes, he did.'

Paniatowski came to a halt, which made it hard for a natural gentleman like Baxter to carry on walking.

'What is it, Monika?' he asked.

'I need you to say it again – and this time I need to be looking into your eyes,' Paniatowski said.

'In other words, you're accusing me of lying?' Baxter said – and though he was not angry yet, he was heading that way. 'You always push things too far, don't you? You just can't help yourself.'

'I've got my people out in the field, and if there are any KGB assassins out there as well, I have to know about it,' Paniatowski said. 'It's not that I don't believe you – but I have to be sure.'

'It's not that you don't believe me, but you don't believe me,' Baxter said. He bent his head slightly. 'Can you see into my eyes?'

She used to look in those eyes and try her hardest to make them hypnotize her into loving him.

She really did.

'Are you ready?' he asked.

'Yes, sir.'

'No . . . Russian . . . agent . . . nor . . . any . . . agent . . . from . . . any . . . other . . . Iron . . . Curtain . . . country . . . is . . . connected . . . in any way . . . with the murder of Arthur Wheatstone. Is that clear enough for you, Chief Inspector?'

'Yes, sir, it is,' Paniatowski said. 'Thank you.'

There were three cars in the lay-by off the ring road. In one of them, a middle-aged man was snoring quite loudly. In the second, a couple in their twenties were having an argument which had already reduced the woman to tears twice. And in the third, a detective sergeant was talking to police headquarters or, more specifically, to a clerical officer called Linda, who thought she was wonderful.

'So DCI Paniatowski is in a press conference at the moment, sarge, but she'd left the information on your desk for you,' the girl said.

'And do you have it?'

'In my hot little hand.'

'Then let's hear it.'

'According to this, there was the dead man and four other people involved in the project. A Dr Horrocks, a Dr Jennings . . .'

'Yes, I've seen them.'

'And a Dr . . . no, wait a minute, I must have that the wrong way round, yes that's it, according to this there's a Mrs Rosemary Pemberton who's a senior technician and a Dr Roger Pemberton, the head of department, who has the same address as her, so is probably her husband . . .'

'Unless she's his mum.'

'It'd be a miracle if she was, because, according to this, they're the same age.'

'According to that, where do they live?' Meadows asked.

'According to this . . .' The clerical officer paused. 'You're not, by any chance, taking the mickey out of me, are you, sarge?'

'Of course not, Linda,' Meadows said, transmitting a warm friendly smile over the airwaves.

'That's all right, then,' Linda said, mollified. 'Well, according to this, they live at number 11 Park Rise.'

Two or three years earlier, the ground from which the Park Rise Residential Area had risen had been occupied by two very gloomy Victorian mansions, originally built at the behest of two very gloomy Victorian mill owners. Everyone agreed that the project which replaced the mansions had been of benefit to the area – that the dozen detached houses added an air of lightness and contemporary ambience which could only be an improvement.

They weren't bad houses at all, Meadows thought, studying number 11. In fact, it would be fair to say that a lot of people would consider them their dream houses. But they were primarily intended for young people on the way up – teachers and officer workers who had just got their first promotion – and the head of a project in BAI should have been able to do much better for himself.

She rang the bell, and through the frosted glass saw a figure approaching down the corridor.

When she opened the door, the figure was revealed to be a woman in her late thirties who could have served as the perfect model for 'before' shots in 'before and after' advertisements.

She was a natural blonde, but her hair had been neglected and grown scraggly. Her skin could use a moisturizer, her teeth could do with a polish, and a little make-up wouldn't have gone amiss.

She was wearing baggy trousers and a baggy jumper, which effectively hid what was, Meadows suspected, a rather good figure.

So what was her game? Meadows wondered.

There were women, it was true, who were trapped in sloppiness like an insect in amber. Some of them did not even notice it. Others did, but had no idea how to escape. Rosemary Pemberton didn't fall into either category, Meadows thought, because neither of those sorts of women would have examined her outfit the way Rosemary was doing – not in awe, but with the cold calculating eye of an experienced fashionista.

'I'm here to ask you a few questions about Arthur Wheatstone,' Meadows said, holding out her warrant card for inspection.

'You'd better come into the lounge, then,' Rosemary Pemberton answered, without much enthusiasm. 'My husband's just watching his sport.'

The television was certainly on in the lounge, but there was no sign of Roger Pemberton.

'Roger?' Rosemary Pemberton called up the stairs. 'Are you up there? The police are here.'

Meadows looked around the room. The furniture, like the house, was more than acceptable, but she would have expected better even if the household's only source of income had come from Roger Pemberton. So maybe they used his wife's salary for living expenses, and were saving his much larger salary to buy a beach house in the Bahamas.

The other thing that was interesting about the room was the decoration on the walls, which seemed to consist almost entirely of photographs of football teams of which, presumably, Roger Pemberton had been a member, since there was also a trophy cabinet full of cups and shields in the corner of the room.

There was the sound of footsteps on the staircase, then Roger Pemberton appeared in the lounge. He was wearing a smart blazer and a tie. His wife had obviously not been expecting this. She opened her mouth to say something, then bit the comment back.

Now why would she have done that, Meadows wondered.

The sergeant took a closer look at Pemberton's tie. It was a tie
worn by members of a certain gentlemen's club in London.
Meadows herself had, in another life, visited the club, and knew
– as surely as she knew the sun would rise in the morning – that
it would never have accepted Pemberton as a member.

Physically, he was quite an attractive man, Meadows decided,
but she was already starting to wonder if his beauty was any more
than skin deep.

'Who are you?' he asked.

'DS Meadows.'

Pemberton held out his hand. His grip was firm but not painful.
It said, I could hurt you if I wanted to, but of course I'd never do
that.

'Well, I expect you're here to talk about Arthur Wheatstone,'
he said. 'Do take a seat.' He turned to his wife. 'Have you offered
Sergeant Meadows a drink, Rosemary?'

'No, I . . .'

'Well, come along then – chop, chop!'

'I don't want a drink,' Meadows said, bending slightly forward
to switch off the television, 'but thanks for volunteering your wife,
anyway.'

Pemberton flashed her a look which said this was not the way
he'd envisaged things going at all, then said, 'Well, let's get this
over with – some of us have busy lives to lead you know.'

'Yes, I can see that,' Meadows said, giving the television a
backwards glance. 'I suppose the first question I should ask you
is whether Dr Wheatstone had any enemies that you knew of.'

'We hardly knew him at all, so we're not really in a position
to say,' Pemberton told her.

'You hardly knew him!' Meadows said incredulously, 'How
long have you been working together?'

'Five years, but we didn't socialize with him, did we, Rosemary?'
Pemberton asked.

'No,' his wife replied. 'We don't really socialize with anybody.'

'But surely you must have known something about him,' Meadows
persisted. 'Dr Horrocks had quite a lot to say about him.'

'Dr Horrocks would.'

'And what does that mean?'

'It means that Arthur liked to bait him for being queer, and

Horrocks – being as thin-skinned as the rest of his tribe – reacted badly, making it even more fun for Arthur.'

'But Wheatstone didn't try to get under your skin, too?'

'How could he? I provided him with no ammunition.'

'Besides which, he'd probably think twice before having a go at his head of department,' Meadows said.

An embarrassed silence which lasted for perhaps fifteen seconds followed the comment. Then Rosemary Pemberton said, 'Actually, I'm the one who is head of department.'

Meadows thought about what Linda, the clerical officer had said to her.

'*And a Dr . . . no, wait a minute, I must have that the wrong way round, yes that's it, according to this there's a Mrs Rosemary Pemberton who's a senior technician and a Dr Roger Pemberton, the head of department, who has the same address as her, so is probably her husband . . .*'

Linda had seen it written down that the woman was a doctor, and had assumed that it had to be a mistake.

She was a very nice girl, Meadows thought – but she'd make a lousy dominatrix.

Pemberton laughed uncomfortably. 'Well, yes, I suppose I could have got my doctorate, just like my swotty wife did, but I was far too busy living life to worry about things like that. And I was right, too, wasn't I, Rosemary? You wish you'd done the same, don't you?'

'Yes,' Rosemary Pemberton said, in the voice of a robot, 'I wish I'd done the same.'

Meadows wondered if it would be possible to fake losing her balance and to contrive to break Pemberton's nose as she grabbed it for support. It was a sweet dream – a pleasing fantasy – but, unfortunately, that was all it was.

'So you know nothing about Arthur Wheatstone's private life, *Dr* Pemberton?' she asked.

'No, nothing.'

'And how about you, *Mr* Pemberton?'

Pemberton glared at her. 'Nothing,' he said.

'Did either of you ever hear him mention his allotment?' Kate Meadows asked.

And suddenly she had their full attention, as if she'd pronounced the magic word.

'His allotment?' Pemberton repeated.

'Yes, he had one on Old Mill Road,' Meadows explained.

'Old Mill Road? That's the one you go to, isn't it?' Pemberton asked his wife.

'Yes, it is,' Rosemary Pemberton admitted.

'And who does it belong to, did you say?'

'My cousin Jane.' Rosemary turned to Meadows. 'Well, she's not strictly my cousin,' she explained, 'but when we were growing up she called my mum "auntie" and I called her mum the same. I help her out, now and again. It makes a nice change, being out in the fresh air.'

'Have I ever met Jane?' Pemberton asked.

'No, I don't think so.'

'And why is that?'

'You don't normally like spending time with my friends, Roger,' Rosemary said.

'That's right, I don't,' Pemberton agreed. 'Did you ever see Arthur Wheatstone when you were down at the allotments?'

'No.'

'That's strange, don't you think?'

'It's a big place,' Rosemary said – and Meadows thought she could detect a hint of panic in her voice. 'If his plot is right at the other end from Jane's, it's unlikely our paths would ever have crossed.'

'What about Horrocks and Jennings?' Meadows asked. 'They've got a plot down there as well.'

'Oh yes, I've seen them,' Rosemary Pemberton said – and the sergeant knew not only that she was lying, but *why* she was lying.

'Well, thanks for your help,' Meadows said. 'I'll call again if there's anything more I need to ask.'

'Ring first,' Pemberton said.

Rosemary accompanied her up the hallway.

'Listen,' Meadows said when they reached the front door, and her foot was already over the threshold, 'if you have any problems, call me, and if I can't get here right away, I'll make sure someone else does.'

'Problems?' Rosemary said. 'What kind of problems are we talking about, Sergeant?'

'You know what I'm talking about,' Meadows insisted.

'You're wrong. I really haven't a clue,' Rosemary said firmly.

And then she closed the door with just enough force to dislodge a little of the mortar.

Jack Crane was a great believer in the maxim that if a horse threw you, you needed to get back in the saddle right away. Mrs Wheatstone, he felt, had not only thrown him over her head at their last meeting, but had then pranced around his sprawling body to complete the indignity. She had made a fool of him, but he didn't blame her – because he'd had an idea about the absence of ladders, and if he was right, then all her aggression had been in self-defence.

She was staying in the Prince Alfred suite at the Royal Victoria Hotel, and when she met him at the door she said, 'Ah, my pet policeman. Won't you come into my parlour, said the spider to the fly.'

The Prince Alfred suite was decorated in the style of Balmoral, the Queen's Scottish residence, and from the walls hung claymores, bagpipes, paintings of dark glens, and the mounted head of a glassy-eyed stag.

Mrs Whitestone giggled.

'Isn't it hideous,' she said. 'Truly hideous.'

'Then why are you staying here?' Crane wondered.

'I'm staying here because your chief inspector won't allow me to stay in my own house,' Mrs Wheatstone said.

'That's almost a lie, but not quite,' Crane said.

'What do you mean?'

'You're staying in *town* because you can't go back to your own house,' Crane said. 'You're staying in the Prince Alfred suite because your insurance company is paying, and it's the most expensive room in town.'

'Second most expensive,' Mrs Wheatstone said. 'The most expensive is the Princess Beatrice, but unfortunately that was already occupied.' She paused. 'But God, even if it was a hole in the ground, it's so good to be back in town.'

'Do I take that to mean you don't like living in the countryside?' Crane asked.

'Do I take that to mean you don't like living in the countryside?'

Mrs Wheatstone repeated, pulling a face as she spoke. 'What kind of sentence construction was that? Listen, lad, you're allowed to be posh *and* live up here, but it's got to be *northern* posh, which means that you say what you want to say without taking us for a trip round the houses.'

'I'll try again, then,' Crane said. 'So the countryside gets up your nose, does it?'

'It gets *right* up my nose!' Mrs Wheatstone said approvingly.

'So why do you live there?'

'Why *did* I live there, you mean, because there's no chance of me going back – but there's no need to tell the insurance that.'

'I won't,' Crane promised. 'So why *did* you live there?'

'I lived there because I thought it might help save my marriage.'

'It must have been very hard for you, married to a man like that,' Crane said, sympathetically.

She gave him a hard stare, as if suspecting he was laughing at her, then, deciding he wasn't, she said, 'Arthur called that thing between his legs "Excalibur", and, credit where credit's due, it was a mighty weapon. He tried to get his end away with every passing woman – but there are fewer passing women available in the countryside.'

'You thought about killing yourself, didn't you?' Crane asked.

'How the . . .?'

'When I said your husband had been found hanged, you said straight away that it had to be murder, because he could never have reached the beam without a ladder.'

'Yes, well, that's obvious.'

'No, it isn't. My inspector's a very practical man, and he thought he could do it until he actually tried it.'

Mrs Wheatstone bowed her head.

'It seemed like an easy way out for me,' she said. 'I put the ladder against the beam and I threaded the rope through.' She paused. 'I didn't make the noose. I never got that far.'

'What stopped you?'

'I think it was the thought of letting him win. You see, it wouldn't have stopped him if he'd come home and found me hanging there. He'd have felt guilty for a while, and then he'd have shrugged it off.'

'So you got rid of the ladders, just in case you ever felt the urge to do it again?'

'Yes.' She sighed. 'As I was climbing the ladder, I think I still loved him. When I came down, I knew I didn't. With love gone, it just became a game. I did all I could to stop him, not because I was jealous any more, but because I knew it would make him miserable. And I at least got the satisfaction of knowing I was better at the game than he was.'

And now I'm about to take even that away from you, Crane thought – and I'm *so* sorry.

'We need your permission to search your husband's potting shed, Mrs Wheatstone,' he said.

'What potting shed?'

'The one on his allotment.'

'I think you must have the wrong person,' Mrs Wheatstone said. 'Arthur wasn't the man who grew the lettuces – he was the randy little rabbit who nibbled at them when no one was looking.'

Crane shook his head. 'He had an allotment on the Old Mill Road site, and he put a potting shed on it.'

Mrs Wheatstone's expression changed from puzzlement to understanding – and then to blazing anger.

'The devious little bastard,' she said. 'There was me thinking I was running rings round him, and all the time he was running rings round me. God, I don't think I've ever hated him so much. Do you know what's in that shed?'

'Not for certain – but I think we can both guess,' Crane said.

SIXTEEN

One of Irene Clark's earliest childhood memories was of the next-door neighbour, Mrs Edna Cowgill, tapping on the kitchen window and then – without waiting for an answer – opening the door and stepping into the kitchen itself.

She'd been a very thin, angular woman, and whenever she was spreading salacious gossip about the other neighbours – which is to say, whenever she was awake – she would wave her hands extravagantly through the air, and her pointy little elbows went in and out like pistons.

Irene hadn't known at the time why she disliked Edna so much – she didn't *need* reasons, she was a kid, and it was enough that she did – but later, when she was studying for her degree in sociology, she realized the problem had been that she'd resented Mrs Cowgill invading her space. Now, a graduate and a young mother, she was resolved to be a good neighbour who would willingly help out, but only when requested to.

It was working from this premise that made her try to ignore all the noise that was drifting across her small garden from the house next door.

It was probably a play on the radio, she told herself. Then she recognized Roger Pemberton's voice, and she was forced to accept that unless Roger had gone into acting without telling anyone, he and Rosemary were probably having a row.

This theory gained more credence when she heard a banging sound that could possibly have been furniture being thrown around, but maybe that was how Roger let off steam.

And it wasn't going to lead to anything more violent, was it? After all, they were both highly educated scientists for God's sake!

Though she wasn't deliberately looking, her kitchen window overlooked the Pembertons' back door, so it was almost inevitable that she'd see a furious looking Roger storming out of the house and going straight to his car. And again without being a latter-day Edna Cowgill, she could not fail to observe that he had left the kitchen door ajar, which was not common, even in a nice community like this one.

Deciding the baby would benefit from a little fresh air, she took him out of his cot and carried him to the small back garden, from where she could observe the Pemberton's kitchen door (should she wish to). She stayed there for around five minutes. Then she went back inside, took some clean clothes out of the tumble dryer, fed some dirty clothes into the washer, and got out the ironing board.

With any luck, she thought, she'd be able to snatch half an hour with her romantic novel.

She felt a little ashamed that a woman with her education should be reading such obvious trash, but having given birth to an organism whose only interests seemed to be shitting and puking, she needed all the escape she could get.

The arrival of the four plain clothed police officers and the two civilian SOCOs at Arthur Wheatstone's potting shed caused something of a stir among the allotment holders.

'You'll not find him in,' one old man shouted across three or four allotments, his words not quite as distinct as they might have been since he always took his false teeth out when he was gardening. 'I've only seen him go in there the once, and he must have had it for over two years.'

Ah, but that was because he was a rabbit, rather than a farmer, Crane thought.

'Right, let's get this done,' Paniatowski asked.

One of the SOCOs stepped forward, and placed his bolt cutters over the shackle of the padlock on the door.

Paniatowski caught the padlock as it was falling to the ground, and bounced it reflectively up and down in her hand.

'It's not had much weathering, this,' she mused, almost to herself.

'I didn't quite catch that, boss,' Beresford said.

'Does this look new to you?' Paniatowski asked. 'And by new, I don't mean just newish – I mean not in use until two or three days ago.'

'Hard to say,' Beresford told her.

'Get it checked out by the lab,' Paniatowski said, dropping it into an envelope, and handing it to him. 'Now let's see what delights the potting shed has to offer us.'

The first thing they noticed when they opened the door was the large brass bed which took up perhaps two thirds of the space. Then there was the small dressing table with a mirror. The top end of the shed had been separated from the rest by a Chinese silk screen, and when Beresford moved the screen aside, he revealed a toilet and wash basin.

The wash basin had buttons on top of the taps, and when Beresford pressed one, water came out of the tap.

He stood looking at the toilet for a quite a while before turning the handle.

It flushed.

'How did Wheatstone manage that?' he wondered.

'The man was an applied scientist,' Meadows said. 'He designed aeroplanes. A simple pumping and waste disposal system can't have put too much strain on his brain.'

'Probably not,' Beresford agreed. 'I suppose what I really meant was *why* did he manage it – it seems a bit unnecessary.'

Meadows laughed. 'That's a typical man's reaction, sir,' she said, and, as usual, the 'sir' was tacked on as something of an afterthought.

'And what do you mean by that, exactly?' demanded Beresford – who never learned!

'Women expect more out of this than men,' Meadows said. 'To the women Wheatstone brought here, it won't have been a quick screw in a shed, it will have been a liaison with their lover – and that kind of fantasy can't be sustained if they have to nip outside for a quick pee between the foreplay and the main event.' She turned to Paniatowski. 'Back me up on this, boss?'

'Don't go dragging me into it,' Paniatowski said, with a bitter laugh. 'I live the life of a nun.'

And the moment the words were out of her mouth she thought, Oh God, did I *really* say that?

'The problem is that, if there's no more to this place than there seems to be at first glance,' she continued quickly, 'then all we've done is confirm what Mrs Wheatstone said – and several other people have hinted at. So we know for a fact that he was a randy little bastard – it doesn't get us any closer to finding out who murdered him, now does it?'

The baby had finally fallen asleep, and Irene Clark was looking forward to slipping into the magical world of Regency bucks with leather boots and horsewhips, and Regency ladies with big hair and beauty spots. But before she could – in all conscience – pick up her book, there was something she needed to check up on, and with that end in mind, she opened the door and stepped into her back garden.

The kitchen door to the Pemberton house was still open, which was slightly worrying. Irene really had no desire at all to be a nosy neighbour, but perhaps on this occasion, it wouldn't do any harm if she . . .'

She crossed the tiny lawn and stepped over the low fence that separated their property from the Pembertons'.

She came to a halt at the door.

'Is there anybody there?' she called.

No answer.

'Are you there, Rosemary?'

Still nothing.

She took a step inside, and looked around. The kitchen was clean and tidy – not as clean as hers, of course, but more than passable.

'Rosemary?' she said again, and this time she heard a noise. It was no more than a dull thump, but it showed she wasn't alone in this house.

'I'm coming into the lounge now – I'm unarmed, so hold your fire!' she said.

She giggled, partly because she thought she had been *quite* humorous, and partly because she was nervous.

She stopped giggling the moment she saw the lounge, because that was no laughing matter.

The mirror over the fireplace had been smashed – seven years bad luck for somebody! – two of the armchairs had been overturned and one of the upright chairs lay in splinters in the hearth.

'Rosemary?' Irene said, and now there was a tremble in her voice.

She heard the thumping sound again. It seemed to be coming from somewhere upstairs.

She stepped into the hall.

The noise was definitely coming from upstairs.

That was when she saw the bloodstains on the stair-carpet.

Her heart was galloping, and her vision was blurred. For a moment she was tempted to turn and run, and yet there was another force – like a powerful magnet – drawing her onwards.

As she climbed the stairs, she kept saying the other woman's name – 'Rosemary, Rosemary, Rosemary, Rosemary' – as if she were an exorcist and the name would keep the devil at bay.

She had reached the landing. 'I'm not alone, you know,' she said in the loudest voice she could muster.

Thud . . . thud . . . thud.

The noise was definitely coming from the master bedroom.

'Come on, Cedric, let's go in there, and find out exactly what's going on,' she said.

Cedric!

Whatever had made her choose the name Cedric?

Why couldn't she have called her imaginary companion Brett or Hugo, because if you wanted someone to save you, Brett and Hugo were your men.

Anybody called Cedric would probably be whimpering in the corner.

Thud . . . thud . . . thud.

The noise was coming from the wardrobe. Irene rushed into the room and flung the sliding door open.

Rosemary was in the wardrobe. Her ankles and wrists were taped together, and there was gaffer tape over her mouth. The lower half of her face was covered in a mixture of mucus and blood, and the area around both her eyes was starting to turn blue.

To put it in medical terms – it looked as if she had been hit by an express train.

SEVENTEEN

'Chief Inspector Paniatowski would like to talk to you, but if it becomes too much of a strain you must tell her,' the ward sister said.

'I want to know the full extent of the damage, please,' Rosemary Pemberton told her.

'Now, now, we don't need to think about that, right at this moment, now do we?'

'Don't we?' Rosemary asked. '*I* do. I'm a scientist, and I want to know the full extent of the damage.'

'I think you'd probably better tell her,' Paniatowski advised.

The sister shrugged. 'You've got extensive bruising almost everywhere it's possible to have bruising,' she said. 'Your collarbone is broken, so are two of your ribs. Another two ribs are cracked. Three of your toes have been crushed – we may have to amputate one of them. There now, do you really feel better for knowing all that?'

'As a matter of fact, I do,' Rosemary said. 'It's always better to know the truth.'

'Well, I'll leave you, then,' the sister said. 'Remember, Rosemary, if you feel it's too much, you only have to say.'

'Don't worry, I will,' Rosemary promised, and when the nurse had gone, she said, 'I'm sure the sister means well, but I'm not going to play the compliant child just to keep her happy. In fact, I'm not going to play by anybody else's rules ever again, because this is what happens to you when you do.'

'Do you want to talk about it?' Paniatowski asked.

'Yes, as long as I can do it in my own way.'

'Take your time.'

'When I married Roger, I was very much in love with him. In those days, he was full of ambition. He was going to get his doctorate in record time and produce some amazing research. He thought he could outstrip me.'

'And could he have?'

'I wouldn't have minded if he had. As I said, I was very much in love with him.'

'That wasn't the question I asked,' Paniatowski reminded her. 'Could he have outstripped you?'

'No,' Rosemary admitted. 'He's not a stupid man by any means, but his scientific vision and instinct are pedestrian, at best. He's perfectly competent to do his present work, but that's as far as he'll ever go.'

'And did he realize that eventually?'

'I think so. He says he decided there was more to life than work, and so I think he must know.'

'He pays all the bills, doesn't he – and it all comes out of his salary,' Paniatowski said.

'Good God, how do you know that?'

'My sergeant thought you were living below your means.'

'And she was right. Roger pays the mortgage, Roger buys all the food and cleaning stuff. It makes him feel as if he's the provider.' Rosemary paused, as if thinking over what she'd just said. 'Well, I suppose he *is* the provider, though quite unnecessarily so.'

'What happens to your salary?' Paniatowski asked.

'It goes into our joint bank account. I think Roger likes to pretend we haven't got it.'

'My sergeant also commented on your personal appearance,' Paniatowski said.

'Your sergeant doesn't miss much, does she? I used to be quite an attractive woman—'

'You still are,' Paniatowski interrupted. 'Well, not at the moment, it's true, but I've seen the pictures and you were – and will be again.'

'It started with little things at first.'

'What did?'

'That will become clear as we go along,' Rosemary rebuked her.

'Sorry,' Paniatowski said.

'He'd be annoyed when I put on some of my nicer clothes. He wouldn't say why – just that he wished that I wouldn't wear that dress tonight, not where everybody could see us.'

Not where everybody could see us, Paniatowski repeated silently.

'Then he started to veto all the new dresses I wanted to buy, and suggest I get ones that looked like potato sacks. He got angry when I went to the hairdressers, and when I coloured my hair at home, he went crazy. What did I want to do that for, he demanded. Why couldn't I let my hair be its natural colour? And it occurred to me that what he really wanted was for me to be unattractive to other men.'

'But you *weren't* unattractive, were you?' Paniatowski guessed.

'No, I wasn't. I don't know if *many* other men were attracted to me, but Arthur Wheatstone certainly was.' She paused for a moment. 'Let me tell you about Arthur. He could pretty much have any woman he wanted, not because he was particularly handsome or well-built, but because he loved women – and they could sense it.'

'You had an affair in that shed of his?'

'Yes, but it started long before that – before, even, Arthur moved out to the countryside. In fact, it was *because of* the affair that Arthur moved out to the countryside. You see, Roger found out about it, and he told Arthur's wife. They made us swear that we'd never see each other again outside work, and then Arthur was moved beyond reach.'

'And that's when he came up with the idea of the shed?'

'Yes. I tried to tell myself that he'd done it just for us, but I knew it wasn't true. He'll have had any number of other women there – he just couldn't help himself. And it didn't matter, you see, because even if I ceased to exist once I walked out of the door, while I was with him, he really loved me.'

'Did Roger find out about the shed today?'

'Yes.'

'How did he find out?'

'It was something your sergeant said.'

'Oh God, I'm so sorry,' Paniatowski told her.

'It's all right, it wasn't Sergeant Meadows' fault. When she told Roger that Arthur had an allotment, she had no way of knowing that I'd used an imaginary cousin and her allotment as an excuse to be with Arthur.'

'You've been seeing him down at those allotments, haven't you?' Roger screams, once Meadows has gone.

'No, I . . .'

'Don't lie to me.'

'I'm not lying.'

'You're so ashamed that you can't tell the truth even when it's obvious.'

'Ashamed!' she repeats. 'Do you think I'm ashamed of what we did in that shed?'

'So now you admit it?'

'Yes, we did it – and if he was still alive, I'd do it again.'

'Last time, before they moved to the country, we could keep it quiet,' Roger says. 'This time, everybody will know because of the murder.' He clamps his hands to the sides of his head in despair, almost as if he were modelling for The Scream. *'Everybody will know. I'll look like a complete fool.'*

'Is that all you care about?' she demands. 'Appearances?'

'What else is left for me?' he asks. And then suddenly he is much calmer, and there is a maniac gleam in his eye. 'I knew you'd never finish with him. That's why I had him killed.'

It would be funny if it were not so pathetic, she thinks.

'You had him killed?' she says. 'You?'

He has never hit her before, and the fact that he does now is almost as much of a shock as the blow itself.

She collapses, and he is standing over her.

'Yes, I had him killed,' he says.

He kicks her in the ribs. She tries to wriggle away and he kicks her again. She realizes how vulnerable her head is, and raises her arms to protect it.

'I was there,' Roger said. 'There was a gap between the beam and the ceiling, and the killer threaded the rope through it. I could never have reached it, but he was such a big man that he didn't even need to stand on tiptoe.'

He lashes out with his foot again, and this time he is aiming at her head. Her arm shields her precious brain, but not without cost – not without an excruciating pain that runs the length of her body.

'When he'd threaded the rope through, he hauled Arthur up like he was a sack of vegetables,' Roger screams. 'He'd been drugged, so he couldn't struggle, but he knew what was happening all right. There was terror in his eyes. And do you know what I did when I saw that terror? I laughed.'

He brings the heel of his shoe down hard on her toes, and she feels a pain which she knows must be greater than any human being has ever felt before.

'I laughed,' *she hears Roger saying, dribbling as he speaks.* 'I bloody laughed.'

She passes out, and when she regains consciousness, she is tied up inside a wardrobe, and can hear a distant voice saying, 'Are you there, Rosemary?'

There was nothing like a victory celebration in the Drum and Monkey, Crane thought, and, as the old joke went, that was what this was – nothing like a victory celebration in the Drum and Monkey.

All the necessary elements were there – the team itself, an unlimited supply of alcohol and a result. Admittedly, Roger Pemberton was still on the run, but even though he had a great deal of money in his pocket (his next act, after beating his wife half to death, had been to draw all the money out of their joint account), he had none of the skills a hardened criminal employs to avoid detection, and he could not possibly remain at liberty much longer.

So what *was* the problem?

'There are so many loose ends,' Paniatowski said.

'There always are,' said Beresford, 'that's because this is life, and there are no Hollywood script writers about to round things off nicely before the final credits roll.'

But Paniatowski was not about to be so easily mollified.

'How did someone like Roger Pemberton manage to contact a hit man in the first place?' she asked.

'Maybe he subscribes to *Contract Killers' Monthly* (Motto: We give it our best shot),' Crane said, in an effort to lighten the mood, then seeing the look in Paniatowski's eyes, he quickly added, 'Sorry.'

'Why did they want to make it look like a suicide?' Paniatowski asked.

'Perhaps because Roger Pemberton worried that any murder investigation would immediately zoom in on him as a prime suspect,' Crane suggested.

'In which case, why did they make such a bad job of faking it?' Paniatowski countered.

'The hit man could reach the gap between the beam and the ceiling easily,' Beresford said. 'Maybe it didn't occur to him that most other men would have difficulty.'

'It should have done – if he was a professional.'

'Then perhaps he wasn't. Perhaps Pemberton chose him because he was cheap – and the reason he was cheap was because he was just learning the business.'

'Or maybe they were working with two audiences in mind, and they wanted one audience to think he'd killed himself, and the other to think he'd been murdered,' Meadows suggested.

'They?' Paniatowski repeated. 'Exactly what "they" are you talking about, Kate?'

Meadows looked quite startled – and no one at the table had ever seen *that* expression on her face before.

'I have no idea where that came from!' she admitted, a little shakily. 'And I certainly have no idea who "they" might be. But if there was a "they", what I just said would have made perfect sense, wouldn't it?'

'If the moon was made of cheese, astronauts would make sure they took a jar of pickled onions up there with them,' Beresford said.

'Very witty, sir – one of your best,' Meadows countered. She shivered. 'For a second back there, it felt like somebody was walking over my grave. Then I remembered I've asked to be buried at sea,' she concluded, with a grin which looked only partly forced.

'What about the American – Proudfoot?' Paniatowski asked, partly to shatter the unexpected – and inexplicable – tension that had suddenly built up, but mostly because it was a question that had to be asked. 'What the bloody hell was he doing there?'

'Maybe checking up that the hit man had done what he and Pemberton had paid him to do,' Beresford said, out of the blue.

'Go on,' Paniatowski told him.

'We keep forgetting how important Wheatstone and Pemberton are,' Beresford said.

'Pemberton's not important,' Crane said. 'He's a technician – a high-level technician, admittedly, but still no more than an assistant.'

'But Dr Pemberton, his wife, *is* important,' Beresford said.

'Agreed.'

'And he will have been invited to all the things that she was invited to, won't he?'

'Like what?' Paniatowski asked.

Beresford waved his hands in frustration. 'I don't know. I'm nowt but a simple bobby from the sticks. Ask Crane and Meadows. It's more their world than it is mine.'

'Scientists do get invited to a lot of international conferences,' Crane said.

'And foreign embassies often throw receptions so their visiting nationals who have distinguished themselves in one way or another can meet the local bigwigs,' Meadows added.

'All right,' Beresford said, 'Proudfoot and Pemberton meet at some sort of conference or reception. Wheatstone is there, too, and Pemberton notices that Proudfoot is glaring at him. What's that all about, Pemberton asks, and Proudfoot says it's nothing. But later, in the bar, when they've both had too much to drink, Proudfoot admits that he met Wheatstone at a previous conference – and Wheatstone slept with his wife!'

'So they agree to kill him?' Crane says.

'That's exactly what they do. They decide to hire a hit man, and they also agree that they'll both be there when Wheatstone is executed.'

'Why do they do that?' Meadows wondered.

'Two reasons. The first is that they both really want to see Wheatstone die. The second – maybe more important – is that it gives each one a little more security by tying the other into the act.'

He looked around the table to see how they were all taking it.

'We're still listening,' Paniatowski said.

'With bated breath,' Meadows added.

'It's supposed to happen when it did actually happen – the night before you found the body, boss. But then Proudfoot's flight is delayed. That creates a lot of problems at this end. The first is that they've already drugged Wheatstone, and there's a chance that if they leave it too long, the drug will wear off. Secondly, the longer they stay there, the more risk they run. And thirdly, the hit man can't wait around, because he needs to be somewhere else.'

'So Pemberton decides to go ahead with the murder without Proudfoot?' Paniatowski asked.

'So Pemberton decides to go ahead with the murder without Proudfoot.' Beresford agreed. 'Once that's done, Pemberton and the hit man leave. They think about meeting Proudfoot at the airport, and decide it's too dangerous. They rule out the idea of leaving him a message, for the same reason.'

'So when Proudfoot lands – hours later than he should have done – he doesn't know what's happening?' Meadows asked.

'Exactly. Maybe they've already killed Wheatstone – or maybe they're waiting until he arrives. They might even have abandoned the plan altogether. He has to know, and so he picks up his hire car and drives up to Barrow Village, where you catch him in the act.'

'Brilliant!' Meadows said. 'Absolutely brilliant.' She held up her hands in front of her, to silence Beresford before he spoke. 'I'm not taking the piss, Colin, I promise you I'm not. I really do think it's brilliant.'

Yes, it was very clever, Paniatowski agreed, but it still didn't explain how the American Embassy knew Proudfoot had been arrested without him even making his phone call. Yet that could probably be explained away too, given a little more thought and a little more information.

Roger Pemberton could provide that information, she thought. He was out there now, but he could not stay out there for long.

They would catch him, and all the loose ends would be tied up.

And if they didn't catch him?

It was not a question that really needed to be asked, because it was impossible to imagine him disappearing off the face of the earth.

But he did.

PART THREE
The French Connection

September 1978

EIGHTEEN

'*Is it possible that one day in the near future, when all your team are gathered around you, you will open your mouth and say "Arthur Wheatstone"?*'

The unexpected appearance of Forsyth in the room in which she was lying – perhaps, indeed, the room in which she was *dying* – had cast the Wheatstone murder case in an entirely new mould. Now she knew he had been hovering in the background, like a great evil goblin, throughout the entire investigation, every word that had been spoken needed to be re-examined, and every incident viewed from as many angles as possible, in order to establish whether it had actually happened or only *appeared* to have happened.

She had to discover what it was he thought she knew – or could work out – that might be a danger to his operation.

But what *was* his operation?

Had he come to Lancashire just to execute Wheatstone?

Nah, a simple execution was way below the pay grade of someone like Forsyth. Besides, he would have found it crude and offensive and – probably most importantly of all – boring. If he had been in charge of such a monochrome job, he would just have phoned it in.

But that wasn't to say that Wheatstone's death had nothing to do with the mesmeric net which Forsyth wove and then used to capture those he needed to use.

What else?

Chief Superintendent Snodgrass had been one of Forsyth's creatures.

'*You thought you'd go and find a simple suicide, and turn it into a murder,*' he'd said, without ever having been anywhere near the crime scene itself.

Snodgrass – or someone else Forsyth could trust – was supposed to get to the garage first, and make it look like suicide.

Then, when Dr Shastri . . .

No, not Shastri! She wouldn't have been there, because an unknown admirer – who probably went by the name of Forsyth – had sent her a ticket for her favourite orchestra.

Baxter had assured her Wheatstone hadn't been spying for the Russians, and she believed him, because why would *anybody* lie about that?

So why had Wheatstone been executed – and why did it have to look like suicide?

She wished she knew what Forsyth thought she knew. She wished she knew why he thought she was such a danger.

She wished, too, that the lights in the ceiling weren't quite so bright, because it was hard to think with them blaring down on her.

And then her brain all but exploded.

The lights! it told her. You can see the bloody lights.

I know I can, she thought.

She wondered if she could speak, because if she could, she was going to shout as loudly as she was able.

She wondered if she could move her arms, because if she could, there must be a button somewhere, and she would press it and press it until the nurses came running in, and she could give them the good news.

And then she thought of Forsyth, and realized that if he found out what had happened, she was as good as dead.

Colin Beresford was aware that the water in baths in the northern hemisphere drained clockwise, and that in the southern hemisphere it drained anti-clockwise, but he had no idea why it should happen that way. He knew that Leonardo da Vinci's *Mona Lisa* was a much more valuable painting than Edvard Munch's *The Scream*, but he couldn't understand what made it more valuable – or, come to that, what made either of them so much better than the rather pleasant picture of a hay wain which he could have picked up for twenty quid in his local furniture store.

It didn't bother him that he didn't know the answer to these and a myriad other questions, but there were a few which did bother him – which would suddenly appear like an itch, and would not be content until he'd scratched them – and one of those which recurred the most was why he – Shagger Beresford – did not fancy Dr Shastri.

It was not that he was racially prejudiced – he'd never bedded a Pakistani or Indian woman, but he'd certainly lusted after them. It was not that she was unattractive – she was film star gorgeous. And if, because of her work, a little of the scent of death clung to her, well, it clung to him, too, because of the nature of his work. So could it be . . .

'Unless you learn to concentrate, you may remain an *acting* DCI for the rest of your career, Colin,' said a sharp female voice.

'Sorry, Doc, I was miles away,' he confessed.

'Well, you have not missed much – just me spouting out reams of scientific gobbledygook, which I do to make people think I am clever.'

'But you *are* clever!' Beresford protested.

'Thank you, Colin, I will treasure your kind words to my dying day.' Shastri paused. 'And speaking of dying, would you like me to talk about Leeks and Carrots Man now?'

'Err, yes,' Beresford agreed, and then, seeing the glint in Shastri's eyes, added, 'please – yes, please.'

'Leeks – I feel I know him well enough now to call him by just his first name – was in his late thirties to early forties.'

'When was he killed?'

'It's difficult to pin down exactly,' Shastri said cautiously, 'but I would say between two and six years ago.'

'You can't be more precise than that?' Beresford asked, disappointedly.

'Would it make you happy if I was?'

'Very happy.'

'All right, then, he was killed on the 7th of July 1977, at eight thirty-five in the evening, so he may – or may not – have just seen a particularly exciting episode of *Coronation Street*.'

'You're taking the piss,' Beresford said.

'Forgive me,' Shastri said penitently, 'but I have just bought a book entitled *101 Ways to Annoy a DCI*, and I just had to try it out.'

'So, two to six years?' Beresford said.

'Two to six years,' Shastri agreed. 'To continue, as you know, his fingertips had been sliced off . . .'

'Would you say they were removed professionally? I mean, is there any indication that the killer had medical training?'

Shastri laughed. 'The killer didn't remove a heart or a lung, you know,' she said. 'He snipped the fingertips off. A child could have done that. Now where was I? Oh yes. He was buried quite deeply, and, I would say, quite soon after death. That is a factor in our favour, as is the fact that all this took part in Lancashire, where – as you know yourself – it can be as cold as a witch's tit. These and other factors have slowed down decomposition, and enabled me to say with some certainty that whilst he was quite a heavy drinker and smoker, he was in very good health up to the point at which he was struck on the back of the head. A micro-second later, of course, he could not have been in worse health,'

'What was the weapon?' Beresford asked.

'From the dent in his skull, I would say it was a hammer, but there has been some deterioration over the last four years and . . .'

'You said the last four years,' Beresford said, homing in on the words. 'You think he's been in the ground for four years.'

Shastri sighed. 'My gut feeling is that it is four years,' she said, 'but I knew that if I told you that, you would latch onto it as a certainty – and it isn't. My advice to you is to give all possible years exactly the same amount of attention. Do you hear what I'm saying?'

'Of course I hear you,' Beresford snapped. He pulled a repentant face. 'Sorry, Dr Shastri, I did hear what you said, and the point is taken.'

'Good boy,' Shastri said, encouragingly.

On his way out of the mortuary, Beresford did a quick mental review of how things had gone.

On the personal front, he now knew why he didn't fancy Shastri – it was because she spoke to him as if he were her little boy, which was very annoying, but also – confusingly – rather pleasant.

On the professional front, it was an almost dead certainty that the body had been in the ground for four years.

Archie Eccleston was sitting on the narrow bed in one of the holding cells, looking thoroughly miserable.

'They say they've found a body on my allotment,' he told Crane, through the bars.

'They have.'

'It's nothing to do with me,' Eccleston said – and it was obvious to both Crane and the custody sergeant that it wasn't.

'Can't you just kick him loose?' Crane suggested.

The custody sergeant shook his head regretfully. 'He's been arrested, and before he can be released, he needs to go through the proper procedures with the arresting officers.'

'And where are the arresting officers?' Crane asked.

'Out,' the custody sergeant said.

'My boss needs to talk to him about this murder, but he's not here, so would you mind if I talked to him instead?'

'Who is your boss?' the sergeant asked. 'Shagger Beresford?'

'That's right.'

'Has he asked you to do it?'

'No.'

'But he won't mind?'

'He won't mind at all,' Crane promised.

The custody sergeant nodded. 'All right, I'll have him sent up to Interview A.'

'I think I'd get more out of him if I took him to the canteen for a cup of tea,' Crane said.

'I'm sure you would,' the sergeant agreed, 'but it's not going to happen.'

'Oh well, at least I tried,' Crane said philosophically.

Interview Room A had a skylight window which hadn't been cleaned on the outside since the Coronation, and a table that wobbled unless a doubled-over cigarette packet was positioned in just the right spot under one of its legs.

'I know you didn't bury that body on your allotment, but some bugger must have, mustn't they?' Crane asked, across the table.

'I suppose so,' Archie Eccleston replied.

'How long have you had the allotment?'

'Fourteen years, since my son . . . since before my son . . . fourteen years.'

'Hmm, the body's not been there that long,' Crane said. 'So how do you think they'll have managed it?'

'I'm not sure I know what you mean.'

'Well, say I'd got a body I wanted to bury there. My first job would be to dig up all your vegetables, wouldn't it?'

'But they probably wouldn't be ready,' Archie Eccleston said, anguish in his voice at even imagining such a tragedy. 'If they had been ready, I'd have dug them up myself.'

'So say I dug them up, then dug much further down, put the body in my new deep hole, covered it with soil, then put your vegetables back where I found them. Would you be able to tell I'd done it, the next day?'

'Well, of course I'd be able to tell. It would be obvious right away.'

'So how will they have done it without you noticing it, do you think?'

'They'll have done it just before a replanting,' Archie Eccleston said, as if he'd just had a revelation. 'That's the only way they *could* have done it.'

'What's a replanting?'

'It's what I call it when I clear out part of the allotment and start again from scratch.'

'Clear it out?'

'There's nothing left by the time I've finished, except for the soil, of course – and even some of that's new.'

'So if you were doing a replanting and you went home at night and somebody buried a body, you wouldn't notice when you came back in the morning.'

'I might not notice,' Archie Eccleston said.

'Might not?'

'I probably wouldn't notice,' Eccleston said, grudgingly.

'How often do you do these replantings?'

'Not very often at all. Only when it really needs doing. It's a big job, you see.'

'How often is not very often?' Crane asked, with just a hint of desperation in his voice.

'I couldn't really say.'

'Don't you keep a gardening record?'

'There's them that does – but I've never bothered.'

They were going to have to rely on the memories of other allotment holders whose plots adjoined Archie's, Crane thought.

He imagined the perfect witness.

It's all here in my gardening records, young man. "4th of October 1975. Planted daffs and tulips. Noticed that silly sod Archie Eccleston is digging up half his allotment again."

'There is one I can remember,' Archie Eccleston said. 'I couldn't tell you the date or anything . . .'

'Then it's not likely to be of much help.'

'But you've probably got a record of it yourselves.'

'Now why would we have a record of what you were doing?'

'No, not what I was doing – what *you* were doing.'

'You're not making much sense, Mr Eccleston.'

'I was replanting, and you were going through the stuff in Arthur Wheatstone's potting shed.'

As he stood at the bar of the Drum and Monkey, Colin Beresford felt a sudden urge to add a double vodka to his order of two pints and a soft drink, even though there was no one at the table who would want it.

Don't be so bloody soft, he told himself angrily. You're a down-to-earth sort of feller – well-known for it – and that kind of fanciful thinking is best left to lads with degrees, like Jack Crane.

He walked over to the table and laid down the tray.

'You're looking like the cat who got the cream, Jack,' he said to Crane.

Crane grinned. 'Am I, sir?'

Not 'boss', Beresford noted, but 'sir'. And quite right, too – because the *boss* was lying comatose on a bed in Whitebridge General.

He sat down and took a swig of his beer.

Thwaites' Best Bitter – one of the very few things in life that never disappointed.

He wiped froth off his top lip with the back of his hand.

'All right, let's hear it,' he said.

'I've got two things,' Crane said. 'I'm fairly confident I know when the victim went into the hole – and I've got a lead on who might have put him there.'

Beresford whistled softly. 'If you're right about both things, you'd better have my job,' he said. 'Let's start with the date.'

Crane explained the way his thoughts had been running before he'd talked to Archie Eccleston, and what conclusions he'd reached during their conversation.

'The Wheatstone case was four years ago, and that's also Dr Shastri's best bet as to when our fingerless stiff was buried,' Beresford said when he'd finished. 'Tell us about your suspect now.'

'Whoever buried our victim had to either have an allotment of his own or a reason to visit the allotments every day,' Crane said.

'Because he had to know there was an allotment suitable for his purposes,' Meadows said.

'Exactly. He couldn't wander around the allotments with a corpse slung over his shoulder on the off-chance there'd be a suitable plot available. He had to know in advance that Archie had prepared part of his allotment for replanting.'

'I'm still waiting for the name of your suspect,' Beresford said.

'Dick or Richard Judd.'

'And what made you suspect him?'

Crane grinned. 'The fact that he was behaving suspiciously,' he said.

There is one cardinal rule at the allotments – and the fact that it is not written down in no way diminishes its importance or significance. That rule is 'Each man's allotment is his and his alone, and no other man shall give it the barest touch without his consent.'

Thus, when Archie Eccleston sees Dick Judd standing on his allotment with a spade in his hand, his first emotion is incredulity, and his second is rage.

'What the bloody hell do you think you're doing?' he demands.

Dick Judd turns towards him with a look of surprise on his face. 'This part that you're replanting,' he says.

'What about it?'

'You've missed bits, but you mustn't blame yourself, because two pairs of eyes are always better than one.'

'I was brought up to keep my nose out of other people's business,' Archie Eccleston says, and the anger is still evident in his voice.

'Look,' Judd says apologetically, 'this isn't the first time it's happened, and I'm sorry.'

'The first time what's happened?' Eccleston asks, curious despite himself.

'Me annoying people by trying to help, when they don't want

*help at all. It's just that when I've got too much time on my hands,
I start thinking about Janice.'*
    'Janice?'
    'My daughter.'
    'What happened to her?'
    *'She died.' Judd fights back a sob. 'She was only nine.'
Eccleston is assailed by waves of guilt and pain.*
    *'You're right, two pairs of eyes are better than one.' He pauses.
'Would you like to help me with the replanting?'*
    Judd sniffs. 'Only if I'll not be in the way,' he says.
    'You'll not be in the way,' Eccleston promises.

'Judd wants to make absolutely sure Eccleston doesn't notice there
have been any changes. That's why he's there with his spade, so
if Eccleston says, "Somebody's been interfering with this allotment," he can reply, "Yes, that was me – you saw me doing it just
now".'
    'What do we know about this Judd feller?' Beresford asked.
    'Only what I've been able to find out in the last hour or so,
since my chat to Archie Eccleston,' Crane said.
    'Then let's hear it.'
    'He's a clerk at the town hall. He's had his allotment for six
years.'
    'That's how long Jennings and Horrocks have had their allot-
ment,' Meadows said.
    'Meaning . . .?' Beresford asked.
    'Meaning the two things may be connected.'
    'You're saying it might be his job to watch them?'
    'Yes.'
    'That squares up nicely with what most of the fellers down at
the allotments say about Judd as a gardener,' Crane said.
    'And what do they say?'
    'That he's competent.'
    'What's wrong with that?'
    'It's damning with faint praise. It means his allotment is not *so*
bad that they feel the need to report him to the committee.'
    'Where does he live?'
    'He's got a flat on Burnley Road.'
    'Did he really lose a daughter?' Meadows asked.

'I'm not quite sure, yet,' Crane admitted. 'What would your guess be?'

'My guess would be it's too much of a coincidence that they've both lost a child,' Meadows said. 'My guess would be that he's a lying, manipulative bastard.'

'If we pick him up and he refuses to say anything – which, given the cool customer he appears to be, is more than likely – then we've got nothing, because we're lacking any hard evidence,' Beresford said. 'On the other hand, if we just keep him under observation, he might notice, and try to do a runner.'

'So what are *you* going to do?' Crane asked.

Beresford took a long sip of his pint. 'I think I'll sleep on it,' he said.

'Am I the only one who thinks she knows who the dead man is, or is it so obvious to you two that neither of you have bothered to mention it?' Meadows said.

'Who *do* you think it is?' Beresford asked.

'I think it's a man who went missing at the same time the body was buried – a man who had no criminal background, yet has managed to stay on the run for over four years.'

'Roger Pemberton!' Crane said.

'Yes, it really has to have been him,' Beresford agreed. 'But the question is, just what did he do to merit such obvious dislike?'

Middleton Terrace was a row of late Victorian houses in what had once been the better part of town, and had provided homes for people who, had they been born seventy or eighty years later, might well have bought a detached dwelling in Barrow Village.

The terrace was no longer fashionable, but neither had it slipped far enough down the scales to have become a slum. In fact, since the houses had four floors (including a servants' attic), they had become much sought after by businesses which could not quite stretch to the rent demanded for the modern – steel and plate glass – offices in the new city centre.

It was the fact that Middleton Terrace was virtually deserted after dark which had made it so attractive to Mr Forsyth's people.

The first three floors had become a bed-and-breakfast business – breakfast room and landlady's quarters in the basement, guest rooms on floors one and two. The landlady was, in fact, a service housekeeper, but in keeping with her cover could serve up heart-attack-inducing fried breakfasts for eager long-distance lorry drivers.

The top floor was the safe house, and was reached by an entirely independent entrance. It was not exactly to Mr Forsyth's taste – when he was in Whitebridge, he preferred to stay in one of the suites at the Royal Victoria – but given the low profile nature of his current mission, he supposed that he could tolerate a little squalor if he had to.

He was sitting in the armchair, enjoying a malt whisky. He shouldn't have been drinking the whisky – his doctor had told him it was a definite no-no – but there seemed little point in avoiding icebergs when two-thirds of your hull had already been damaged beyond repair.

There was a coded knock on the door.

'Enter,' he said.

Downes came in.

'I've just got a report from mobile unit two,' he said.

'Which one is that,' Forsyth asked, not because he didn't know but because it would deflate Downes' sense of drama.

'It's the one outside the Drum and Monkey,' Downes said.

'And what has it got to report?'

'Beresford's team think that it was Roger Pemberton who was buried in that hole on the allotments,' Downes said.

'Is that what all of them think?'

'Yes.'

'Even that smart young Oxford graduate Jack Crane?'

'Even him.'

Forsyth chuckled. 'Then they are going to be disappointed in the morning, aren't they?'

He usually left his vehicle in the Drum's main car park, next to those of Meadows and Crane, but tonight he had left it in the supermarket car park, which was a five-minute walk away.

A big supermarket was easier for her – a new girl in town – to find than a grotty little pub, he'd told himself, although he knew that was a load of bollocks, because there wasn't an adult in Whitebridge who couldn't have directed her towards the Drum and Monkey if she'd got lost.

What was it, then?

Didn't he want to be seen with her?

Of course he wanted to be seen with her. What man wouldn't?

But he didn't want to be seen with her by Crane and Meadows – at least, not yet, anyway.

Adolescent! he told himself.

Big bloody baby!

You're an acting chief inspector, for Christ's sake.

He turned onto the car park, and saw her leaning back luxuriantly over the bonnet of his car.

'I should have given you my key, then you could have opened the car and been comfortable,' he said.

'Or I might have stolen the car, sold it on the black market, and been on the next plane to Thailand,' she said.

He wondered if he should kiss her, then told himself that a supermarket car park was not the most romantic spot for a first kiss, and there would be other opportunities later.

'So where shall we go?' he asked.

'I'm the new girl in town, so it's pretty much up to you,' she said.

'There are a couple of nice cocktail bars on the other side of Whitebridge,' he said, tentatively.

'Isn't it a bit late for that?' she said.

He glanced at his watch. The meeting with Crane and Meadows had run on longer than he'd imagined.

'Yes, it is a little late,' he agreed. 'But there's this nightclub called the Blue Note . . .'

'It sounds absolutely horrid,' she said dismissively. 'I'll tell you what – why don't we just go back to my place?'

'Yes,' he agreed, 'why don't we?'

NINETEEN

Colin Beresford had long ago come to the conclusion that Man was never intended to be happy, and that this was especially true in the case of *Northern* Man.

Jack Crane agreed with him. He said Northern Man was driven

by a *philosophie froide*, and when Beresford had accused him of showing off, he'd said no, no, he wasn't showing off at all, he was merely using *le mot juste* (which was probably a good joke if you understood French).

Anyway, be that as it may, Man was never intended to be happy, but there were moments – like this one, lying in bed, a cigarette in his right hand and his left arm draped over Ward Sister Diana Sowerbury – when life felt rather more than tolerable.

'I have to go,' he said, stubbing his cigarette, disengaging his arm, and swinging his legs onto the floor.

And now he faced the inevitable question – what the bloody hell had he done with his clothes?

He'd find his jacket near the front door. He was fairly sure of that.

And his trousers?

He would have thought the trousers must have been gone by the time that he and Diana had tried that incredible manoeuvre with the Victorian hat stand in the hallway, but he supposed he could just about have managed it with them still round his ankles.

He looked around the bedroom, and into the living room that lay beyond it.

'It's a very nice place,' he said. 'You were lucky to get it at such short notice.'

'It belongs to the woman who was the ICU ward sister before me,' Diana said.

'And what happened to her?'

'She was offered this fantastic job in Singapore, but she had to leave immediately.'

'I shouldn't imagine the hospital was very pleased about that.'

'It wasn't at first – but then they found out they could get me, and realized what a favour she'd done them.'

He could see his tie on the floor of the living room, but what he really needed to find first was his underpants.

'Couldn't you stay a little longer?' Diana pleaded, as he stepped into the living room. 'I'm not on duty until ten o'clock.'

It was tempting – after the night they'd spent together, it was *very* tempting – but he knew he was going to have to turn her down.

'I'm in the middle of an investigation,' he said, pulling on one of his socks and looking around for the other one.

'Is this investigation you're in the middle of the one that I read about in the papers?' she asked. 'The body on the allotments?'

'Yes.'

'How exciting! Do you have a suspect?'

His underpants were poking out from under the sofa, his shirt was draped over the back of one of the armchairs, like an antimacassar.

'I can't talk about the case,' he said.

'Of course you can,' she replied.

Her voice sounded closer than before, and he turned around. She was standing in her bedroom doorway – gorgeous and naked.

'I talk about my patients all the time,' she said. 'I have to. It's a release. I've seen some terrible things, and if I don't talk about them to somebody, my head will explode.' She mimed an exploding head, and the way her breasts moved was most disturbing. 'But what I do,' she continued, 'is talk in very general terms. Do you think you could manage that?'

'Maybe,' Beresford conceded. 'We do have a suspect. He works for the council. But we've got nowhere near enough evidence to even pull him in for questioning.'

'So it's a "he",' Diana said. 'How disappointing. It's always so much more exciting when it's a woman.' She hesitated for a second before speaking again. 'This isn't just a one-night stand, is it?'

'God, no!' Beresford said.

His words surprised him, because one-night stands were his speciality – yet even the thought of not seeing this woman again made his stomach contract into a tight, angry ball.

'Will you come round tonight?' she asked.

'If I can,' he told her.

'Ah, the start of the classic brush-off.'

'It's not that at all. It depends on how the investigation is going. But I'll see you at some point during the day, anyway.'

'Yes?'

'Yes, you'll be on duty, and I'll be coming to visit Monika.'

'Do you always visit her on a Tuesday?'

'I visit her every day of the week.'

'And what do you do?'

Beresford shrugged. 'I talk to her. Sometimes it's about the past – when the two of us were working for Charlie Woodend. Sometimes it's about whatever case I'm working on that day. I don't know if she can hear me, but I talk anyway.'

Tears were forming in his eyes. He turned his back on her and pretended to be searching for clothes, though by now he had located everything he'd been wearing when he arrived.

'So that's it,' he heard her say. 'You're not sure you can find time for me, but you'll make time for a woman who probably doesn't even know you're there.'

She was speaking lightly – as if making a joke – but he could tell that she was hurt.

It would be best to say nothing, he thought.

'The difference is that I love her, and I don't love you,' he heard himself say.

She gasped, and then – after a slight pause – she said, 'Yes, well, I suppose I asked for that.'

He turned around, not caring that she would see the tears in his eyes.

'But I think I could learn to love you,' he said.

The two boys were constantly warned by their mothers to stay away from Smugglers' Cove.

'One minute it can be as calm as you like, and the next minute you'll find yourself surrounded by a roaring, bubbling torment,' said Will's mother, who had a great love of words, even if she didn't always use them correctly.

'It'll do you no good to come crying to me when you've been swept out to sea and drowned,' said Tommy's mother, who had a more prosaic view of life.

The two styles of warning were equally effective, which is to say, neither of them had any effect at all.

After all, how could you expect two young lads of spirit to ever stay away from somewhere called Smugglers' Cove?

Besides, there were rewards to be gained from the cove.

In the old days, Tommy's and Will's ancestors had stood on the beach at night, holding out a lantern. The hope was that passing ships would mistake it for a distant lighthouse and, thus disorientated, would crash onto the rocks. It was not, as they would probably have been the first to admit, the most honourable of trades, but, when combined with rum smuggling, it was *their* trade – and, by God, it beat gutting fish for a living.

There weren't wreckers in Cornwall any more, but interesting things were still washed up on the beach occasionally. Tommy and Will had found, at various times, a sodden armchair, a large fridge, a dozen cricket balls and a large wooden box which had contained (rather disappointingly) something called the *Encyclopaedia Britannica*. They did not know where any of these things had come from, nor how they had got into the sea in the first place, but that only served to add to their fascination. And every time they went down to the sea, they hoped (and secretly half-expected) to find that the waves had washed ashore a Japanese motorcycle, which they could hide in the caves and ride when there was no one around.

That very early morning when they arrived at the beach, they saw something long and thin at the far end, half-in and half-out of the water.

'I hope it's a roll of lino,' Tommy said.

They'd found a roll of linoleum once before. It had been heavier than they'd imagined, and difficult to manoeuvre up the twisting path to the top of the cliffs, but once they'd got it back to the village, they'd managed to sell it to the mad old lady at Rose Cottage for a pound, so that was all right.

As they got closer, they could see it wasn't a roll of lino at all.

'I think it's a man,' Tommy said.

'He's asleep,' Will said, with a worried edge creeping into his voice. 'Don't you think he must be asleep?'

'Yeah, he's asleep,' Tommy agreed, in what came out of his mouth as a high-pitched squeak.

And then they both turned and ran as fast as they could away from the dead body.

It had been four years since Meadows last saw John Horrocks and Philip Jennings, and she was rather looking forward to it. She arrived at their flat at eight-fifteen, so she was hardly surprised to find them both still in their dressing gowns. She did, however, raise an eyebrow when she noted that both dressing gowns were shot silk.

'Oh, come on, give us a break, Kate,' Philip Jennings said, when he caught her reaction. 'We live most of our lives like "normal" people. Surely we're to be allowed to swathe ourselves in a few old queen clichés.'

'They're beautiful dressing gowns, and you are two of the most normal people I know,' Meadows said.

Horrocks beamed at her. 'Flattery will get you nowhere. Would you like a cup of coffee?'

'I'd love one.'

They sat down in the living room, pretending to enjoy their coffee whilst conducting surreptitious inspections of each other.

In four years, Horrocks had got a little heavier and the odd white hair lay uncomfortably in Jennings' dark thatch, but other than that, time had been very kind to both of them, Meadows thought. She hoped in their furtive assessment they were being as charitable about her.

'So how are things at work, boys?' she asked.

'Oh, you know, there've been ups and downs,' Horrocks told her.

'One of the ups being that we no longer have to work with that awful little prick Arthur Wheatstone or that equally objectionable arsehole Roger Pemberton,' Jennings said.

'Now, now,' Horrocks admonished him.

'And Dr Pemberton has really come into her own,' Jennings continued. 'She's much happier in herself, and that makes her an even better boss.' He turned to his partner. 'See? I can do nice when I want to.'

'The downside is the Americans,' Horrocks said. 'The place has been flooded with them since the murder. They're supposed to be "security advisors" but if they were just advisors, they wouldn't have the right to boss us around, would they?'

'One of them was particularly rude to me,' Jennings said. 'He kept calling me fag or faggot, which is the American term for . . .'

'I know what it's the American term for,' Meadows said.

'Anyway, he was always using the word. "Where are you going, fag?" "Don't you know you're not allowed in here, fag?" In the end, I went and complained to Dr Pemberton.'

'And what did she say?'

'She said that she was very sorry, but after what had happened,

we couldn't really object if the Americans wanted us to beef up
our security a bit.'

'"After what had happened"?' Meadows repeated. 'Do you think
she was talking about Arthur Wheatstone's death?'

Jennings shook his head. 'No, she was talking about something
that had happened at the plant.'

'Like what?'

'I don't know, I tried to push her, but she wouldn't be specific
– just told me there were some things I'd be better off not
concerning myself with.'

Meadows took another sip of her coffee. It really *was* very good.

'I'm interested in a man called Dick or Richard Judd,' she said.
'John may have come across him in his capacity as secretary of
the allotment society, but I was wondering if you, Philip, knew
him too.'

'Does Philip know Dick Judd!' Horrocks said.

'Do I know Dick Judd,' Jennings echoed. 'Oh yes, we both
know our spook very well.'

And then they both broke into a chorus of 'Me and My Shadow'.

Chief Superintendent Crouch of the Cornish Constabulary was on
the phone to Dr Dalton, the police surgeon, who was never an
easy man to get on with at the best of times.

'What the bloody hell were you doing sending me a cadaver?'
the doctor demanded.

'The man was thrown up by the sea. He was dead, I thought
you might be interested,' Crouch said.

'But you knew I was just about to set off on my fishing trip.'

'Then hand him over to your locum,' Crouch suggested. 'Oh,
wait a minute, what was it you said when I suggested you hired
a locum? Wasn't it something like, "It would be just like pouring
money down the drain, because nothing's likely to happen that
will be so urgent it can't wait until I get back".'

'Oh, well, that's fine, then. If it's not urgent, I'll just put the
cadaver on ice, and then, when I—'

'Those were your words, not mine,' the chief superintendent
interrupted.

'What are you talking about?'

'"Nothing's so urgent it can't wait until I get back." "If it's not urgent, I'll just put the cadaver on ice." I never said either of those things.'

'Well, maybe you didn't in as many words, but . . .'

'There's a family somewhere waiting for news of this missing man, and I'm not prepared to keep them waiting for another two weeks.'

'The autopsy won't tell you who he is.'

'True, but it will tell me what he died of, won't it?'

'Well, yes. But so what?'

'The thing is, say I find his wife tomorrow, for example. I'm sorry, but your husband's dead, I tell her. That's terrible, she says. How did he die? I don't know, I say, but in a couple of weeks Dr Dalton will be back from his holidays, and I can tell you then.'

'Look, I'm afraid I'm going to have to say no.'

'Oh yes?'

'What does that mean?'

'It means "oh yes".'

'What will you do if I refuse to do this autopsy now?'

'I'll feel obliged to inform the police authority that I don't think you're the right man for the position of police surgeon.'

'They won't listen to you. I went to school with two of the members of the authority, and I was on the same staircase as the chairman at Oxford.'

'You're probably right,' the chief superintendent agreed. 'After all, what chance does a humble copper, who worked his way up through the ranks, have against people who went to the same school and university?'

'That's a very sensible attitude to take,' the doctor said. 'And on that other matter – the humble thing – I think you should feel very proud of yourself for getting as far as you have.'

'Thank you,' the chief superintendent said. 'And while I'm on the phone, can I take this opportunity to invite you to my celebratory dinner next month.'

'What will you be celebrating?'

'Didn't you know? Next year, I'm going to be Grand Master of my lodge, which is the same lodge, coincidentally, as most of the members of the police authority belong to.'

There was a sharp intake of breath on the other end of the line, then the doctor said, 'I'll have the autopsy report to you by this afternoon.'

'Thank you,' the chief superintendent said. 'I'd appreciate that.'

The personnel manager at the Whitebridge town hall was called Howard Barnes. He wore a tweed suit and sported a large salt and pepper moustache. Crane guessed he was near retirement and that he considered every hour not spent on the golf course an hour wasted.

'I got the job of deputy personnel officer just after the war,' he told Crane, in a booming voice. 'Ted Cobb was personnel manager then, and one afternoon, when we were sinking a few drinks at the nineteenth hole, he said to me, "Tell me, Howard, is it true you were a wing commander in the last show?" I admitted I had been. "So you know about handling men," he said, and I said I supposed I did. "Right," he said, "come and work for me in the town hall".'

Crane smiled.

'I know what's going through your mind,' Barnes said. 'You're thinking I'd not get the job nowadays.'

'Actually, I wasn't,' Crane said. 'What I was thinking was that it might be interesting if there were more people like you in personnel.'

'That could never happen. Even I can't be like me.'

'What do you mean?'

'I used to judge a man by how clean his braces were.' He paused. 'Incidentally, did you know the Americans don't even call them braces – they call them suspenders.'

'Yes, I did know that,' Crane admitted.

'Extraordinary people! Now where was I?'

'Judging men by their braces.'

'Ah yes. Now you might laugh at that, but I think it's a pretty good test. You see, a slob will always smarten himself up for an interview. He'll polish his shoes till you can see your face in them, and he'll make sure he's got a clean white collar. But it's only as he's getting dressed for the interview that he thinks about his braces, and by then it's too late. The kind of man I'd be interested in, on the other hand, will have blancoed his braces every day.'

'The problem is that today most people wear belts,' Crane said.

'The problem is that even if I like the cut of a man's jib, I still have to give him psychological aptitude tests thought up by some long-haired weirdo in one of our so-called universities,' Barnes said. 'But you've not come to hear me gripe, have you? So what is it you want to know?'

'Everything we say in this room must remain confidential,' Crane said. 'You must not even mention that this conversation has taken place.'

'Understood,' Barnes said.

'I want to ask you about Richard Judd, who works in your invoicing department.'

The change in Barnes was dramatic. One moment he was jovial and open, the next, it was as if invisible steel shutters had suddenly encased him.

'Can I ask you what this is all about?' he said.

'No,' Crane replied, 'I'm afraid you can't. How long has Richard Judd worked here?'

'I'd have to look at the files to be sure, but I'd say six or seven years.'

'And have there been any complaints about him?'

'None.'

'You could check his file to make sure,' Crane suggested.

'That won't be necessary,' Barnes said firmly.

'Judd isn't here at the moment, is he?' Crane pressed on.

'No, he's taken a few business days off.'

'Do you have an address at which I can contact him?'

'I really have no idea where he is.' Barnes glanced at his watch, stood up, and held out his hand. 'Look, DC Crane, I really think I've given you all the help I can, and I have a very busy day ahead of me.'

Bowing to the inevitable, Crane stood up and took the proffered hand.

'Thank you for your help,' he said.

The town hall had a canteen for its workers, and no doubt most of the married men with kids and mortgages would be grateful for the subsidized institutional stodge available there, Crane thought. The 'lads' however – the free-as-a-bird young invoice clerks and trainee bookkeepers – would probably head for the Dog and Partridge (conveniently situated just across the road) for a pint and a sandwich. Thus, by the time the big hand and the little hand of the bar clock were as one over the twelve, Crane had already positioned himself at the back of the room, from where he had a clear view of everyone entering.

Half a dozen clerks suddenly burst through the swing doors, jostling each other in a way that could not possibly be interpreted as anything but good natured. The landlord, noting who was there, began pulling pints – two mild, three bitter, one black-and-tan – without them even having to ask.

Crane gave them a few minutes to settle in, then sauntered casually over to then and said, 'Sorry to disturb you, but I'm waiting for a mate of mine – name of Richard Judd – and I wondered if you'd seen him.'

He could feel the wave of resentment run through the group the moment the name was mentioned.

'If you're waiting for Rarely Round Ricky, then your wait could be a long one. Nobody's seen him since the end of last week.'

'Do any of you happen to know . . .?'

'None of us have got a clue where he is. We never do. When he goes off on one of his little excursions, it's like he's vanished into thin air.'

Crane grinned. 'Yes, he is quite a character,' he admitted. 'But you can't stay mad at him for long, can you?'

'Can't you?' one of the other men asked. 'Well, maybe *you* can't, but then you don't have to work twice as hard because he's not pulling his weight, do you, pal?'

'I really don't know how he gets away with it,' a young man with ginger hair said.

'I do,' said another. 'After every time he's been away, he drops his trousers and lets Mr Barnes do what he wants with him.'

'Now then, now then,' said the landlord. 'We'll have none of that mucky talk here.'

TWENTY

Colin Beresford strode across the personnel department, directly to the head of personnel's door.

'You can't do that!' gasped Howard Barnes' secretary, whose desk was just by the door.

Beresford turned the handle and stepped inside.

Barnes, startled, instinctively rose from his desk. 'What . . .?' he began.

'You've been giving one of my young officers the run around,' Beresford said.

'Then you're a policeman?'

'DCI Beresford.'

Barnes sank back into his seat. 'Do sit down, Chief Inspector, and could you please, if at all possible, show a little respect.'

'A little respect,' Beresford repeated after he'd taken his seat. 'For what? Because you're older then I am? Because you're a war hero? Because you're head of personnel?'

'Or simply because I'm another human being,' Barnes said mildly.

'Fine,' Beresford said. 'But in return, I want you to show some respect for the police.'

'I *do* respect the police,' Barnes said.

Beresford shook his head. 'No, you don't,' he said. 'Not really – otherwise you'd never have lied to my officers.'

'I lied to *one* of your officers,' Barnes corrected him. 'I didn't want to, but I had no choice.'

'Great defence!' Beresford said. 'I expect everybody will be using it soon. "I didn't kill the whole family, your honour, just the youngest daughter." "And why did you kill her, Mr Homicidal Nutter?" "I didn't want to, but I had no choice." "Oh, that's all right then, Mr HN. You're free to go, and here's a book of complementary luncheon vouchers".'

'I do not like being ridiculed,' Barnes said.

'And I don't like being pissed about when I'm trying to catch a killer. Why did you lie?'

'I can't tell you that.'

'Then I'll tell you,' Beresford said. 'And the reason I know is because this is the second time we've had M15 . . .'

'I never said anything about M15,' Barnes interjected.

'Please listen,' Beresford said. 'A man visits you. He tells you he represents the security services, and he asks you to ring a number – the Ministry of Defence or 10 Downing Street, for example – and the person on the other end will vouch for him. Which he does.'

'I'm saying nothing,' Barnes said.

'This man tells you to employ Richard Judd. He says that Judd will have the skills to do the work you assign him, but sometimes he will be absent from work, and when he is, you will find someone to cover for him.'

'I can't comment,' Barnes said.

'You don't need to – the fact that you've not said that what I've told you is bollocks is comment enough.'

'You can't infer . . .'

'Of course I can,' Beresford said. 'I'll be needing Richard Judd's personnel file.'

'You can't have it.'

'I'm investigating two murders and a possible security leak.'

'I'm sorry.'

Beresford sighed. 'Tell me, Mr Barnes, when you were flying Spitfires, what was the one thing that kept you in the air?'

'Well, fuel, I suppose.'

'We're just trying to do a job like you were just trying to do a job,' Beresford said. 'Please don't deny us our fuel.'

Barnes got up from his desk and walked over to his filing cabinet. He was moving like a much older man than he had been only a few minutes earlier. He extracted a thin file.

'There's not much there, I'm afraid,' he said.

Beresford smiled. 'It's probably a bit like the war. You have to make do with what you've got.'

The team were sitting in the office when the call came through.

'This is Inspector Green of the Cornwall Constabulary,' the man said. 'I've been asked by Chief Superintendent Crouch to contact a DCI Pam Something-or-other.'

'Paniatowski.'

'That's right. But they tell me she's not available.'

'I'm DCI Beresford filling in for her,' Beresford said, clicking on the speakerphone. 'What can I do for you, Inspector Green?'

'A few years ago, you issued an arrest warrant for . . . let me see, I've got the name here somewhere . . . for a Roger Pemberton.'

'Yes, we did, but . . .'

'Well, the good news is that we've got him for you – and the bad news, I'm afraid, is that he's dead.'

It would have difficult to say which of them looked the most shocked.

Green couldn't possibly have Pemberton (alive *or* dead) because they had him – they'd dug him out of the ground at the allotments, and they had him sitting in the mortuary.

'Tell me more,' Beresford said cautiously.

'He was washed up onto one of our world famous Cornish beaches yesterday morning.'

A mistake! Beresford thought. It just had to be a mistake!

'How did you identify him, Inspector Green?' he asked. 'Was it from the photograph?'

Green chuckled. 'Oh dear me, no, we couldn't have done that. His face took a battering on the rocks, and once the skin was broken and it was opened up a bit, there were half a dozen sea creatures who took that as an invitation to a free buffet.'

'Then how?'

'He didn't have any driving licence or library ticket on him, either, so my bright spark of a sergeant suggested we checked his fingerprints. Well, as it turns out, he doesn't have a criminal record, but apparently he'd done some work for the Ministry of Defence, and they had his prints.'

Beresford was beginning to wish he was dead himself.

'Have you established the cause of death?' he asked.

'No, not me personally. We have a police doctor for that,' the amiable Inspector Green told him.

'Is that a joke?' Beresford asked.

'No, we really do have a police doctor,' Green said, sounding puzzled. 'Don't you?'

At long last he'd met a real actual yokel, Beresford thought. How lucky was that?

'So what *was* the cause of death?' he asked patiently.

'It would have been an overdose of drugs if he'd lived long enough,' Green said, 'but before they had time to kill him, he'd drowned in the sea.'

'Is there any suspicion of foul play?'

'None as far as we can tell. And a couple of the barmen in town have given statements to the effect that a chap dressed just like him has been hanging around the pubs for the last couple of days and drinking himself stupid, but that's as far as we've got.'

'You couldn't find out where he's been staying, could you?' Beresford asked hopefully.

There was a slight pause, then Green said, 'We're a bit short on manpower down here, to tell you the truth. Is it very important?'

'No,' Beresford admitted. 'Thank you for your help, Inspector Green.'

'It's been my pleasure, DCI Beresford,' Green said.

Beresford hung up.

'So what are we left with to investigate?' he asked Meadows and Crane.

'We're left with an unidentified –and probably unidentifiable – body, and a man called Richard Judd, who may or may not have killed him, but who almost certainly buried him,' Meadows said.

'The body's a dead end,' Crane said. He gave the others a weak grin. 'No pun intended.'

'Good, because if there had been, I'd probably have had to kill you,' Meadows said.

'And if we rule out the body, then all we're left with is Richard Judd,' Crane continued.

'Does either of you think that's his real name?' Beresford asked. The other two shook their heads. 'Does either of you think he's still in Whitebridge – or that if he's left, he's coming back?' Again, Meadows and Crane shook their heads. 'That's what I thought.'

Beresford opened his drawer, took out a folder, and slapped it down on the desk.

'This is Richard Judd's personnel file, for what it's worth,' he said despondently. 'Why don't you two spend a pleasant afternoon seeing what you can extract from it.'

'Where will you be, sir?' Crane asked.

'I'll be out of the building.'

'Could you be a little more specific?' Meadows asked.

'Since I won't be contactable, there doesn't seem to be much point in being specific,' Beresford said, with an edge to his voice which would have been ample warning to most people not to push it further.

'I'd still like to know,' insisted Meadows, who was not most people.

'All right, then, if you must know, I'll be visiting Monika,' Beresford snapped.

Meadows looked at Crane, and Crane looked at Meadows. Neither of them spoke a word, but their eyes said, 'Oh, it's as bad as that, is it?'

The listeners' shift changed at four and first thing the new man heard when he got into the van was the sound of someone singing.

'Who the bloody hell's that?' he asked.

'It's Beresford,' the other man said. 'He's singing to Paniatowski.'

'He's got a terrible voice.'

'I think you're being a little charitable there. Personally, I've heard better sound coming out of concrete mixers. But that's not stopped him. He's been at it for over an hour and a half.'

'It's a good job she's unconscious, or she'd have gone barmy by now,' the new man said.

'Ain't that the truth,' the other man agreed. 'As a matter of fact, if I'd had to sit through another half hour, I think I'd have been about ready for the funny farm myself.'

'Why do you think he's doing it?'

'Maybe it's the pressure. Maybe that phone call from the Cornwall police finally pushed him over the edge.'

'We can only hope,' the other man said.

It was half-past seven, and they were back in the Drum and Monkey.

'So what do we know?' Beresford asked, reaching for his pint of best bitter and taking a swig. 'We know that just after Arthur Wheatstone was killed, somebody else was murdered and buried on the allotments. Do we have any idea who that somebody might be?'

Meadows shook her head.

Crane said, 'I've checked the records. There was no one else reported missing in central Lancashire that week – or the week before, for that matter.'

'Let's call him Wilfred,' Beresford suggest. 'Does anyone have any idea who might have killed Wilfred?'

'Richard Judd,' Crane said. 'We know that he works for the government, and that he had an allotment just so he could keep his eye on Arthur Wheatstone, John Horrocks and Philip Jennings. We know that Archie Eccleston actually caught him in the act of digging on Archie's allotment. It has to be him.'

'*Why* did he kill Wilfred?'

'Since Wilfred's not from Whitebridge, maybe he was a Russian spy,' Crane said.

'But if Judd had killed a Russian spy, he surely wouldn't have had to dispose of the body himself, would he?' Beresford asked. 'They have a special department for that. You know the sort of thing – a black van pulls up, the two men inside it load the dead man on a stretcher, and he's never seen again.' He paused. 'Or maybe I'm starting to confuse real life with what I've seen on the television.'

'They really do have departments like that,' Meadows said, and when saw the two men were looking at her oddly, she added, 'I used to know a man involved in that kind of work.'

Of course she did, Crane thought. Take an Eskimo drug dealer, a South American gun runner, a Kalahari bushman and a Tibetan butterfly collector to a party, and chances were that Meadows would have cracked a whip over all of them at one time or another.

'So let's assume the murder was a private matter – absolutely nothing to do with spies at all,' Beresford said. 'Did Judd lure his victim to Whitebridge and then kill him? Or did he – for some insane reason – kill Wilfred somewhere else, and then bring him here?'

'We've no way of knowing,' Crane said. 'And more to the point, we've no way of finding out, because we don't even know who Judd is. That's right, isn't it, Sarge?'

'That's right,' Meadows agreed. 'It says in his file that the last place he worked before he had his job at the town hall was a supermarket warehouse near Salisbury, which, as I'm sure you've both already worked out, is very close to Boscombe Down air force base.'

'A Ministry of Defence test and evaluation centre,' Crane said.
'Exactly.'

'The BAI and Boscombe Down,' Beresford mused. 'Now that's
hardly likely to be a coincidence, is it?'

'And before that, he worked at a paper mill near Bradford,'
Meadows said, 'except that no such paper mill exists or ever has
existed.'

'So what did Richard do before that?' Crane asked.

'There was no Richard before that – at least, not this one. I
checked his national insurance number, and it belongs to a Richard
Judd who died in a car crash fifteen years ago.'

'If we could get a warrant, we could search his flat to see if
we could find anything that might tell us who he really is,' Beresford
said.

'It wouldn't do any good,' Meadows said. 'There's nothing
there.'

'How do you . . .?' Beresford began. 'Kate, don't tell me
you . . .'

Meadows shrugged. 'I had an hour to spare,' she said. 'And it's
not as if I got caught, is it?'

'I suppose it doesn't matter anyway,' Beresford said. 'We've
got two murders to solve, and the only people who could help us
are Richard Judd – who's disappeared and is probably called
something else by now – and Roger Pemberton, who witnessed
the first murder and may have witnessed the second, but can't tell
us about either, because they fished him out of the sea this morning.'

'So what do we do?' Crane asked.

'So tomorrow I go and see the chief constable and tell him it's
hopeless. He'll ask me if I'm sure, and I'll say I am. Then he'll
see to it that we're assigned to something else, and we'll agree
that we'll review this case when things are a little less hectic –
except that we both know we won't.' Beresford sighed. 'It's a
failure, and since this is my team, it's my failure.'

'No, it isn't,' Crane said.

'Don't talk pissed up,' Meadows told him.

Beresford sighed again. 'Perhaps if Monika had been in
charge . . .'

'If you go self-pitying on me, I'll rip off those bollocks you're
so proud of, and wear them as earrings,' Meadows threatened.

Beresford grinned weakly.

'Does anybody want another drink?' he asked.

Meadows shook her head, and Crane said, 'No thanks, I've had enough and I think I'll just drift off home.'

'Thank Christ for that!' Beresford said. 'Apart from Monika, I don't think there are two people in the world I'd rather be with – but I don't want to be with you right now.'

'God, but you look rough!' Diana Sowerbury said, as Beresford stood in the doorway to her flat.

'I feel rough,' Beresford admitted.

'Well, sit down,' she said, taking his arm, 'and I'll get you something restorative.'

She led him to an armchair and eased him down into it.

'Now what shall it be?' she wondered. 'Beer? Or whisky?'

'I don't really . . .'

'I wasn't asking you. I think I'll make you cocoa.'

She must have already had the milk near to the boil, because no sooner was she gone than she was back again, with a steaming cup of cocoa. She gave him the cup, then sat on the arm of the chair, stroking his hair.

'My nurses tell me you spent a long, long time with Monika today,' she cooed.

'That's right,' Beresford said, taking a slurp of his cocoa.

'Do you know how long it was?'

'Nearly two hours.'

'What did you find to do for nearly two hours?'

'I sang to her.'

Diana giggled, then gasped with horror.

'I'm sorry,' she said. 'That was most unprofessional.'

'We're not at work now,' Beresford said. 'If we can't be human with people we care about, when can we be human?'

'You're right,' Diana agreed. 'So you sang to her?'

'Yes.'

'What sorts of songs?'

'Anything that came into my mind. This week's top ten, songs from when I was a kid – even a few advertising jingles.'

'And have you got a good voice?'

'Very – if you're fond of the sound of a spade scraping on

gravel. But Monika didn't care how well or badly I sang. She didn't even care *what* I sang.' His voice started to crack. 'I must have gone through "Happy Birthday to You" half a dozen times, and it's not even her birthday. But it doesn't matter . . . it doesn't matter . . . because she can't bloody hear me!'

Tears were streaming down his face.

She hugged his head tightly to her breast.

'Would you like to go to bed?' she asked softly. 'Do you think that would help?'

'I don't know,' he said.

They turned the bed into a raging battlefield on which no quarter was expected or given.

Three times, the neighbours banged on the wall, and three times they ignored them.

They discovered a power within themselves which was both exhilarating and frightening, and when it was over they lay side by side, sweating and gasping for breath, and not saying a word.

Slowly, the world of normality began to penetrate the world of fire and lust they had created.

They heard footsteps on the street outside, and a man whistling. They heard a dog bark, and tyres screeching.

'When are you planning to see the chief constable tomorrow?' she asked.

'How do you know I'm planning to see him?' he wondered.

'You mentioned it earlier.'

'I'm almost sure that I didn't.'

'You must have done, or how would I know?'

'That's true.'

TWENTY-ONE

I f Mr Forsyth had had a personal motto (as distinct from the one he inherited on his family crest), it would have been that a man should be bold and courageous whenever the need arose, and as cautious as a field mouse whenever it didn't.

He would have added, as a caveat, that the time to be especially cautious was when an operation was in the process of being wound up, as this one was. Thus, even though he had heard Beresford himself say to his team in the Drum and Monkey that he was planning to go to the chief constable and admit failure – and even though the DCI's sobbing the night before had been indicative of a man on the verge of a nervous breakdown – he had resisted the temptation to draw down resources, because it was at precisely this stage that the people manipulating events could get careless and things could go seriously wrong.

And so it was that morning (which he hoped and believed would be the last morning of this not-exactly-official operation), he had assigned an agent to each member of Beresford's team, just to make sure they didn't come off the rails.

Monika herself was a different problem, for while he was sure he had blindsided her team, and they would never grasp the truth if they lived to be a hundred, it was possible that if she came out of her coma . . .

He was going to have to terminate her, he decided. It was a pity, but there it was. And while there would no doubt be an internal service inquiry which would probably find against him, he would almost certainly be gone to his grave by then, knowing, as he drew his final breath, that he had done what was best for his country.

The agent who'd been drafted in to watch Meadows went by the name of Wilson, and he was outside her flat at seven o'clock, when she emerged wearing rather a smart grey suit – much more expensive and stylish-looking than the clothes he'd seen her wearing the day before – and carrying a cylindrical cloth bag.

She must have a change of clothes in the bag, he thought. It was something women did. His wife – and all her friends – travelled to dances and events in casual clothes, and changed into their posh frocks when they got there. But Kate Meadows was wearing the posh things now, which didn't make sense.

Maybe she was doing a runner, and had grabbed the first thing that came to hand, but he couldn't think of anything she needed to run *from*, and she seemed neither furtive nor cautious as she walked to her car, got in, and pulled carefully away from the curb.

His first thought was that she would get onto the ring road, and from there join the motorway, but then she turned left instead of right, and he decided that despite her wearing a fancy suit, she must be going into work.

He was wrong about that, too. Instead of heading for police headquarters, Meadows took the Boulevard to the railway station.

Beresford rolled over onto his back, scratched the thick black hairs on his belly, and grunted like the satisfied creature he was.

'Have you seen the time?' Diana Sowerbury asked.

Beresford raised his arm, and glanced at his wristwatch.

'Oh yeah,' he said.

'Oh yeah? Is that all you've got to say?'

'What else do you *expect* me to say?'

'I expected you to say, "Bugger me, I'd better be going",' Diana said, in a fair imitation of his voice.

'I don't feel like going.'

'But you're leading a murder investigation.'

'True, but we're all agreed it's going nowhere.'

'I still think you should put in an appearance. I think you owe it to your team.'

Beresford chuckled. 'Yesterday morning, you've have done just about anything you could to stop me leaving – and I mean just about anything, you dirty, dirty girl.'

Diana giggled. 'Maybe I am a dirty girl – but I've never heard you object,' she said.

Beresford grinned. 'So what's different about this morning?' he wondered. 'Why can't you wait to get me out of the flat? Is there something you need to do – but won't be able to do until I've gone?'

'Like what?'

'Like make a phone call, for example.'

'A phone call?'

'One you didn't want me to overhear.'

'Whatever made you say that?' Diana asked.

'I really don't know,' Beresford lied.

Wilson was standing in a telephone box in which vomit, urine and cigarette smoke fought with each other for the title of dominant smell.

'She's bought a ticket to Manchester,' he said.

'When was this?' Forsyth asked.

'Five minutes ago. She's out there waiting on the platform now.'

'Is she alone?'

'Yes.'

'Then you'd better get a ticket yourself, and follow her.'

'And what happens at the other end?'

'How long's the journey to Manchester?'

'Thirty-five minutes.'

'Shit!' Forsyth said. 'I can't possibly get people to Victoria Station by the time she arrives, so you're on your own. Try not to get spotted, but whatever you do, don't lose her.'

He hung up. There was no reason for Meadows to go to Manchester, he told himself, no reason at all.

And it was extremely worrying that she had.

It was four o'clock in the morning EST. The moon was emerging from behind a cloud, and as it did, it cast a pale light on the brick house on a street just off Zulette Avenue. Houses exactly like it (or houses that were a variation on that theme) could be found in large clusters all over the Bronx. It was the sort of house in which three families could lead comfortable and independent lives, each with a floor of their own.

This house may once have served just that function, but not anymore, because, as the discreet brass sign by the doorbell announced, it was 'Pelham Bay Gentlemen's Social Club: Members Only'.

The man who approached that door along the empty street looked easily well-dressed enough to be a member of a club that had its own brass plate, but the clothes were not his own, and had only been borrowed for the occasion from the department's wardrobe.

He rang the bell and waited. His ring was answered by a large man in a tight-fitting tuxedo.

'Yes?' the doorman said.

'You must be Gregory,' the visitor said.

'What if I am?' the doorman growled.

'I was told your name by my very good friend, Orville James III. He said you knew him.'

'I do know him. He's a member of the club.'

'Exactly so. And he said if I were to mention his name to you . . .'

'You're not a member,' Gregory said flatly, as if he were reading from a script. 'This is a members' only club.'

The visitor – whose breath smelt of alcohol thanks to a whisky gargle, took a step forward.

'I want you to think long and hard before you offend a man like my very good friend Orville James III,' the visitor said.

But Gregory was no longer listening to him. Instead, his eyes were following the large black van which had its lights off and seemed to be almost crawling up the street.

Gregory made an effort to slam the door closed, at the same moment as the visitor was pushing in the other direction.

'Don't!' the visitor said, holding up a small leather wallet, containing a shiny metal shield, in his free hand.

Gregory relaxed his muscles. What was going to happen would happen whatever he did, and his best plan was to leave as little of it sticking to him as was possible.

The van came to a halt at the front entrance, its back doors were opened, and half a dozen men emerged. They all ran towards the club, and before they'd even reached the door, two vans full of uniformed cops came round the corner with tyres screeching.

The predominant ambience of this phone box was curry, and looking down at the aluminium box by his feet, Wilson guessed it was vindaloo.

'Sergeant Meadows is at Piccadilly Station now,' he told his boss, back in Whitebridge.

'How did she get there from Victoria?' Forsyth asked.

'She walked.'

'And you followed on foot?'

How else did you expect me to follow her? Wilson wondered. In a taxi?

Might he not have looked just a little suspicious in a taxi that was travelling at walking speed?

'Yes, I followed her on foot,' he said.

'How far is it between the two stations?'

'Just under a mile.'

'Did she spot you?'

'I can't say – one way or the other. She didn't make a habit of turning round, she didn't stop to look in shop windows, and she didn't use any of the standard evasion techniques, but if she'd been looking out for a tail, she couldn't have missed me.'

'Has she bought another ticket?'

'Yes.'

'Where to?'

'London.'

'Make absolutely certain that she gets on the London train, and then report back here.'

'You don't want me to follow her?'

'No. She has probably made you, so I'll introduce a couple of fresh faces on the journey down, and have two more waiting for her at Euston station.'

Forsyth put down the phone. She might just have gone on a shopping trip, he told himself. But from what he'd seen of her, he was surprised she hadn't stayed in Whitebridge, in case Beresford needed support.

He wondered – given what Beresford was planning to do – why he hadn't heard from Beresford's minder.

The final car involved in the operation drew up just after the uniformed officers had entered the house just off Zulette Avenue, but neither man made any move to get out of the vehicle.

'I reckon you owe me big for this, Fred,' said the man behind the wheel, who went by the name of Harvey James Boone, and who was head of the vice squad in the Bronx.

'Oh please! We've known each other a long time – and done things for each other that are probably best forgotten – so don't start bullshitting me now,' said his passenger, Fred Mahoney, who was the captain of the One-Four. 'You've been planning this raid of yours for weeks. It would have gone ahead even if I hadn't come along for the ride.'

'Two things you should appreciate,' Boone said. 'One: I may have been planning this raid, but it wasn't supposed to happen until next week. Two: I go out of my way to avoid tangling with people of influence like state assemblymen.'

'So what you are saying is that if somebody's got a seat in

Albany, it's like having his own personal "get out of jail free" card?'

'You are never going to wipe out vice,' Boone said, 'so what you do is, you work out which bits you can mop up that maybe might help a few people at least, and when you go home, you can say to yourself, well, things are a little better than they used to be.'

'I know it isn't easy,' Mahoney said, with a mixture of sympathy and encouragement.

But Boone had not finished.

'Do you know what happens when you tangle with the rich and powerful?' he asked 'You find yourself locked in a battle which takes all your resources, which means even your little bits of mopping up go by the board. And even if you manage to get a conviction, you've not just made an enemy of him – it's his prep school buddies and country club friends you gotta look out for. Are you sure you still want Proudfoot?'

'I want him,' Mahoney said.

'Well, I guess it's your ass that you're kissing goodbye,' Boone said.

Living in the shadow world of Zelda had probably been good training for a spy, Meadows thought, because it taught you never to take your environment for granted, and to be on the constant lookout for both dangers and opportunities.

True, she'd been expecting to be followed when she left her flat, but even if she hadn't been, she reckoned she'd have spotted her tail by the time she reached Whitebridge railway station.

And now she'd left him behind. Looking at him standing on the platform at Piccadilly, trying his best to appear inconspicuous, she'd had to fight back the temptation to wave to him.

So when would the next lot appear? Her guess would be at Birmingham, which meant she had plenty of time to select the ground on which she would fight the next battle.

She chose a carriage halfway down the train. It had two advantages. The first was that one end of it was quite empty, and would give her the manoeuvring space she might need. And the second was that at other end of the carriage were a group of young men who could only be – from their build and general demeanour– a team of rugby players.

She sat down close to them, but facing away. Then, when she heard the sound of beer can tabs being pulled, she turned around and said, 'Look, I know this is being a bit cheeky, but I'm spitting feathers, and if one of you could spare me a sip of your beer, I'd really appreciate it.'

Six fit, square men were instantly on their feet, jostling each other for space and holding their cans out to her.

'Goodness!' Meadows gasped.

'What do you want to do, smother the lady?' asked a deep authoritative voice. 'Get back in your seats now.'

The young men slunk reluctantly back, and Meadows got a clearer view of the speaker. He was around forty, and as square as his team. Meadows quite fancied him, and on another day might have suggested they inspect the toilet together.

'I'm Sid Harris, the manager of the Rochdale Irregulars,' he said.

'And my dad,' chipped in one of the boys.

'And his dad – or so his mother informs me,' Harris said. 'Why don't you come and sit with us?'

'I don't think there's any room,' Meadows told him.

'Nonsense,' Harris said. 'There's space where Dockleaf's sitting. You don't want to sit there, do you, Dockleaf?'

'No, Dad,' the boy said, so the matter was settled, and by the time the train reached Stafford, Meadows had learned that they were indeed a team of amateur rugby players, and were on their way to France for a series of friendly games with French teams.

Her new tails got on at Birmingham, as she'd expected them to. They were both nondescript men – again to be expected – though there was no question that they were both fit. They quickly assessed the carriage, and sat down. One chose a seat four rows behind hers, and to the left of the aisle. The other selected a seat eight rows back, and to the right.

It would have been easier if they'd sat together – but hell, they weren't about to do her any favours.

Inside the house just off Zulette Avenue, half a dozen men were engaging in some kind of conversation with the police officers who brought with them such an unpleasant and unexpected end to the evening.

Some of the men were angry – or at least using anger as a shield to hide their fear.

'This is still a free country and I can go where I like, and the fact that I happen to be in the same house as a number of perverts does not give you the right to tar me with the same brush.'

Others were attempting to mitigate their situation.

'This is the first time I've been here, and I haven't done anything. I wouldn't have done anything. I swear it. I was just curious to see for myself, but I'd never have done anything.'

And some were just begging for mercy.

'Please, I know I've done wrong, but I swear I'll never do it again. Please help me. Think of my wife! Think of my children!'

And the officers they were talking to listened to them stony-faced and then said, 'Your name. I need your name. You give it to me now, or we can sweat it out of you back at the precinct. I don't care which.'

The one man not being questioned was sitting huddled in the corner. He was horrified at the thought of being interrogated, but even more horrified that he had been singled out not to be.

'You wait over there,' one of the officers had said to him.

Why him?

Was it because they were going to be even harder on him, because of who he was?

Or could it be – a splinter of hope here – that because of who he was, they were just waiting for the opportunity to sneak him out of the back door, and away from this nightmare?

A police sergeant entered the room, with a small photograph in the palm of his hand. He looked at the man in the corner, then the photograph, then back at the man in the corner.

And then he beckoned.

Oh God, the man in the corner thought.

Beresford did not emerge from Diana Sowerbury's flat until ten o'clock. Even then, he did not head for police headquarters, but drove to the hospital instead.

'Diana won't be in today,' he told the ward sister on the early shift. 'She's got a shocking migraine headache.'

'Hmm!' the ward sister said.

'Is something the matter?'

'I don't know how things worked in Miss Sowerbury's last
hospital,' the ward sister said stiffly, 'but in this hospital we're
required to phone in to administration when we are unable to work.'

'She must have thought that me telling you was enough,'
Beresford said cheerfully. 'I'll tell you what – I'll ring her now
and tell her to ring you.' He clicked his fingers. 'No, that won't
do, because after I put her to bed I took the phone off the hook.
Maybe I could drive round and . . .'

'Forget it,' the ward sister said. 'I'll ring administration myself.'

'That is kind of you,' Beresford said. 'Would it be all right if
I spent a bit of time with my boss now I'm here?'

'Yes,' said the ward sister, 'that would be fine.'

The listener in the van heard the door of the hospital room open,
and then a voice he'd come to recognize as Beresford's.

'Good morning, Monika,' said the voice. 'I've brought my
cassette player with me today, so you don't have to listen to my
horrible voice.'

'Thank God for that, at least,' the listener said to himself.

'I've got all sorts of music, but the jewel in the crown is this
album by my absolute favourite American group of the moment.
Can you guess who it is?'

He sang 'Sugar, Sugar' five times yesterday, the listener thought.
Please let it not be the Archies.

'Can't guess?' Beresford asked. 'Well, I suppose I'll just have
to tell you, then. It's the Archies.'

'Sweet Jesus,' the listener moaned.

The woman who walked into St Neames police station was in her
early forties, but had the same effect Marilyn Monroe might have
done if, for some strange reason, she'd suddenly turned up in a
small Cornish town.

It was hard to say why she should have such a dramatic effect.
She was beautifully dressed, it was true. Her legs were long, her
hair was blonde, her breasts seemed firm and pleasantly shaped.
But that was still not enough to explain it. Perhaps it was simply
that because *she* thought she was gorgeous, *you* did, too.

No, even that was not *quite* right – it was that because *she*
thought she was gorgeous that she *was* gorgeous. Yes, that was it.

She walked up to the counter.

'I'm Dr Rosemary Pemberton,' she said. 'I believe you've got my husband here on ice.'

'Well, yes, he's in the police mortuary,' the sergeant admitted, 'but I don't have the forms here—'

'The forms?' the magnificent lady interrupted him. 'What forms are you talking about?'

'The forms you need to fill in to claim the body.'

'Why would I want to claim him?' Rosemary Pemberton asked. 'He was a dead weight round my neck when he was alive – he'd be even worse now he is actually dead.' She grinned. 'Get it? Dead weight!'

The sergeant did not appreciate humour, even when, as on this occasion, it came from the mouth of a vision of loveliness.

'So if you don't want to claim the body, then why are you here, madam?' he asked.

'Because I want to make sure that the bastard really is dead.'

'I think you'd better talk to my inspector,' the sergeant said.

The train had been rattling along at a fair old rate, but as it approached Watford Junction it started to slow down.

Meadows stood up and, squeezing between several sets of thick young-manhood knees, negotiated her way to the aisle.

'Are you going to the loo, Carole?' asked Sid Harris – rugby coach and all-round nice guy. 'I'm only asking because, if you are, then I'll get one of the lads to go with you.'

Meadows grinned. 'To tell you the truth, Sid, I don't think there'd be room for both me and one of your lads in a single cubicle.'

Although if it was you and me, we might just squeeze in, she thought.

Harris had gone a little red in the face.

'I wasn't suggesting that you and the lad . . . that you and the lad . . .' he began.

'I know,' Meadows said, reaching across and stroking the top of his head. 'You just want to make sure I'm protected, don't you?'

'Well, you can never be too careful,' Harris mumbled.

The lads were delighted with the performance and especially with their manager's discomfort.

'Put him down, Carole – you don't know where he's been,' one of them shouted.

'Hey, Dockleaf, your dad's getting married again,' another one called out. 'Hadn't somebody better tell your mum?'

'Can I be a bridesmaid?' asked a third.

The whole team was having a good time, but the performance hadn't been staged for them. It was aimed at the watchers, and it said, 'You can relax, fellers, because nobody having this much fun is planning anything dramatic in the next few minutes.'

The train was entering the station, and platforms had appeared on both sides of it.

Meadows had already worked out two plans, and now was the time to choose between them.

Plan A: she would move quickly into the next carriage, and get off the train from there. If her tails followed her through to the carriage, she would have a start of something between twenty seconds and half a minute on them. If they worked out she was getting off, and got off themselves from *this* carriage, she would have a ten-to twenty-second lead.

Not enough!

Plan B then.

She grabbed her bag and walked quickly down the aisle towards the watchers. The movement caught them off their guard, and the closest one was only starting to rise to his feet when, with no warning at all, she threw herself sideways right on top of him.

For three or four seconds they were a single creature – a confusion of arms and legs – with her screaming at the top of her voice, and him silent as he processed what was happening.

Then she pulled herself free.

'How could you!' she moaned. 'How could you?'

The rugby players now filled the aisle, and as the watcher attempted to regain his balance, one of them planted a mighty fist in the centre of his face.

The other watcher was on his feet, but seemed unsure whether to go to his partner's aid or to stick with Meadows.

While he was making up his mind, Meadows kicked him as hard as she possibly could in the crutch.

He made a whooshing sound and sank to his knees. Meadows stepped round him.

The rugby team were still roaring at the first watcher, but it was not clear whether each roar was being accompanied by a punch or not.

Meadows stepped off the train and walked quickly towards the entrance to the London Underground. She did not look back.

TWENTY-TWO

He was taken to an interrogation room in the One-Four, where a burly man in a blue uniform had clearly been waiting for him.

'You are Assemblyman Robert Proudfoot,' the burly man said, and it wasn't a question. 'I am Captain Fred Mahoney.'

'I demand you release me immediately,' Proudfoot said. 'I have important state business to conduct in Albany.'

Mahoney chuckled. 'Have you seen how, on all those cop shows on the television, the police captain gets thrown into a panic because the squad's got a senator or some other high-up in the cells?'

'I am a state assemblyman. I don't have much time to watch television,' Proudfoot said haughtily.

Mahoney slammed his huge fist down on the table. 'Have you seen it?' he demanded.

'Maybe once or twice.'

'Well, that's all made up – and this is real life. You were caught in a male brothel where most of the sex workers were underage.' Mahoney smiled. 'Did you notice that? I said "sex workers". That's because I've been sent on a course where they teach you to be nice and clinical. It's called being politically correct.'

'I demand to see my lawyer!' Proudfoot said.

Mahoney scratched his head. 'Well, you can certainly do that, but it may turn out to be one big fat mistake,'

'What do you mean?'

'See that recording machine over there? Mahoney told him. 'The reel isn't turning, because it's not recording. You can check that out for yourself, if you want to.'

'I'll take your word for it.'

'So why am I not recording it, you ask yourself. It's because I want it all to end here in this room – done and dusted, all forgotten, it never happened. Once your lawyer enters the picture, however, it's all a matter of record, and that takes it out of my hands.'

'Let me see if I've got this straight,' Proudfoot said. 'If we keep this just between us, it will be like my arrest never happened.'

'Nearly right,' Mahoney said. 'If you give me the answers to the questions I'm going to ask you, it will be as if your arrest never happened.'

'So what do you want to know?'

Mahoney stood up. 'Not yet,' he said.

'What do you mean, not yet?' Proudfoot asked. 'I'm here, you're here, let's do it.'

'If we started now, you'd just feed me bullshit for the first half hour, so while I'm away, I'd like you to tell all that bullshit to yourself – get it out of your system. Then, when I come back, we can get right down to the real nitty-gritty straight away.'

'You can't treat me like this,' Proudfoot said. 'I am entitled to some respect, you know.'

'You think?' Mahoney asked.

There were those in the stylish and artistic circles who regarded the Rivoli Bar of the Ritz Hotel as a masterpiece of Art Deco, but Kate Meadows was not one of them. Nevertheless, that was where she'd arranged to meet Farhad at exactly twelve o'clock.

She entered the Rivoli at half-past eleven, walked over to the bar, and said to the nearest of the two barman on duty, 'I am meeting Prince Farhad bin Wahid here. I believe he has reserved a table.'

'You do realize, Madame, that strictly speaking, we don't reserve tables for anybody,' the barman replied, running his eyes approvingly over Meadows' smart grey suit.

'Yes, I do realize it,' Meadows agreed.

'That said, your table is over there, Madame.'

The barman pointed to a table under a bas-relief of Zeus (disguised, on this occasion, as a swan) in sexual congress with Leda.

'Perfect,' Meadows said.

'Would Madame like me to take her bag to the cloakroom for her?'

Meadows shook her head. 'Madame will be needing her bag.'

She went straight to the ladies toilets. When she emerged again there was no sign of her stylish grey suit, and instead she was wearing a metallic purple dress with a neckline that plunged, and had a slit up the side almost to her waist. She was also wearing a piled-high purple wig that Medusa would have sold her soul for, and had applied mascara in industrial quantities.

The two barmen were alarmed to see that a whore had managed to worm her way past the doorman, then horrified when they realized she was the classy-looking lady who was due to meet a prince.

Meadows read their expressions with some amusement, but also with a great deal of sympathy.

What do we do, they were asking each other.

If we throw her out, the prince will be furious with us.

But if we let her stay and other customers complain – and they were almost bound to – then the bar manager will be furious with us.

Meadows walked over to the bar. Her movements were much more catlike, now that she was in costume.

'Don't worry,' she said to them, 'if you get any grief from this, I'll tell Farhad to buy this place and promote you both. And he would do it, if I told him to, you know.'

'Of course he would,' said the first barman, who could no longer imagine anybody not doing what she wanted them to do.

Dr Pemberton and Inspector Green sat facing each other across the coffee table. Green was doing his best not to look at Rosemary's knees, which he had already established were everything that a man could hope a woman's knees would be.

'There's really no need to put yourself through all this, Dr Pemberton,' he said. 'The fingerprints are quite enough to have him declared legally dead.'

'I want to see him,' Rosemary said.

'And his face is a real mess. It will only distress you.'

'Before my husband left me, he beat the shit out of me and emptied my bank account,' Rosemary said. 'I could see him after he'd been fed through a jigsaw puzzle cutter, and it still wouldn't distress me.'

'I just can't understand how any man could ever leave you,' Inspector Green said.

And then he thought – Oh my God, I didn't intend to say that. I honestly didn't.

'I'm so sorry . . .' he began.

Rosemary laughed. 'There's no need to apologize. I enjoy being admired by men. Ah, but if you could have seen me before he left me, you would not have admired me then. Since he's been gone, my hair has turned quite gold with grief.' She laughed again. 'That's Oscar Wilde, you know.'

'No, I didn't know, actually,' Green confessed.

'So I have to see Roger, you see,' Rosemary said. 'I need to convince myself that he's never coming back. It's not logical at all. It's right down here,' she began to rub her stomach, slowly and sensually, 'in my gut.'

I wish she wouldn't do that, Inspector Green thought.

'I'm sorry, Dr Pemberton, but for your own protection . . .'

'Call me Rosemary.'

'. . . for your own protection, Rosemary, I really must insist . . .'

'I wouldn't like to have to go to all the time and trouble of hiring a lawyer,' Rosemary said sweetly. 'I wouldn't like things to get messy – in the legal sense, of course.'

There was no fighting her.

'Very well, Dr Pemberton . . .' he began.

'I asked you to call me Rosemary,' she pointed out.

'Very well, Rosemary, I will allow you to see your husband's body – but on your own head be it.'

At exactly midday, Farhad entered the bar. Had he been in a smart suit, he would have turned women's heads. Dressed in robes, as he was, he was accompanied by a train of admiring gasps.

He had always been a handsome man – a distinguished man – but in the several years since they had last met, his looks had, if anything improved.

Kate had once heard a society hostess (the wife of an important cabinet minister) try to flatter him by saying that he was Omar Sharif's double.

Farhad had not taken it well.

'You think I look like an Egyptian?' he'd asked, in a voice as cold as the desert at night-time.

'No . . . I . . .' the hostess had replied, completely flustered.

'Besides,' Farhad had interrupted her, 'if anyone is anyone's double, then Sharif is mine.'

Farhad came to a halt by Meadows' chair, and when she held out her hand, he caressed it with his lips.

'Zelda, my dear, you look wonderful,' he said.

'You're late,' she told him.

He looked at his watch.

'No . . . I . . .' he began.

Meadows seemed to swell to twice her normal size.

'Do you dare to contradict me?' she demanded.

'No, I . . .'

'Then sit down!'

There'd been a time when she'd found his predilections so amusing that it had been hard not to laugh. After all, Farhad came from a society in which men ruled supreme – in which most women would regard being treated as second-class citizens as a promotion.

In Saudi Arabia, a woman could not leave the house unless in the company of a male relative, could not have a job (which must be in an all-female environment) without the permission of a male relative, could not travel in a vehicle unless accompanied by a male relative – and could not even have an operation for a serious illness unless a male relative agreed.

And this male relative could, in some circumstances, be her son. Yes, the child she'd given birth to – who could be thirty or even forty years younger than her – had the power of life and death over her.

It would have been a dream-come-true for macho shitheads all over the western world, and yet this prince – this member of the Saudi Arabian royal family – had been so wired genetically that he obtained his sexual pleasure from being ordered about by a woman in thigh-length boots.

'May I speak?' he asked.

'You may.'

'When you disappeared, I spent thousands of pounds on private detectives, looking for you.' Farhad paused. 'Did I do wrong?'

'Yes.'

'Will you forgive me?'

'We shall see. I want you to do something for me.'

'Anything.'

'Do you have good contacts in the Saudi Air Force and the Ministry of Defence?'

'I have three brothers in the Ministry, and one in the Air Force. I share a mother with the one in the Air Force.'

'Do you get on well with all of them?'

Farhad shrugged. 'I cannot remember. When you have fifty-three brothers, as I have, it is sometimes hard to keep track.'

'Then let me put it another way – will they all do favours for you?'

'Oh yes.'

'How can you be so sure?'

'I work for the ministry which watches our people when they leave the Kingdom. All of those brothers have gone abroad at one time or another. I have no idea what they will have done that they would prefer to keep buried, but there is bound to be something.'

'Where are these brothers of yours now? In Saudi?'

'No, at my father's villa in the south of France. It is his birthday in three days' time.'

'All fifty-three of them are there?'

'Fifty-four, including me. No, I lie. It is only fifty-three, because one of my brothers was executed last year.'

'What had he done?' Meadows asked.

'In the Kingdom, it is sometimes wiser not to ask that question.'

Jesus, Meadows thought – but back to business . . .

'Fifty-three of you,' she said. 'And how do you manage it? Do you sleep in bunk beds?'

'Of course not! Don't be so disgusting. We all have our own rooms, though some of my less important brothers have to share a bathroom.'

'So it shouldn't be too difficult to have some time alone with the ones you need to talk to?'

'No problem at all.'

'And how long should it take you to get back to your father's villa, Farhad?' Meadows asked.

'Two or three hours,' the prince replied.

It wouldn't do to look impressed, Meadows warned herself. It would be fatal to look impressed.

'Two or three hours!' she said scornfully. 'Is that the best you can manage?'

'I don't see how I could do it quicker,' Farhad said. 'I will fly back to France in my own jet, when I land there will be a helicopter waiting to take me to the villa, and . . .'

'If it's the best you can do, it's the best you can do, and we'll just have to learn to live with it,' Meadows said.

'I am sorry,' Farhad said.

'What matters most is not how long it takes you to get there, but how quickly you can find out what I want to know once you're there,' Meadows said briskly.

'What *do* you want to know?'

'I'll tell you, if you'll only be silent.'

'I am sorry again.'

'I want to know about the deal your country signed with BAI and Roussillon Aéronautique for the Faucon fighter plane. Specifically, I want to know why it took so long to negotiate, and what finally tipped the balance.'

'Am I allowed to ask what my reward will be if I succeed in doing what you've asked me to do?'

'You're allowed – and I will tell you. When it's over, we'll spend a night together – perhaps even two.'

'Will it be dangerous, Zelda – this thing you're asking me to do?' Farhad asked.

'It could be.'

'Might I be arrested and tortured?'

'It's possible.'

'Is there a chance that, even though I am a prince, I might be executed – like my brother was?'

'Yes.' Meadows smiled. 'But I don't think that bothers you, does it?'

'No.'

'In fact, it excites you.'

'It does,' Farhad admitted. 'It excites me very much.'

Rosemary had told them that she could identify Roger in the drawer, so there was no need to go through all the palaver of getting him out, but they insisted, and would not even let her into the room until he had been neatly laid out on a trolley.

Rosemary looked down at the face. 'Well, I can't tell anything from that,' she said.

'I did warn you,' Green said

'So let's see the rest of him, then.'

'I beg your pardon?'

'The rest of him. The part that's hidden by the sheet.'

'I don't think you're quite aware . . .' Green began.

'Of course I'm aware. I'm not a medic, but I am a scientist. At the very least, there'll be a big Y-shaped incision down his front that's been roughly sewn back together again, and if you think that will send me running from the room, you haven't learned much about me in the last half hour.'

'Pull back the sheet, please,' Inspector Green said to the attendant.

'Right down to the feet?' the attendant asked.

'Right down to the feet,' Rosemary Pemberton said.

The attendant pulled back the sheet.

Rosemary examined the body for less than ten seconds, then said, 'Shit, that's not my husband.'

Green wondered if he dared put his hand on her shoulder, and decided that the circumstances justified it.

'It's natural to deny that your husband is dead,' he said. 'I've seen it happen so many times. You may tell yourself that you hate him, but there must still be love for him in some small part of your heart, and that part refuses to let him die.'

'It's not him,' Rosemary said firmly.

'There was a perfect match with the prints.'

'Then someone screwed up.'

'Mistakes are made, but they are so rare that . . .'

Rosemary brushed the comforting hand aside, and stepped away from the table.

'Listen very carefully, because I will not be repeating this,' she said. 'My husband was circumcised, and unless he had a foreskin transplant while he was on the run, this is not him.'

Dr Pemberton glanced at her watch. She couldn't ring Colin Beresford for some time yet, so she thought she might as well go to the nearest hotel and treat herself to a bottle of champagne.

Captain Mahoney was only gone for twenty-five minutes, but it seemed to Proudfoot – with only an unresponsive patrolman in the corner for company – to have been at least three or four hours, so that when the captain did return, Proudfoot was surprised to discover that he was pleased to see him.

Mahoney sat down.

'So you used to be in the CIA, didn't you?' he asked.

Proudfoot had not been expecting this, but he was surprised, rather than worried.

'Yes, I was in the CIA,' he said. 'I couldn't admit it while I was operational, but I've made no secret of it since I left.'

'Now that is one hell of an understatement,' Mahoney said. 'Made no secret of it? Man, it was splashed all over your campaign literature when you ran for the Assembly.'

'I'd done my duty while I served the Company. I saw no reason to be ashamed of it.'

'Quite so. Good for you, I say. And while you were working for the CIA, did you ever come across an English police officer called Detective Chief Inspector Monika Paniatowski?'

'No.'

Mahoney shook his head. 'It's a pity you're taking that attitude. Still, since you're here, I suppose we might as well press on. I met Monika at a couple of international police conferences, and we got on like a house on fire. No sex, you understand, and she spoke a special kind of English called Lancashire English, so I'm not sure we even understood each other half the time. But like I say, we hit it off.'

'What's the point of all this?'

'That will become clear real soon now. A couple of years ago, Monika asked for my help on a case because it involved a New Yorker – a very famous New Yorker, as things turned out. You may have read about it.'

'I didn't,' Proudfoot said.

Mahoney made a face. 'You want to consider changing your name to Sourpuss,' he said. 'So, I do Monika this little favour, and then I read in the *New York Times* that I'm the one who's cracked the case. And where do you think the reporter got that information from?'

'I don't know.'

'Take a guess.'

'I couldn't possibly . . .'

'Take a guess.'

'I know what you're doing,' Proudfoot said. 'In the CIA, I was taught how to resist interrogation.'

'If you don't answer my question right now, I'm going to come round that table and pull your head off,' Mahoney growled.

'It was her who probably told the reporter,' Proudfoot said sulkily.

'Yep, that's right,' Mahoney agreed. 'So instead of her being in my debt, I'm pretty much in hers. So when she calls me up, yesterday . . .'

'She couldn't have called you up,' Proudfoot said. 'She's in a coma.'

His face froze.

'Yes, she is in a coma, and it was one of her friends who made the call,' Mahoney said. 'But how would someone who's never even heard her name before know that?'

'No comment.'

'Now you're talking like a criminal,' Mahoney said. 'Anyway, this friend asks me if I know anything about a Robert Proudfoot, who she tried to arrest a few years back, but who turned out to have diplomatic immunity. Well, it doesn't take me long to find you, and it's almost as quick to get something on you, because you perverts are never as smart or discreet as you think you've been. So here we are. I've got you over a barrel, and I want to know what you were doing in Barrow Village that early morning four years ago. I believe it's your move.'

Proudfoot took a deep breath, 'I feel under a certain obligation to the Company not to say anything about that incident,' he told Mahoney.

'Fine,' the captain said. 'In that case, call your lawyer – and while we're waiting for him to arrive, I'll throw you into the cage with four or five guys who are just going to love you.'

'If I . . . if I tell you about that morning . . .?'

'Yes?'

'. . . what do I get in return?'

'I'll kick you loose.'

'Why should I believe you?' Proudfoot asked.

'Because I've just given you my word,' Mahoney growled.

He'd always been going to kick him loose. What choice did he have? He couldn't charge Proudfoot, because it hadn't been his operation. And if he sent him back to Vice, then Boone would kick him loose, because Proudfoot was a state assemblyman, and as far as Boone was concerned, that gave him the right to jam his dick into little boys' assholes.

'The reason I went to Barrow Village that morning was to check with my own eyes that a man called Arthur Wheatstone had been terminated,' Proudfoot said.

'Who sent you?'

'The short answer to that is my boss sent me.'

'And what's the long answer?'

'Somebody in State? Somebody in Defence? Maybe even somebody in the White House? I wasn't told.'

'And that was all? You just had to check he was dead?'

'No, not just dead – terminated. I was to check there was no possibility that he'd killed himself.'

'Why would you need to do that?'

'If you ask yourself why in the Company, you'll last maybe a week.'

'OK, you can go,' Mahoney said.

'Just like that?'

'Just like that.'

Proudfoot rose unsteadily to his feet.

'Thank you,' he said.

'Don't thank me,' Mahoney said. He paused for a second. 'Oh, by the way, say hi to the reporters for me.'

'What reporters?'

'The ones waiting outside. Somebody must have told them you'd been arrested in a brothel full of under-age sex workers.'

'But . . . that . . . will ruin . . . me,' Proudfoot gasped.

'I should hope it would,' Mahoney told him.

'I'm not going down alone,' Proudfoot said. 'I'll find a way to drag you with me.'

That was a possibility, Mahoney thought, but it was a long-term possibility. In the short term, he still had to look at his own face in the shaving mirror each morning.

It was early evening, and nothing had gone as Mr Forsyth had expected it to that day.

Colin Beresford, who had announced in the Drum and Monkey that he would be seeking a meeting with the chief constable to tell him that it was the end of the road for his investigation, had spent most of his day by Monika's bedside, playing her songs which, in Forsyth's opinion, were more likely to induce a coma than pull someone out of one.

Then there was Kate Meadows. There was no doubt that she had targeted the two men on the train, which meant she knew they were connected with the security services in some way, but that didn't necessarily mean her trip to London had anything to do with the case. It might simply be – and knowing Kate Meadows as he did, probably was – that she had just decided that she didn't want to be followed around by a couple of spooks, and had not been too particular about how she got rid of them.

The other concern was Diana Sowerbury. He had brought her to Lancashire with the sole purpose of her keeping an eye on Monika, and the fact that she'd already struck up a relationship with Beresford by the time he'd briefed her on her mission had been a real bonus.

And it had all continued running like clockwork until nine that morning, which was when the transmitter in her flat had gone down. Sowerbury herself couldn't have known that, of course, but the protocol was that whether you were wired up or not, you checked in by phone, as a safety measure, at given pre-set times – and she hadn't been doing that.

It was when Sowerbury had missed three of those check-in calls – and still not made an appearance in public – that Forsyth reluctantly decided that even though it might compromise her cover, he had better send Wilson up to her flat.

Wilson rang back ten minutes later.

'She's here,' he said. 'I found her on the bed, bound and gagged.'

'Who . . .?' Forsyth began – and then realized what a stupid question he was about to ask. 'Has Diana Sowerbury said *why* Beresford tied her up?'

'No. He came at her from behind. She thought he was starting some sex game at first, and even when he put the tape over her mouth . . .'

'All right, I get the picture,' Forsyth said. 'Does she need medical care?'

'It might be wise for her to have a check up.'

'Then ring the number, and they'll send an ambulance.'

'Beresford's been back, sir,' Wilson said.

'Then why in God's name didn't you tell me before? When was this?'

'Diana thinks it was about three quarters of an hour ago.'

'Thinks!'

'Yes, it's hard to look at your watch when your hands are taped behind your back.'

'Did he do anything to her – or say something which might give us a clue about what he might do next?'

'He asked her if she'd like some water, and he gave her a massage.'

'He did what!'

'You've been tied up like that for hours, and it's not good for you,' Beresford says. 'So what I'm going to do is, I'm going take some of the tapes off, so I can massage you. Please don't take advantage of the opportunity to try and escape, because you won't make it, and I'll probably have to hurt you. Do you understand?'

Diana Sowerbury nods.

Beresford strips off some of the tape, and goes to work on her legs.

'I used to do this for my mum,' he says. 'She had Alzheimer's disease. I'm not sure it did her much good – she'd given up any sort of exercise by then – but I think she recognized it as a kind act, if not a loving one, from this stranger who was always around. And that has to count for something, doesn't it?'

He starts to work on her other ankle.

'I'm sorry about this, I really am,' he says, 'but we're on different sides, and that's just the way it is.'

He finishes the massage, and tapes her ankles together again.

'I'm expecting some phone calls,' he says. 'The way we figured it, you'd have all our phones bugged, but you probably wouldn't have bugged your own,' he said. 'Is that right?'

She glares at him.

He grins back.

'Well, there was always a chance you might tell me,' he says.

The phone rings in the living room.

He walks through and picks it up.

She hears him say, 'Hello Captain Mahoney . . . Yes, sir, that is very good news.'

'How many other calls did he receive?' Forsyth demanded.

'Two.'

'And who were they from?'

'Diana doesn't know.'

One of the other phones rang – the one from the van outside the hospital.

Forsyth picked it up.

'Yes,' he said, irritated.

'I really think you should hear this, sir,' the man in the van said.

There were a few seconds of a screeching song – something about sugar, honey and candy men (as far as Forsyth could work out), then the cacophony was gone and a voice that he recognized as Beresford's said, *'I'm Col the Pol and that was the Archies singing "Sugar, Sugar". You're listening to Radio Monika, broadcasting to all blue vans in the vicinity of Whitebridge General Hospital. And now, a word from our sponsors.'*

There was a few seconds' silence, then a voice which was very weak – but also instantly recognisable, said, *'I think that it's about time we had a talk, Mr Forsyth.'*

TWENTY-THREE

'Will there be cricket on the radio?' Forsyth asked Downes, as they crossed Whitebridge on their way to the hospital.

Downes checked his watch. 'There'll be no match coverage at the moment, but you might catch a summary on the news.'

'Well, see if you can find it for me,' Forsyth said.

He enjoyed his cricket, and it annoyed him when he heard racists shout unpleasant things at the Indian and Pakistani players. He was a racist himself – if you were born white, you were born superior, and there was just nothing you could do about that, was there? – but it seemed to him that if these chaps batted or bowled well, they deserved the credit for it, and if they did happen to win, well, you just gritted your teeth and accepted the result, because when all was said done, damn it, you were *English.*

'. . . *and that is the end of the sports results,*' said the news-reader. '*Here are the closing headlines. The Chancellor of the Exchequer, in a major speech . . .*'

The Chancellor of the Exchequer was a windbag, Forsyth thought. He had been a windbag at school, and he was a windbag now.

'. . . *raised an objection with the International Monetary Fund. It has been announced that the chairman of British Aircraft Industries, Sir Henry Tavistock, is stepping down next month. His replacement is Mr Thomas Carter, who has been a senior executive with the Boeing Corporation for a number of years. On the stock market . . .*'

Well, well, well, Forsyth thought, that really is what the Americans would call a game changer.

Beresford was standing outside Paniatowski's door as Downes and Forsyth approached.

'Not you,' Beresford said to Downes, 'just him.'

Downes bristled. 'Now look here,' he said, 'I'm a government official, and if you think I'm going to be ordered about by a provincial copper, you've got another think coming.'

'You're a sordid little spy,' Beresford said, 'and if you get close enough for me to touch you, I'll break your arm.'

Forsyth came to a halt, so Downes did, too.

'Go to the canteen, and get yourself a cup of tea,' Forsyth said.

'Look, sir, I don't think—'

'An excellent quality in a subordinate, especially at a time like this,' Forsyth said. 'Go!'

Downes went.

'You left Diana Sowerbury tied up all day,' Forsyth said.

'Yes, that way I knew where she was.'

'It was most uncomfortable for her.'

Beresford shrugged. 'She should look at it as an occupational hazard.'

'Her occupation is nursing – and she's very good at it,' Forsyth said.

'Until you need her for something else.'

'Yes, until I need her for something else,' Forsyth agreed. 'How did you get onto her?'

'There were a lot of little things. She arrived very suddenly. She seemed very interested in my work, and she knew things about me that I hadn't told her.'

'Plus the fact that she was willing to leap into bed with you hours after you first met.'

'No, she did that because she wanted to,' Beresford said. 'You'd be surprised how often something like that happens.'

'You have a very high opinion of yourself,' Forsyth said.

'Yes, don't I just,' Beresford agreed. 'Anyway, the little things on their own meant nothing, but when I found out you were here, they all fitted together.'

'I think I'd like to see Monika now,' Forsyth said.

'Of course,' Beresford agreed, 'but a word of warning before you go in there – if you hurt her, I won't just break your arm, I'll break your bloody neck.'

*   *   *

Forsyth walked over to the bed and looked down at Monika.

'I must congratulate you, my dear,' he said. 'It can't have been easy to contact your gorilla without me finding out about it.'

Not easy? It had been bloody hard!

Timing, she'd realized, was everything, and not just in the way it mattered to a comedian, because if he got it wrong all he would lose was a laugh, whereas if she got it wrong she would be bloody well dead.

What she had to do was to let Colin know that she was conscious at the same moment as she warned him to show no reaction at all.

She'd practiced moving her hand. At first, it had seemed unwilling to respond, as if it had got used to a sedentary existence, and resented these calls to action from the brain. Or perhaps it was the brain which had forgotten how to issue commands. Then, slowly, the movement had come, the commands were obeyed.

There was a part of her which had wanted to delay alerting Colin until she had more control, but caution was not a luxury she could have afforded when – at any moment – Mr Forsyth might have decided the time had come to silence her forever.

And so, the previous afternoon, she had waited until Colin was looking out of the window, then raised her finger to her lips.

He had turned – and frozen.

Please, please, her eyes had begged him, say nothing.

When he'd nodded to show that he understood, she gestured that he should go over to the bed and put his ear to her mouth.

'Sing,' she had whispered, in a voice that sounded like a brittle dry flower being crushed.

And Colin – good old reliable Colin – had done just that.

'Ye tek the high road, and I'll tek the low road, and I'll be in Scotland afore ye . . .'

It was not until he'd reached 'the bonny bonny banks of Loch Lomond,' that she'd dared speak again, and this time she'd said, 'The room is bugged.'

'Yes, it must have been hard,' Forsyth said, 'but I've long been impressed by your ingenuity.' He glanced down at his watch. 'Shall we get to the point of this meeting, Monika?'

'I'm not talking to you as a police officer who wants to arrest you for what you've done,' Paniatowski said. 'Even if I did want to arrest you, I don't think I'd ever have enough evidence to make it stick.'

'So if you're not talking to me as a police officer, then why am I here at all?' Forsyth wondered.

'You're here so I can convince you to spare my life,' Paniatowski said.

'You think I might kill you?'

'I know you would, if you thought it necessary.'

'I have to say, Monika, that if you really do believe that, you seem remarkably calm.'

'I'm not calm at all,' Paniatowski said, because there was no point in lying to a man like Forsyth. 'I'm absolutely terrified, because if you kill me, who will take care of my baby boys? And who will be there to cry at Louisa's wedding?'

'I can see why that might concern you,' Forsyth agreed.

'You'd decide to kill me if you thought I might be able to piece together what happened,' Paniatowski said, 'but if I'd already pieced most of it together – and had it written down – I'd have insurance.'

'Only if you'd got it right,' Forsyth pointed out. 'If you'd got it wrong, it wouldn't be worth the paper it was written on.'

'It all starts with the Anglo-French fighter plane,' Paniatowski said. 'It would be a big boost to the economy if we could sell it to the Saudis.'

'The treasury was gasping for that money.'

'But before the Saudis would buy it, they wanted the planes equipped with the Z-13 missile guidance and detection unit.'

'How in God's name do you know about that?' Forsyth asked, shocked.

'It came to me in a dream,' Paniatowski said. 'At any rate, the Z-13 was an American system which they were perfectly willing to share with their NATO allies – at a price – but were never going to give to France, under any circumstances.'

'Are you sure about that?'

'Certain. France had left NATO, and the Americans were so angry that they wouldn't have pissed in France's mouth if its throat was on fire. So, the Saudis were insisting on the Z-13 or something just as good, and the French could come up with nothing. And that left you with a big problem.'

'Are you saying that we found ourselves in a Henry II situation?' Forsyth asked.

'I've no idea – because I haven't got a bloody clue what you're talking about.'

'Then I'll explain. Henry II was always having trouble with his archbishops of Canterbury, so when he saw the chance to put his best friend, Thomas Becket, in the post, he took it. The only problem was that Becket turned out to be even more of a troublemaker than his predecessor.'

'I'm not here for a history lesson,' Paniatowski said angrily.

'You should be,' Forsyth told her. 'History teaches us what mistakes we have made in order that we can better understand why we are repeating them.'

'Does this have anything to do with why we're here now?'

'It has *everything* to do with why we're here now.'

'Then get on with it, for Christ's sake!'

'It was December. Henry was in France, at a banquet, when news reached him that Becket had excommunicated some of his allies. "Will no one rid me of this turbulent priest?" he asked. And four of his knights immediately set sail for England. They found Becket in Canterbury Cathedral, kneeling before the altar. They surrounded him. In their hands, they had broadswords, huge, heavy weapons which, if used correctly, could decapitate a horse with a single stroke. Can you picture it, Monika?'

Yes – and worse than just picture it. The room was suddenly as cold as the great cathedral in winter, and though she was lying in bed, she could feel the hard stone flags pressing against her knees.

'They killed him, of course,' Forsyth said matter-of-factly. 'The king was delighted with the result – without their leader, the rebels in the church were silent – but unhappy with how it had been attained, and it was not long before he started saying that he had never wanted Becket killed at all. In other words, he wanted the cake, but he would rather not have known how it was baked. Anyway, four years ago we had a minister at the Treasury cast in much the same mould. He told us we desperately needed those aircraft sales, and he didn't care how we got them. Of course, if we'd told him what we actually *did* . . .' He paused. 'I'm sorry, Monika, I seem to be doing your work for you.'

'Or rather, you're cutting into my audition for my right to continue living,' Paniatowski said.

'Whatever,' Forsyth said airily.

'My guess is that getting hold of the Z-13 wasn't a problem,' Paniatowski said. 'Dr Pemberton's team probably had access to it through the project they were doing for the Americans. But you couldn't just hand it over to the Anglo-French project, so what you had to do was to pretend to steal it, and sell it to the French through a third party. Once it became known that the French had it, someone in the government will have gone over to the States and grovelled to someone in the White House. It was a shocking lapse of security, he will have said. Left to ourselves, we would never use it, but now the French had got their hands on it, and they were insisting. As a sweetener, he probably also promised to pay a royalty on every plane sold.'

'Interesting,' Forsyth said.

This was even harder work than she'd thought it would be, Paniatowski told herself.

It was like climbing the steps to a scaffold, with each step becoming steeper and more difficult. She wondered where the image had come from – wondered if all that talk about Henry II and his knights had been partly calculated to plant such thoughts in her mind.

Focus, Monika! You need to focus! Focus or you're dead!

'But that wouldn't have been enough, would it?' she asked. 'The Americans will have wanted the guilty party – the person in the lab who committed the actual theft. But you couldn't give him to them, because under interrogation, he'd be bound to confess who was behind it.'

'There are very few people who can withstand prolonged interrogation,' Forsyth said.

'So you said that you'd questioned Wheatstone and were convinced he'd worked alone and had nothing more to tell, and since he was your traitor, you reserved the right to execute him yourself.'

'Very good,' Forsyth said.

'So once they'd . . . once they'd . . .'

'What's the matter, Monika?'

The matter was that Forsyth had agreed far too easily.

'It wasn't Wheatstone, was it?' Paniatowski said shakily. 'I can tell from the way you reacted.'

'The whole purpose of this meeting is for you to tell me what you know, so that I can assess whether or not we dare let you stay alive,' Forsyth said. 'If we've hit a roadblock at this early stage, then clearly you can have nothing else to tell me, and I should go.'

He turned and walked towards the door.

She felt as if she had reached the scaffold, and could see the spot on which she was to die.

'*Why* wasn't it Wheatstone?' she asked.

Forsyth reached out for the door handle.

She could almost see the axe – glinting in the light, stained with the blood of countless others who had gone before her.

'*Why* wasn't it Wheatstone?' she repeated desperately.

Forsyth turned around. 'Do you know, I'm enjoying this game so much that I think I'm going to tell you,' he said. He walked back to the bed. 'It wasn't Wheatstone because our psychologists didn't think he'd do it. It seems that while he had no morals to speak of, he had an ample sufficiency of principles.'

'So who was it who you persuaded?'

'Roger Pemberton. I don't think it was so much the money as the promise that if he did it, we'd kill Wheatstone for him. That was rather convenient for us, since we were planning to do it anyway.'

'If Pemberton did the deed, why not kill him and leave Wheatstone alone?'

'Think about it, Monika,' Forsyth said.

'Because . . . because Pemberton might have written something down as a form of insurance.'

'As you claim you have.'

'As I *have*.'

'Good for you. Now carry on.'

'But Wheatstone wouldn't think he'd need any insurance, since he knew nothing about it.'

'Exactly,' Forsyth smiled awkwardly. 'Actually, Pemberton

didn't take that routine precaution, which just shows what a
complete fool he was.'

'Yes, it does,' Paniatowski agreed.

Forsyth frowned. 'You've missed a trick there, Monika,' he said.

'Have I?' Paniatowski asked. 'Ah yes, I get it now.'

'Get what?'

'I'm supposed to ask you how you know Pemberton didn't leave
any papers behind him. I'm supposed to point out that since it's
less than two days since his body was washed up, the person
holding his papers may not even know he's dead yet. Isn't that
what you were expecting?'

'Yes, it was – but it seems you're not quite as sharp as I anticipated you'd be,' Forsyth said.

'Or it may be that we both know it wasn't Pemberton who was
washed up in Cornwall,' Monika said.

Forsyth smiled. 'Nicely played,' he said.

'Thank you,' Paniatowski replied.

'Why don't you tell me about Arthur Wheatstone's termination,'
Forsyth suggested.

'Don't you mean Arthur Wheatstone's murder?'

'If that's the term you prefer.'

'There was someone in the States – someone calling the shots
– who was adamant he shouldn't take his own life, wasn't there?'

*I was to make sure there'd been no possibility of him having
killed himself,* Robert Proudfoot had said.

'Yes, there was,' Forsyth agreed. 'He was, I believe, a middle-
ranking member of the State Department, which – if we're honest
about it – means he had more clout internationally than virtually
anybody in our own Foreign Office. His grandparents came from
Sicily, and brought with them a Sicilian code of honour which
includes – along with many other quaint notions – the idea that
you never give your enemy the easy way out.'

'So Proudfoot was here to make sure that the traitor wasn't
given the soft option.'

'Just so. The plan was that he was there to witness the elimin-
ation, but his plane was delayed. By the time that message got through
to us, Pemberton and the terminator were in Wheatstone's house.
Pemberton was already a nervous wreck, and terminators as a breed
don't like taking unnecessary risks, so they went ahead as planned.'

'But why hang him?' Paniatowski asked. 'Why not shoot him? Or knife him?' She thought for a second. 'Ah!'

'Ah?'

'If Henry II's knights had told the king that Thomas Becket had committed suicide, they might just have got away with it.'

'Precisely so. The man in the Treasury wanted matters clearing up, but he didn't want a murder on his conscience. And we are, after all, the *British* secret service – a rather gentlemanly organisation. We don't want to be thought of as assassins.'

'Even if you are.'

'Especially if we are.'

How was she doing? Monika wondered.

No – she couldn't afford to ask herself that, because she was no longer on a gallows, she was on a tightrope – and if her mind wasn't focussed purely on moving forward, she would fall off into the darkness below.

'I would have loved to have seen the looks on their faces when they realized they were missing an essential piece of equipment for staging their little drama,' she said.

'I don't know what you're talking about,' Forsyth said.

'Yes, you do.'

'Perhaps so – but I would still like to hear it from you.'

'There were three things they needed. The first was a syringe of some kind of dope to knock Wheatstone out, which the killer brought with him. The second was a rope. There was one of them hanging on the garage wall, but even if there hadn't been, that was no problem, because the killer could have used a bed sheet instead. The third component was a ladder. Now the killer had all the reason in the world to expect to find one, hadn't he?'

'Had he?'

'Of course he had. Every house has at least one ladder – but Mrs Wheatstone had got rid of hers after her suicide attempt. All that was left was a set of steps, slightly higher than a chair, and no help in reaching the beam unless the person using them happens to be an exceptionally tall man.' She paused. 'Why do you employ such a tall killer? Isn't he a bit conspicuous?'

'I do not employ killers at all,' Mr Forsyth said, with a sudden chill edge to his voice.

'Not your department?'

'Not my department. However, I am told that this particular terminator compensates for his conspicuity by being extremely good at his job.'

'So the whole thing was a fiasco right from the start,' Paniatowski said.

'What do you mean?'

'I worked out almost immediately that Wheatstone couldn't have hanged himself using only that small stool, and so would any other bobby who'd discovered the body.'

'Unless that other bobby was Chief Superintendent Snodgrass,' said Forsyth, clearly stung at what he took to be criticism.

'Snodgrass was supposed to be the first police officer to arrive at the scene of the crime?'

'Yes.'

'Did he have a reason for calling on Wheatstone?'

'Of course he did. The day before he was found hanging, Wheatstone witnessed a robbery in the centre of Whitebridge.'

'What kind of robbery?'

'The Lord Mayor's wife had her handbag snatched. Since she is so important municipally – though on the stage of real life she would scarcely merit a walk-on part – Chief Superintendent Snodgrass himself was going to interview Wheatstone.'

'You dragged the mayor's wife into this?'

'Literally. She was pulled to the ground, and her knees were scraped quite badly.'

'Why would Snodgrass play along with all this?'

'He's a good policeman, but he's an even better ex-soldier – not to mention a fiery evangelical Christian. Which is why, when we told him he needed to cover up the death of a traitor and notorious fornicator for the good of his country, he readily agreed.'

No wonder the killer had been careless enough to let Inspector Cole see him, Paniatowski thought. He must have been told in advance that any mistakes he made would be squared away by a senior police officer.

'I assume that Snodgrass would have taken a ladder of the appropriate length with him,' she said.

'Yes. He also had an artfully crafted suicide note in which Wheatstone confessed to spying. And to support that, we'd left some semi-secret documents in his potting shed on Old Mill Road.'

'There *were* no documents there,' Paniatowski said.

'There were no documents there by the time you arrived,' Forsyth said. 'We'd removed them again, because after you'd blundered into Wheatstone's garage, we needed a new script.'

'Snodgrass made a big mistake in bawling me out,' Paniatowski said.

'He did,' Forsyth agreed. 'It made important people start to question his judgement, and once that happened, he had to go.'

'What about the autopsy?' Paniatowski asked. 'How did you hope to get round that? Oh yes, you managed to get hold of a ticket for an orchestra that Dr Shastri liked, so she wouldn't be in Whitebridge that day.'

'Managed to get hold of a ticket!' Forsyth repeated. 'How you still under-rate us, even after all these years.'

'What do you mean?'

'It wasn't just any old orchestra that the estimable Dr Shastri likes, it was her absolute favourite. And we didn't buy a ticket – we printed it, because we were the promoters.'

'So you brought an orchestra to Manchester from where – London? – specifically to distract Dr Shastri for two hours on Tuesday lunchtime?

'No, we brought an orchestra across from India specifically to distract Dr Shastri for two hours on Tuesday lunchtime, though no doubt it gave others pleasure, too. Are you beginning to appreciate what a very complex and well-resourced operation you barged in on, Monika?'

Don't be impressed! And don't be intimidated!

'The moment you found out I'd discovered the body, you handed the autopsy back to Shastri.'

'There didn't seem to be much point in using our man to tell the truth. Better to hold him in reserve for when lying is necessary.'

'Why did the man who was washed up in Cornwall yesterday have Pemberton's prints? Had you switched around two sets of prints in the Ministry of Defence?'

'Yes, it was the easiest thing in the world.'

'And you did it to make my team think that they hadn't already got Pemberton?'

'Yes.'

'Whereas, in fact, it was Pemberton who was buried on the allotment?'

'Yes.'

'Who killed him? Judd?'

'What makes you say that?'

'Judd was the man who knew where he could bury him without it being detected.'

'Yes, it was Judd.'

'Why did he kill him? Was it because Pemberton had already confessed to his wife that he'd been there when Wheatstone was killed?'

'Yes, although that was merely indicative of just how unstable he'd become. But just to set the record straight, Judd did that on his own initiative – he'd had no authorisation from the centre.'

'So I suppose it's Judd whose body is in the Cornish mortuary.'

'Yes.'

'And who killed him?'

'No one. He killed himself.'

'Oh, come on, it's a little too late to start bullshitting me now,' Paniatowski said.

'Judd was told that we could no longer shield him from the consequences of killing Pemberton. We also pointed out the location of a large supply of tranquilizers. And finally we told him that if he still wanted to be of service to his country, we were very much in need of one dead body at that point in time.'

'You bastard!' Paniatowski said.

'It was his choice,' Forsyth said mildly. 'A footnote to this story – and the main reason you may sleep peacefully in your bed from now on – is that . . .'

'What was that you just said?'

'You mean about you being able to sleep peacefully in your bed from now on?'

'Yes.'

'It's quite true. Your life was in danger when there was a chance that you might be responsible for the Americans finding out that we stole the Z-13. That, it now seems, is no longer a problem.'

'What do you mean?'

'On the way here, I heard on the radio that Sir Thomas Tavistock,' the chairman of BAI has resigned, and is going to be replaced by Robert Carter, an American.'

'So?'

'*An American!*' Forsyth said. 'Come on, Monika, I know having your sentence of death withdrawn might knock you back for a while, but it's time to move on.'

'The Americans know what *really* happened.'

'Yes. Some minister must have deemed it necessary to confess to what we did, and now the Americans are extracting a heavy penalty.'

'Everything you've just put me through was totally unnecessary, wasn't it?' Paniatowski demanded.

'Yes, but I didn't know that the option of killing you was off the table until I was nearly at the hospital, and it seemed a pity to waste the journey.'

'And have you enjoyed yourself, listening to me beg for my life?'

'You're being too self-critical, Monika. You didn't beg. You have too much spirit to ever be able to beg.'

'*Have you enjoyed it?*

'It has been a pleasant diversion for a man who does not have too many pleasant diversions left to him,' Forsyth admitted.

'And doesn't it bother you that three men have died in order to keep a secret which some spineless politician has decided is no longer worth keeping?' Paniatowski demanded.

'Oh for God's sake, Monika, grow up!' Forsyth said, and there was real anger in his voice. 'We are selling weapons which we know will be responsible for the deaths of thousands – maybe hundreds of thousands – of innocent women and children. Do you really think I should feel any guilt for my part in the deaths of a roué, a wife beater and a burned-out spy?'

EPILOGUE

I t was a perfect – almost emblematic – English April afternoon. The sun, attended by a few wispy clouds, shone down benevolently on the churchyard, and the spring flowers basked in its glory. Bees buzzed in the hedgerows, birds chirped in the trees, and in the distance there was the clip-clopping sound of horses' hooves.

The Norman church – according to Pevsner, one of the finest in the country – was full, and the vicar was just delivering his eulogy.

'George Harrington-Maud was not a poor man, as anyone who has been fortunate enough to be entertained in his lovely home can attest. That he worked was not through need, but because he felt it was his duty to his country. If he had entered the world of politics, he might have become prime minister – indeed, those of us who knew him well are convinced he would have been. But that was not his way. He did not seek the limelight, but chose to immerse himself in the intricacies of life in the higher civil service. Most of us would have found his work dry and dusty. I suspect that he did, too – but he knew it was necessary work that few men could have handled, and so he did it without complaint.'

In one of the pews close to the back of the church, a blonde woman leant over to her dark-haired daughter, and said, 'I've had enough of this shit – anyway, I need a cigarette.'

They were standing by the lychgate.

'You smoke too much, Mum,' Louisa said.

'I was unconscious for months, so I've a lot to catch up on,' Paniatowski replied.

Louisa sighed. 'Explain to me again why we're here,' she said.

'We're here because George Harrington-Maud – as we now know him to be – invited me to his funeral.'

'Why did he do that?'

'Perhaps he wanted me to find out if I was brave enough to come.'

'And why *are* you here?'

'Perhaps because I wanted to find out if I would be brave enough to come.'

The wake was at the family home, an Elizabethan manor house a short walk from the church.

Since it was a lovely day, the reception was held in the garden, and uniformed waiters were kept busy with plates of canapés and trays of Pimm's No. 1 Cup.

Paniatowski was halfway down her second Pimm's when the tall, elegant woman in her early sixties approached her.

'You must be Monika,' she said.

'That's right.'

'You do realize you're one of the select few, don't you?'

'I beg your pardon?'

'You're one of the few people here who know what George actually did.'

'I see.'

'George rather liked you, you know. In fact, he had a sneaking admiration for you. He wanted you to know that.'

There was a pause, and then Paniatowski said, 'Mrs Harrington-Maud . . .'

'Lady Harrington-Maud.'

'Lady Harrington-Maud, if you knew how much I would like to say – for your sake – that I felt the same about your husband. But I can't.'

The other woman smiled. 'Don't distress yourself, my dear,' she said. 'George thought you might say that, and so there was a second message, which he asked me to repeat accurately. He said, "The advantage of being born into my station in life is that approval from someone born into your station in life is of no interest to me." I have to say that I agree with him. Have a pleasant trip home.'

Prior to leaving, they strolled down to the end of the garden. There was a stream running through it, and they stood looking into the water.

'Mum?' Louisa said, with a mischievous edge to her voice.

'What?'

'Were you being quite honest back there? Isn't there a small corner of you which is quite going to miss not dealing with Mr Forsyth?'

'Oh, for God's sake, we're not living in some cosy detective novel, where the murders are antiseptic and the murderer isn't quite scary enough to keep you awake at night,' Paniatowski said. 'Forsyth was a ruthless bastard. You could say he did what he did for his country – but the country he did it for was one in which a few people drink Pimm's No. 1 Cup in the middle of the afternoon, and the rest of us just scrape by. I'm not sure I quite believe in hell yet, but I'm trying my hardest so I can picture him burning in it for all eternity.'

'Do you know, I'm rather sorry I asked,' Louisa said.

Lightning Source UK Ltd.
Milton Keynes UK
UKHW041832270820
368936UK00004B/90

9 781847 519993